LOVE ME NOT

LOVE ME NOT

A HIDDEN SPRINGS NOVEL

LISA MCLUCKIE

The Betty Press LLC
PO Box 241
Williams Bay, WI 53191
www.thebettypress.com
(262) 729-3231

ISBN-13: 978-1-941744-04-8
ISBN-10: 1941744048

For Charley, who never doubted I could do it.

CHAPTER ONE

Kat licked the last of the marshmallow from her fingers and debated making one more s'more. Already starting to buzz from the sugar high, she decided against it. Truth be told, she really should have stopped at two.

The bonfire had mellowed to a warm glow. Firelight flickered on the split log benches surrounding the fire pit, while the rest of the commons had faded into semidarkness. Teenagers clustered together, caught up in the end of summer and the imminent return to school. Younger children raced around in the dark, flashlights bobbing wildly. Adults stood around in groups of two or three or five. Looking out across the grass toward the lake, the pinpricks of light on the far side of the water felt awfully far away. It was easy to imagine herself at a camp in the remote north woods.

In reality, though, they were all too close to civilization. The twenty or so houses that comprised The Gardens circled the edge of the commons. This swath of lakefront property served as a haven for summer people up from Chicago. A handful of families lived here full time, but most were weekenders, and most of these families had been coming up to the lake for generations. The tight-knit community reflected those bonds.

Kat had never felt more like an outsider.

Her lawyer brain did not let her get away with a sweeping statement like that, even in the privacy of her own mind. Technically, she had felt like more of an outsider on multiple occasions, including the first time she had come to a barbecue at The Gardens, not even three months ago. Or her first day of kindergarten, when she had understood that she belonged to no group—not the milk-pale farm girls, or the already-friends town girls, or even the Spanish-speaking Mexican girls, daughters of immigrant farm workers, who puzzled over the girl who looked like them but couldn't understand them.

Mentally scrolling through the years between kindergarten and today, Kat concluded that she had spent more of her life as an outsider than an insider. No wonder she was so comfortable in the role. She had trained for it her whole life.

So why had she accepted another invitation to a gathering here in The Gardens, knowing that she would always be on the outside looking in? She didn't even socialize in her own neighborhood, not that the tidy row of townhomes where she lived could really be considered a neighborhood. She wrinkled her forehead, considering the possibility. Maybe, if you used the term loosely. They certainly didn't have barbecues. They exchanged friendly waves as they passed each other going in and out. She knew the names of the people in the next townhome. Did that add up to a neighborhood?

One stark contrast between her tidy group of townhomes and this sprawling neighborhood was the trees. A spindly sapling accented the front "lawn" of each townhome, each the same size and species, although Kat couldn't put a name to them. Perhaps one day they would be as majestic as the trees here on the commons, but Kat suspected they had been chosen for their modest size and good behavior. The trees here in The

Gardens were neither modest nor well-behaved. Scattered randomly across the otherwise open expanse of grass, these trees anchored the neighborhood, bearing witness to generation after generation of tradition.

Kat drained the last of her beer and contemplated heading home. Better to think deep thoughts in the privacy of her own living room. But before she could come to a decision, a girl approached the picnic tables on the edges of the firelight. She was so intent on her goal that she didn't seem to notice Kat sitting quietly in the shadows. Kat watched with interest as the girl filched something from the buffet and began to back away slowly, moving toward Kat and the bonfire. As she inched closer, Kat realized three things. First, she couldn't be older than fifteen. Second, that was a bottle of vodka clutched behind her back. And third, she was about to trip on one of the split log benches surrounding the bonfire.

"Look out," called Kat. The girl jumped, dropping the vodka as she whipped around to see who had caught her. Luckily it landed in the dirt and not on the log. Kat gave her a brisk nod. "Have a seat."

The girl promptly sat down on the bench that had nearly tripped her. Kat didn't recognize her, but then, she really knew only two families here.

"Why don't you pick up the vodka before someone trips over it?"

The girl picked the bottle up gingerly, as if it were a Molotov cocktail about to blow, and set it beside her on the very end of the bench. Both the girl and the bottle were poised for a quick getaway.

Kat waited while a pack of smaller kids ran past, playing some kind of tag in the dark, then she continued. "So, was this your idea, or did your friends put you up to it?"

The girl looked startled before she put her bland talk-to-the-adults face back on. "It's on me," she answered.

The lie was convincing nobody.

"If it was your idea, you wouldn't be so nervous."

"I'm not.... Nobody. It was my idea."

Kat studied the girl for a long minute, but it looked like she wasn't going to give up her friends, and Kat didn't really have jurisdiction here. She was just a guest. She also admired the girl's willingness to stick up for her friends, even if they were being idiots.

"Leave the vodka. You're free to go."

The girl was gone before Kat could say another word, leaving behind the bottle of vodka teetering on the bench. Kat sighed. She hated playing bad cop.

Thank God it was the last night of the summer. Even without kids of her own, the summer wreaked havoc on her schedule. She was looking forward to fall, and to a return to "normal." She made a disgusted sound in the back of her throat. Normal wasn't that great these days. She'd been working crazy hours these past few years building her practice. It was work she loved, but she didn't have anything outside of work that could be called a life.

She had done much better in those first couple of years after law school. There had been an entire cohort of newly minted lawyers all working for the big firms in Milwaukee. Sure, they had worked crazy hours then, too, but they had done it together. She had great memories of late-night after-work drinks, concerts, and comedy clubs—even the occasional weekend away. Not anymore. Ever since she had ditched the big money and the big firm to come home, her world had grown smaller and smaller. Sure, she kept up with friends on Face-book, but on a day-to-day basis, she had no social life. No dates. Nothing but work.

"Hey."

Kat had been so absorbed in her own thoughts, staring into the fire, that she hadn't heard Mel approach. It was weird how she could tell the triplets apart so easily now. Maybe it was because they were all older, or maybe it was just repeated exposure. She didn't expect they would be close friends anytime soon, but over the summer, she and Mel had reached a tentative truce, leaving their high school animosity behind.

"Hey, yourself," she answered.

Mel took a seat beside Kat on the bench and stuck a marshmallow into the fire. They sat in an oddly easy silence while the marshmallow toasted. Only when it was done—a little overdone, in Kat's opinion—did Mel break the silence again.

"This is definitely my last one," she said as she clamped the skewer between two graham crackers (and the chocolate, of course) and slid the pointy end out from the s'more. She leaned her skewer against the bench and took a giant bite.

"That's what I said after my third, but I can feel the fourth one calling my name."

Mel choked on a laugh, then swallowed. "I hear you." She gestured toward the bottle of vodka still sitting on the opposite side of the fire. "Vodka keeping you company tonight?"

"Confiscated," said Kat. "Pretty sure we don't want a bunch of teenagers puking their guts out later."

Mel snorted, her mouth full of the next bite of s'more.

"Are there fewer people than usual tonight?" Kat had been to only two other events here at The Gardens. The group tonight fell far short of the Memorial Day weekend or Fourth of July crowds.

"Illinois kids are already back to school. Not all the families make it back up for Labor Day weekend."

That made sense. "It must be exhausting, living your life in two different places, running back and forth all the time."

"I don't mind. The city revs you up, and then the lake calms you down. It's actually a nice balance."

They sat in silence for a few minutes until Mel asked, "Do you ever think about taking off and exploring the world?"

An unexpected question—one that must be on Mel's mind because it certainly had nothing to do with their conversation so far. It also felt strangely intimate, at least for their fledgling friendship. Maybe Mel had drunk enough wine to be feeling philosophical?

Kat considered her answer, and realized to her surprise that the idea didn't interest her at all.

"I've never had itchy feet," she said. "I guess my mother did, or she never would have left Colombia to come here to school." One of the logs shifted, sending a flurry of tiny sparks into the air. Kat watched them float and fade away as she continued speaking. "I've been on a few vacations—Florida, up north, Canada, even—but I haven't found anywhere else that feels like home." The expression on Mel's face made Kat curious to know what had prompted the question. "I was away for long enough. This is where I want to be right now. It's where I need to be." Her personal life would sort itself out eventually. "What about you?"

A brief silence before Mel answered. "Sometimes I wonder what's wrong with me. Chicago is amazing, and Hidden Springs is one of the most beautiful spots on the planet. The fact that I get to split my time between the two makes me very lucky. I shouldn't be daydreaming about someplace else."

"Why not? Dreams make the world go 'round."

Mel grimaced. "Dreams make me fight with my mother."

"She doesn't want you to travel?" That was a surprise. Mel's mother, Dora, seemed like the kind of person who would be up for any kind of adventure.

"She's been pretty clear about wanting me to settle down here and make some babies."

"You do know that you're an adult, right? You don't have to do what your mother says." Kat delivered the observation with an arched eyebrow and got a dirty look in return.

"You try saying no to my mother and see what happens."

Mel shoved the last of the s'more in her mouth. Kat turned back to the fire to hide her smile. Everyone in town knew Dora, and to her knowledge, nobody had ever successfully told her "no."

This was nice, Kat decided. She and Mel were having an actual conversation, one that wasn't tense or heavy with unspoken baggage. It made her feel less like an outsider and more like a human with a social life. It also made her miss her friends from law school a little less.

It occurred to her that Mel might be lonely, too. With her two sisters neatly paired off and in the throes of "true love," she seemed a bit lost.

Mel stood abruptly. "I need to head home before I eat another ten s'mores."

Kat stood, too, realizing this could be her chance for a graceful exit. "Me, too."

"What should we do with the vodka?"

Kat had completely forgotten about it, but Mel was right. If they left it unattended, the teens would reclaim it in about two seconds.

"Do you want to take it home?" asked Kat.

With a shrug, Mel said, "I could stick it in the liquor cabinet, but I doubt anyone will drink it. You?"

"Same. Why don't you take it?"

Mel grabbed the bottle, and they started walking up the hill, Mel heading home and Kat toward RJ's house, where she had parked her car. They had almost made it to the edge of the firelight when a voice rang out behind them.

"There you are!"

There was too much satisfaction in that declaration for Kat's peace of mind. She turned to face Dora with a tiny sigh. So much for a quiet fade from the party. Beside her, Mel did the same, although she might have hesitated a second longer and turned more slowly.

"Here I am," said Kat.

Mel crossed her arms, the vodka bottle dangling against one hip. "Mother."

Dora was about the same age as Kat's mother would have been, if she were still alive. Maybe a few years older. Kat remembered her own mother as quiet, at least around other people. Dora, in contrast, was never quiet. She was a force of nature. You always knew where you stood with her. No hidden agenda. No games. She was like a giant beating heart that never stopped talking.

"Come with me." Dora claimed Kat with one hand and Mel with the other and led (some might call it dragged) the girls back downhill, veering off toward one of the clusters of adults. "Mary Evelyn and I were just talking about the library project. You remember Mary Evelyn, don't you? The librarian?" Dora paused only long enough to take a breath and hear Mel's and Kat's murmured affirmations that they did indeed remember Mary Evelyn. "Of course you do. Everyone knows Mary Evelyn. Anyway, this mural project at the library is very exciting. They've won a grant to fund an artist from Chicago. He's going to do a mural on the side of the library building, and there's going to be a new garden put in. It will be beautiful." They arrived at a small knot of people, and Dora announced, "I found them."

The group included Mary Evelyn Bennett, the librarian, as well as several other retired ladies who were quite active in the community. Kat began to wonder if she should be nervous.

"Just the women we needed," said Mary Evelyn. "Kat, we're hoping that you know the right person to talk to up at the county. We're wondering if there are any teenagers in need of community service hours who could help on the library project. We thought you would know the right person to call."

Kat breathed a sigh of relief. Dora and her friends weren't

trying to rope her into some huge volunteer project. They just needed help making connections. This she could handle.

"I'm not sure exactly who's running the juvenile programs right now, but I'd be happy to make a few calls. Connect you to the right person."

"That would be wonderful!" said Mary Evelyn.

"See, I knew she would know what to do," crowed Dora. "Thank you so much, honey. There's no way we can do this without some volunteer labor, and kids these days are just so busy. I think the community service angle will be much better than an open call for helping hands."

"Happy to help," said Kat.

"And now you, sweetheart," began Dora, but Mel quickly interrupted.

"Mom, you know I'm swamped—"

Dora interrupted her right back. "I know you're between apartments right now—" She packed a lot of disapproval into that short phrase. Kat was exceedingly happy not to be on the receiving end. "And that you're planning to spend the next few weekends up here."

Mel had the look of a trapped rabbit, and she was making some kind of growling noise in the back of her throat.

"It will be so nice to have your helping hands on Saturday mornings."

They had a brief staring contest. Mel lost, and Kat bit back a smile.

"I'm afraid I have to head out," said Kat, "but I'll make some calls first thing in the morning and let you know what I learn."

She escaped as quickly as she could, their calls of "thank you" following her as she tromped back up the hill toward her car.

Rob was finishing up his breakfast at Lucy's Diner the following morning when Dora breezed in. Everyone knew Lucy, in much the same way that everyone knew Dora. They were always in the thick of things, always up to something. Rob was sitting at the middle of the counter, so he could overhear very clearly as Dora ordered doughnuts to go and the two women started chatting.

His ears perked up when he heard them mention Kat. As far as he knew, there was only one Kat in town, and that was Katherine Rodriguez, attorney-at-law, whose offices happened to be right next door to this very diner. Kitty Rodriguez, back in town as if she'd never dropped off the face of the earth in the middle of their senior year of high school, leaving behind dead parents and a lot of unanswered questions. She had opened that office a few years ago, just after he had launched his business, and only the intense pressure and long hours of that startup year had kept him from stopping by to welcome her back to town. Well, that and possibly nerves.

The pressure had eventually eased off, but not the hours, leaving him little opportunity to casually drop by and reconnect. You'd think, living in a small town, that they would have crossed paths at some point, but the universe appeared to be working against him on this one. His least favorite people he saw all the time, but not once had he seen Kat around town. Not at the grocery store. Not at the post office. Not even at the gas station. He didn't really go anywhere else.

Clearly, he needed to get out more.

Last week, as his company marked its three-year anniversary, he had realized that if he wanted to see Kitty sometime this century, he was going to need to get creative and make it happen. Today's breakfast was a first attempt at reconnaissance. His workday started at seven, and he was unlikely to catch Kat in her office this early, but he was hoping that Lucy might drop a hint as to her habits. He didn't dare ask, though, without drawing attention. He would need to play this just right.

"That girl works too hard." This comment was from Dora.

"All the young people do these days. They've lost the ability to have fun. Did you have any luck?" asked Lucy.

"Yes!" crowed Dora. "She's going to make a few phone calls, put us in touch with the right person up at county."

"But is she going to help?"

"Small steps," said Dora. "Small steps."

Dora headed out with her doughnuts, and Rob pondered their conversation. Clearly, they were trying to rope Kat into one of their schemes, and so far she was managing to stay clear. If Dora and Lucy had joined forces, however, chances were that she would end up doing whatever they needed her to do. It was just the way things worked.

Lucy came over to freshen up his coffee and give him his check. When she came back with his change, she paused. He did not like the gleam in her eye.

"You're Rob Murray, aren't you? Peggy's son?"

At his nod, she continued. "And you have a landscaping business, isn't that right?"

"Yes...?" He shifted on the rotating stool, realizing that he was about to be roped into something as well.

"You know my mother, don't you? Mary Evelyn Bennett, the librarian?"

He nodded slowly. It seemed safe enough to confirm this fact.

"Of course you do. I remember seeing you there when you were small. My girls are older than you, but I always chatted with the other mothers while my girls looked for books to check out."

Rob set down some of the change to leave a tip, putting the rest in his wallet and standing to slide the wallet into his back pocket. As he has hoped, this prompted Lucy to get to the point.

"Mom just won a grant to put in a mural on the side of the library building, the side that faces the empty lot that's all full of scrub brush, between the library and the church. You know where I'm talking about?"

He considered saying he had no idea, but he just couldn't bring himself to lie to her. He nodded again despite the sense of impending doom.

"There's some money available in the budget for new plantings, but she doesn't even know where to begin, that lot is such a mess. Do you think you might be able to swing by and give her some advice? She really needs to talk to an expert."

Rob breathed an internal sigh of relief. Advice he could do. He didn't have time to take on a big project—particularly a free one—but he could offer a little advice, especially for Ms. Bennett.

"Why don't I swing by there after work today and see what she's dealing with?"

"That's wonderful of you, sweetheart. I really appreciate it. I'll give her a call and let her know you're coming."

Another customer called for Lucy's attention, and Rob took the opportunity to escape. As he walked out to his truck, he wondered if Kat would be helping with this same project. He had no intention of getting sucked into something big, but if she were involved, maybe he could volunteer a few hours here and there after work. If they happened to cross paths, well, then that was just good luck. He slid into the truck with a smile, started the motor, and turned up the volume on the radio. Today was going to be a good day.

CHAPTER TWO

KAT CLOSED THE FILE AND LEANED BACK IN HER LEATHER CHAIR, stretching her arms high above her head. Her spine cracked a few times in protest and her stomach rumbled. She should take stretch breaks more often, but hated to interrupt the flow when she was on a roll. Leaning her head to the left and then to the right, she wiggled her feet back into her work shoes and grabbed the blazer from the back of her chair.

Definitely time for lunch.

A quick glance at the antique clock on the credenza told her that lunchtime had long since passed. RJ, her upstairs office tenant, semi-colleague, and friend, had knocked off for the day a few hours before, taking advantage of his light client load to squeeze in extra sailing time before the fall weather made it impossible. She should have taken a break then, at a normal lunch hour, but she had wanted to finish drafting her report. Two hours had gone by in a blink.

At least Lucy's would still be open, and she had missed the lunch rush. She snorted to herself as she headed toward the door. Lunch rush. As if she ever had to wait more than five minutes, even during tourist season. It was one of the perks of leaving the city behind and setting up shop in a small town.

She slipped out the front door of her office, the bell jangling a cheery farewell. No need to lock up. Lucy's was literally next door. In the unlikely event that a client dropped by, Kat would see them coming through the front windows.

"I saved your seat," said Lucy with a smile when Kat entered the quirky café. Lucy had gone a little overboard on the lake-themed decor, the walls crowded with anchors, porthole mirrors, intricate knots, and photos and artwork featuring the lake. All of it for sale, of course. Lucy was no dummy, and this was, after all, a tourist town.

Kat slid into her usual spot at the end of the lunch counter. From this vantage point she could survey the street, keep an eye on her front door, and surreptitiously listen in on the police scanner. Lucy's husband, Frank, was a retired police chief who liked to keep tabs on what was going on in town. He had a small outpost at the far end of the counter, over by the kitchen, where he monitored the scanner. He gave her a nod in lieu of hello.

"Any excitement today?"

He shook his head. "Quiet day. Always settles down after Labor Day, once all the tourists are gone and the kids are back in school."

Kat still wasn't all that comfortable around police officers, but Frank was retired and didn't ask for much in the way of interaction. Her therapist, years ago, had told her that her visceral reaction to law enforcement might never completely go away, but she could learn to moderate her response with calming techniques and with repeated low-threat interactions. She still experienced plenty of tense interactions because of her work, but you couldn't get much more low-threat than this.

"Usual?" asked Lucy. Always energetic, she nearly crackled with it today.

"Yes, please."

Kat supposed she should change it up every now and then, but she liked her chopped salad with chicken. Why risk disappointment when you could have a sure thing every time? When Lucy brought the salad a moment later, Kat dug in.

"So I hear you're going to help with the library project."

There was a reason that Lucy knew all the gossip in town. When things weren't too busy, and even sometimes when they were, she loved to chat with the customers. Perhaps a better word would be interrogate. In this case, Kat wasn't sure how to respond, given that her mouth was full of lettuce, so she shrugged and nodded.

"I'm so glad they're finally going to clear out that empty lot. It's been a mess for as long as I can remember. And this muralist from Chicago sounds fabulous. You should google him. He's an architect who does mural projects on the side. Make sure you find an article with a picture. His work looks amazing, and so does he. As far as I can tell, he's single." At Kat's raised eyebrow, Lucy grinned. "Doesn't hurt to look, and honestly, I don't mind screening candidates for you." Kat rolled her eyes, still crunching away on her salad, and Lucy continued to chatter. "And it's not just the mural. There's going to be a garden, too, and outdoor seating. It will be a lot of work, but it will be worth it."

Kat nodded. She really didn't know what to say. If she agreed too enthusiastically, Lucy would try to recruit her to do more than just make phone calls. It seemed safer to focus on the salad.

"I'm glad you're going to help," said Lucy, reading Kat's mind. "They'll need all kinds of help for the garden. Not much grant money for that part of the project, just volunteers. Dora's helping my mother with recruiting, which is wonderful. Hard to say no to Dora. I bet she gets all three of her girls to help. Maybe that RJ, too, now that he's dating Tessa."

It was easy to forget that Mary Evelyn, the librarian, was Lucy's mother. They did have a similar build, both of them on the short side, trim without any extra padding, but Mary Evelyn fit the librarian stereotype to a tee, while Lucy looked like she might be a biker chick in her spare time. Mary Evelyn had to be in her seventies now, and her fluffy curls had gone gray over the years. Her wardrobe was classic librarian, featuring cardigans and reading glasses on a silver chain around her neck. Lucy, somewhere in the neighborhood of fifty, wore a uniform of jeans, black boots, and sassy T-shirts. (Today's said "Bookmarks are for quitters"—clearly a gift from her mother.) Her long hair was dyed a fierce red, for now. The color changed on a regular basis.

"I'm really just making a few phone calls."

Lucy clucked at her. "You should get out there and get your hands dirty. You spend too much time indoors. Don't think I don't notice. Working from first thing in the morning until late at night, forgetting to eat lunch most of the time. Girl your age should have a life. Friends. Not just clients."

"I love my job."

Kat's protest sounded weak, and not just because she had salad in her mouth again. Lucy may as well have been channeling Kat's own inner voice. Now that her business was stable, her total lack of social life had become glaringly obvious. With her law school friends scattered to various parts of the country, Kat spent her (admittedly limited) downtime curled up on the couch watching Netflix. Over the last few years, she'd allowed work to fill every empty nook and cranny of her world, leaving room for little else. It had been a simple and effective way to build her practice, but watching people her age pair up and settle down, she had started to realize that she was lonely.

"I know you do, sweetie, or you wouldn't be doing it, and the kiddos certainly need you. But if you burn out, who will look after them?"

Kat stabbed her salad and took another large bite, declining to answer Lucy's question. She was nowhere near burnout. Lucy gave her a measuring look and then went to get a wet cloth to wipe down the counter. They would be closing soon.

"I'm just saying, it's not healthy to work as much as you do. Why not go help at the library? Get a little sunshine. Meet some new people."

A part of her actually wanted to do it. It had been years since she had her hands in the dirt. Did she even own a pair of ratty jeans anymore? But her caseload wasn't going to magically take care of itself. Each case represented a child who needed her help. She wasn't going to let them down just so that she could catch her breath.

"I wish I had the time to spare," she said. It was the only diplomatic thing she could think of. "Sounds like a cool project."

"You think about it," said Lucy. She wasn't one to give up easily. "Maybe you can make the time."

Kat finished her salad as quickly as she could and escaped back to the sanctuary of her office.

By the time Rob finished work, it was after four, and the library closed at five. He had planned on swinging by the house for a quick shower, but Ms. Bennett would just need to deal with his dusty, dirty self.

Rob couldn't remember the last time he had set foot inside the library. Maybe the year he started his business? He remembered checking out some how-to books about business setup and taking a free night class on how to build a website. Come to think of it, he should probably update his website—or at least make sure it was still working.

He spotted Ms. Bennett immediately. She hadn't changed a

bit, except maybe that her fluffy cloud of hair was more gray now than brown. She was still short, probably no taller than his armpit, and currently occupied with a young customer. He hung back, unsure of whether he should step off the all-weather entry mat and onto the otherwise clean tile floor of the entryway.

She finished and waved him over. He pointed at his boots. Taking one look at the dried mud, she nodded, holding up a hand to let him know he should wait. He stayed where he was as she came out from behind the desk and joined him by the door.

"Rob Murray, I am so glad you're here."

Her enthusiasm made him wonder exactly what Lucy had promised regarding his involvement, and he prepared himself for a lot of backpedaling.

"Good to see you, too, Ms. Bennett."

She gave him a sharp look, and if she had had a ruler handy, he got the sense she would have rapped his knuckles.

"It's Mary Evelyn. I thought we covered this years ago."

"Yes, ma'am."

At that she sighed and shook her head.

"Lucy said you needed some landscape advice, I'm happy to do what I can to help. I should warn you, though, my schedule is tight."

She did the classic librarian finger-wag. "Now, Rob, you need to make time for community projects. It's good for business."

Lots of things would be good for business, but there were only so many hours in a day. He needed to focus on doing excellent work and keeping clients happy, which would lead to referrals, which would lead to more business. This didn't leave a lot of time for volunteering.

Ms. Bennett—Mary Evelyn—caught the attention of another member of the library staff and indicated that she would be going outside. She then gave a stern look to two teenage girls giggling in front of the romance novels. It occurred to Rob that she was probably killer at charades.

"Let me show you what we're planning," she said, leading him outside.

The street in front of the library sloped downhill, gradually revealing the foundation of the building as they approached the empty lot next door. The lower level of the library included several windows that looked out onto the unused side lot, but it wasn't a pretty view. He would guess that the lot was about half an acre, plenty of space for a nice little park, but choked with scrub brush, weeds, and a few invasive tree species. There was one large oak toward the back of the lot, but otherwise not much worth saving. The sidewalk along the street was new and in good shape, but the retaining wall along the back edge, separating the vacant lot from the small cottages on the rise above, was not. He could see only bits and pieces of it, but what he saw did not look good. The right side of the lot bordered the back side of the church.

"What do you know about the project so far?" asked Mary Evelyn. "I don't want to bore you."

"Basically nothing," said Rob. "Lucy said something about a mural."

"That's how it started. I was inspired last year by a photo series showing urban art installations. The work was just so creative and unique. I immediately began researching how we could do something similar here. Not that we're urban, of course, but that doesn't mean we can't be creative. The village has this great little piece of land next door, and it's just going to waste. It could be a real asset to the community—with a little work."

She paused, and he realized she was waiting for a response. "Of course," he murmured, and she nodded briskly.

"I applied for a few grants and won a big one." Both her

voice and her expression were smug. "It was very exciting. Now we just need to make it happen."

Another pause, so he nodded. How in the world had she won a grant without a complete plan?

"We've secured the services of a muralist from Chicago. His work is good, and he always makes sure to involve the community in the design process." Some of Rob's concern must have shown on his face because she quickly moved to reassure him. "Don't worry. I budgeted for improvements to the lot, but I'll admit that I was trying to make the project cost come in under the maximum grant amount. I'll need your help to estimate the actual cost and amount of work required." She smiled up at him, her excitement contagious. "Even if you don't have time to do any of the work yourself, I know you have the right skills to help me make a real plan."

He nodded slowly, surveying the site again.

"I can tell you now, it's going to take a lot of work."

"I know," she said. She didn't sound concerned at all. "My Lucy is already working on volunteers and donations for me. We'll sort it out."

He almost asked about Kat before catching himself. The last thing he wanted to do was alert the gossip circuit that he was interested. They hadn't spoken in years, and he honestly had no idea if she was anything like the girl he remembered, before her parents died and she had basically disappeared. On the other hand, if he didn't ask, he might miss an opportunity to finally cross paths with her. He settled on an indirect question.

"Who have you recruited so far?"

Mary Evelyn had to think about it for a minute. "Mostly the garden club members, couple of folks from the bridge club. I've got Kat—Do you know Kat Rodriguez?—working on some teenagers for me, and I'm hoping that the Mom-n-Tots will help with the finishing touches."

Rob was pretty sure he had kept his poker face on when Mary Evelyn asked about Kat, but she was a sharp lady. The safest course would be to change the subject completely.

"Have you had a chance to talk with the church about the project?" he asked. "It's literally in their backyard. They might have some suggestions, or at least some opinions."

Mary Evelyn's eyes slid away from his. "I don't go to that church."

Rob waited for her to explain how that would prevent her from having a conversation with someone there, but the moment stretched into an awkward silence.

"Maybe we can hunt up a church member to act as a liaison," he offered, stopping short of volunteering to chase them down himself.

Mary Evelyn nodded, but she didn't specifically say she would take on the task. Rob decided that one of them needed to be clear.

"I'm happy to help you with the landscape plan, but I just want to reiterate that my company can't take on the actual work. Our schedule just won't allow it. Are you sure you'll be able to find the help you need?"

She patted his shoulder, and he felt like he was five again. "Don't worry. These things have a way of working out."

CHAPTER THREE

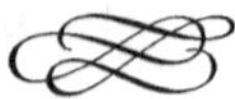

It didn't take Kat long to track down the right contact person for juvenile programs up at county. Of course it turned out to be Joan Haverford. Small world was an understatement in this case. Joan had been the social worker in charge of Kat's own case ten years ago. As Kat had aged out of the foster system and fumbled through the transition to adulthood, Joan had been her rock, and Kat had tried never to let her down. Over the past few years, since Kat had started her practice and begun to accept guardian *ad litem* work from the county, she and Joan had worked together on more than a few cases. Joan had recently been promoted, and as it turned out, she now ran all the juvenile programs for the county.

"Kat, honey, I'm so glad you called. I've just lost the community service coordinator for your area, and I could really use a hand."

"Oh, no. I'm not volunteering." Kat had already overcommitted in terms of her caseload. No way could she add more to her plate, no matter how much she might enjoy it. "I'm just trying to connect you with a group here in town that has a potential project."

"And that's exactly what an area coordinator does. You would be amazing. It's not a full-time gig, just an add-on." Kat made some protest noises, but Joan pretended not to hear. "Just think about it. You're great at the casework, but this would help to counterbalance the stress, get you out into the community."

"Joan, my caseload right now—"

"And who knows? You might meet someone."

Joan had been happily married for more than twenty years, and she had made it her personal mission to scout bachelors for Kat so that she, too, could one day enjoy marital bliss. Unfortunately, Joan's idea of an eligible bachelor did not line up well with Kat's. She had been on several painful blind dates before she learned that the best way to avoid them was to give the impression that she was already dating someone else.

"I let my caseload get too big, to be honest, and I need to cut back. But it's not all work all the time. I have some new friends, and I'm sure I'll meet a great guy through them."

As cover stories go, it wasn't quite as good as an actual boyfriend, but she didn't even have a semi-recent date that she could embellish. Their overlapping professional circles were too small for her to make something up, to say nothing of the fact that she wouldn't be comfortable lying to a friend. Joan just wanted her to be happy.

So instead of creating a fictional love life, Kat exaggerated what passed for her social life. She felt only the smallest twinge of guilt classifying the triplets as her "new friends." Technically, they had known each other since high school, but at least now they were on speaking terms. Sure, Callie and Tessa had scooped up the only remotely eligible bachelors in town, but there was still hope of making her own romantic connection. Right?

Joan's sigh echoed through the phone. "I hope you do meet someone—and soon! And I completely understand how caseloads can get out of control. I'll keep looking for a new coordinator. If you think of anybody, will you let me know?"

"Of course." Kat held back her own sigh of relief.

"Tell this community group to give me a call and we'll see if we can work out a schedule for the kids. I'm hoping Jack will be available to supervise the shifts."

"Jack?"

"Jack Emerson. He's a police officer there in town."

Kat felt her shoulders tense and forced them to relax. "Right. I know Jack," she said. "Are the community service projects usually supervised by police?"

"Sometimes. Depends on the town. Small town like that, there aren't a ton of people available, so I'll take what I can get. Jack is a little stiff with the kids, but his heart's in the right place."

Kat wondered just how much of a disciplinarian Jack would be. Unless she was ready to volunteer, though, she should keep her concerns to herself.

"You should take a look at Jack," said Joan. "He's about your age, and I'm pretty sure he's single."

The chances of her dating a cop were somewhere between zero and hell freezing over, but Joan didn't need to know how much baggage she still lugged around.

"I'll be sure to check him out," said Kat lightly, then quickly moved to change the subject. "So how do you like the new job? Do you miss the casework?"

Joan was quiet for a moment before responding. "I do and I don't," she finally answered. "I was really getting burned out, so a change was definitely in order. I was hoping the new job would involve more kid time, but it's a lot of office work and time on the phone with adults, coordinating things."

"I'm sorry."

"No need to be sorry. I needed the change, and now that I'm not so exhausted I've been volunteering with kids on the weekends. Change is a good thing." Kat wasn't sure who exactly Joan was trying to convince.

They chatted for a few more minutes before Kat signed off. "Thanks again for your help, Joan."

"Anytime. And if you change your mind, let me know. We could really use your help."

"I will."

Kat hung up the phone and rubbed her temples. The tension headache had been brewing all morning, and she could tell by now that it wasn't going to let go. She stood and rolled her shoulders. Definitely time for another break. The antique clock clicked over to the hour and gently chimed five times. Some people actually left their offices at this time of day. They might go home, or to the gym, or to meet friends for dinner. Kat had never really learned how to make that work. Instead, she planned to put in another few hours of work followed by a late dinner at home with Netflix to keep her company.

Starting the brew cycle on a fresh cup of coffee, Kat stared out her window at the view that had sold her on this space. She could see all the way down the boulevard to the waterfront park and the lake beyond. So soon after Labor Day, the trees and the grass were still lush, without even a hint of fall color. The ancient cottonwood, her favorite tree in the whole town, stood proudly in the center of the park, at least double the size of the rest of the trees scattered throughout the open space. Tourists strolled along the boulevard, enjoying the last days of summer. She could even see boats out on the lake. Did nobody have a job anymore?

A knock on the door broke her grumpy train of thought.

"RJ, what are you doing here so late?" The man treated his job like a hobby, not a career.

He shook his head. "Poor planning on my part, or I would have been on the lake all afternoon. There may still be time for a quick sail before sunset. Want to come?"

"No thanks," she said, feeling the disappointment keenly. Not that she wanted to be a third wheel with RJ and Tessa, but one of these days she just wanted to say yes to something. Anything. "Too much work, too little time."

"Don't forget to eat," he called over his shoulder as he headed out the door.

"I won't." Her answer was cut short by the door closing.

As she returned to her desk, she could hear her old therapist's voice echoing in her head. *Your choices are your own. If you want to control your life, you need to make your choices. Don't let anybody else make them for you.*

She growled in the back of her throat. She loved her choices. She had made great choices. Once she cleared out the backlog, everything would be fine.

Later that night, finally showered and fed, Rob sat down to catch up on work email and the August billing. He had kept up with client phone calls during the day but had ignored anything coming in on his personal line. Fifty-fifty the messages were from a telemarketer or from one of his buddies giving him shit for working all the time. Either way, those were not messages he needed to hear right now.

He needed to find a way to grow the business, one that didn't cost much money. He was barely keeping his small crew occupied, and if any of his bigger equipment failed, he'd be in trouble. It felt good to send out the bills each month, but the grand total barely covered his payroll and expenses. At some point he needed to make enough to invest back into the business. He squeezed the back of his neck, trying to get at the semipermanent knot right where his neck met his right shoulder. If he could just make it through the fall, the end-of-season cleanup would give the business enough of a boost to make it through the winter.

As he was about to close out for the day, a new message appeared in his inbox—a reply to a quote he had provided to a prospective client. He couldn't help the surge of optimism. It was a big job. It would be a big win.

Only it wasn't.

The potential client had decided to go with a different company, one not that much bigger or older than his own. He hadn't lost on price, though. He had lost because the other company was "better known." What did that even mean? Had they sent out marketing postcards recently? Radio ads? Or had they just done work for a friend?

He slammed a hand on the desk before reining in his frustration and closing his email for the night. A polite and professional reply would have to wait until the morning. He was in no frame of mind to do it now.

As he reviewed the schedule for the rest of the week, his thoughts kept circling back to that phrase "better known." He could barely stay on top of all the different aspects of his business. How the hell was he supposed to do more? Marketing postcards and radio ads took both time and money. He could find time, somehow, but there just wasn't money to spare. Unless...

He needed to talk with Mary Evelyn again.

Kat woke up gasping for air. Disoriented, she groped for the alarm and managed to hit the snooze button on top. She leaned back against the mountain of pillows and waited for her heart rate to go back to normal and her breathing to slow.

She had fallen asleep working again. The bedside lamp was still on, and her bed was covered with files. A few had slid onto the floor, the enclosed papers spilling out. She would need to make sure they all ended up back in the right file, in the right order, before she did anything else.

The alarm had caught her in the middle of a dream. She tried to capture the details before it faded. Something about a garden. She had been in her "secret garden" from when she was very small. No, that wasn't quite right. In the dream, she had been a part of the garden itself, somehow both the gardener and the garden. She had hacked away at deadwood so that new growth could sprout, but she had felt every single cut. The logical part of her brain knew that the ache in her shoulder came from sleeping in an awkward position all night, but as she massaged the cranky muscle, she remembered the cuts from the dream, and the sap running down her side.

Once, when she was about twelve, she had ridden her bike out to the house where she and Mom had lived before, when her first stepfather was alive. Finding nobody home, she had crept around to the backyard and peeked in the kitchen windows. The new family had changed a lot inside. They had covered the colorful kitchen walls with bright white, and the refrigerator with letter magnets and photos. A high chair sat in the corner and a booster on one of the kitchen chairs. In the backyard, they had added a swing set and ripped out the small raised garden that had once belonged to Kitty.

In that moment, Kat had understood that nothing lasts forever. Not people. Not places. Not even memories. She had left before the new images could overwrite the old, and she had never gone back.

She hadn't thought of her "secret garden" in years. Her stepfather had created the planting bed for her after she had read the book, and she had tried so hard to grow flowers in it. Sadly, her stepfather's green thumb had not rubbed off on her at all, and he had died before they could give it another season.

The garden of her dream had been much larger than her

real-life garden plot, but in the logic of dreams, Kat had understood that they were the same garden. If she knew him better, she could have asked Kevin Archer, the local school psychologist, to help her analyze the dream. With understanding would come control, and maybe she would be able to shake the lingering sense of dread. But she didn't know him that well. The loneliness pinched again, and she pushed it back. She would just have to deal with it herself.

She slid carefully from beneath the covers and collected her scattered work files. Only when they were reassembled and neatly stacked on her dresser did she head for the bathroom in the hope of showering away the grit in her eyes and the fog on her brain.

As she went through her morning routine, she was struck by how automatic it had become. Turn on the shower, set out the towel, pajamas in the hamper, quick check on the scale, check the water temp. Ready. Shower, working top down. Shampoo. Conditioner. Facial wash. Body wash. Extra-hot rinse. Shot of cold water to wake her up, then shut it off and towel dry, finally feeling alert.

Wrap the towel around the hair and move to the vanity. Start on the far left, with toothpaste and toothbrush. Pea-size squeeze of paste onto the toothbrush, then flip the two-minute timer and brush the teeth. Next in line, cooling toner and SPF moisturizer, deodorant, makeup. Check the weather. Get dressed. Dry hair. Pack briefcase. Repeat ad infinitum.

Kat stared at her reflection in the mirror as she brushed her teeth, wondering when her life had switched over to autopilot. Unless something changed, she would be doing exactly the same routine twenty, even thirty years from now. She grimaced, struck by the thought that Kitty, the girl she had once been, would not be impressed by the Kat she had become. Oh, she would have loved the Kat that she showed the world. That Kat was strong and brave and ready to stand up for herself, just as

Kitty had hoped. Sadly, her long-ago vision of the future had focused on the external, never realizing that she could achieve all those things and still feel hollow on the inside.

Her inner snark suggested that maybe she should stop wallowing in self-pity and get a cat or two so that she could have someone to talk to. Or maybe a goldfish. She spat out toothpaste on a laugh. God, she was starting to lose it.

As she stepped out the front door of her tiny town house, she noticed that all the landscaping around her unit was well-tended and perfectly groomed, each plant neatly separated from the next—exactly the kind of garden she hated. How had she never noticed before? Of course, it wasn't as if she had time to do anything about it, and given her track record with house-plants, if she were left in charge of her own garden, her thumb of death would most likely kill everything. Better—and safer—to leave the gardening to someone else, even if she didn't like the results.

During the short walk to work, she tried to be mindful, as Doc Archer had advised on more than one occasion. She tried to appreciate the humidity, even as her blouse began to stick to her back. Six months from now she would be slogging through the snow and wishing she could fly away to somewhere warm just like this.

Kat ducked into Lucy's to pick up her morning coffee. She would brew her own second cup. Much like gardening, however, her coffee-brewing skills needed work. Lucy did a far better job.

"So did you think about it?" asked Lucy. She had seen Kat coming and had the coffee all ready to go. It took a few seconds and a hit of caffeine before Kat decoded what Lucy was talking about.

"You mean the project?" she asked. "I had a great talk with Joan over at county, and she's going to assign Mary Evelyn a group of community service kids."

Lucy snorted. "That was the easy part. I already heard about that. The question is whether or not you're going to get your hands dirty."

Kat took a second slow sip of her coffee while scrambling for a diplomatic response.

"I'm glad I could connect everyone, but my caseload is overflowing. I just can't make time for new projects."

Lucy did not look like she approved. "Well, that's your decision, I suppose, but you know what they say."

"What do they say?"

"All work and no play means a girl never gets laid."

Lucy cackled and wandered down the counter to refill mugs, leaving Kat choking on her coffee. When she had recovered, she left her money on the counter and fled to the haven of her office.

Kat was on her third cup of coffee when RJ finally rolled in. He lived no more than five blocks from the office (in the opposite direction of her own place), but he hadn't walked. Tessa was dropping him off. Their goodbye kiss in the car lasted much longer than necessary, given the fact that they were in full view of both Kat and the breakfast crowd next door. Not that they cared. They were so caught up in each other that they didn't even notice their audience.

The fierce surge of jealousy took Kat by surprise. It's not like she was attracted to RJ. She had written him off as a candidate ages ago. She didn't want *him*, but longed for what he had found with Tessa—only maybe not so wild and overwhelming. She wanted the calm and orderly version, someone strong and steady with a predictable nine-to-five job who paid his bills on time. Someone who would help her draw some boundaries between work and life. Someone who wanted to build a life with her, who loved her like crazy. Was that too much to ask?

The bell gave a happy little jangle as RJ walked in, a satisfied grin on his face and an irritating spring in his step. He paused in the doorway to her office before heading to his own space upstairs.

"Kat, you're looking lovely today, as always." She gave him a look that had him raising his hands in self-defense and backpedaling. "Not feeling lovely, apparently. You okay?"

"Too much work, too little time." It felt like she'd been saying that a lot lately.

"I hear you're going to help with the library project. That's great." He leaned on the doorframe, apparently in the mood to chat. "Tessa and I might help out, too, on the weekends we don't have regattas. I hear even Mel is going to be drafted."

"I just connected Mary Evelyn with the volunteer coordinator up at county. She should have a work crew of sullen teenagers in no time."

RJ didn't bother to hide his amusement. "That's a recipe for disaster. Mary Evelyn has no patience for 'young hooligans.'"

"What are you talking about? I hung out there all the time when I was a teenager, and it was fine."

"Let me guess. You were quiet and respectful and hid out in a corner reading a book."

Kat wasn't sure why his quick assessment embarrassed her, but it was spot-on, and she couldn't help feeling defensive. "The library was a safe haven. Nobody bothered me there."

"Well, let's just say that summer kids looking for air-conditioning and a hangout away from parents were not quite so welcome. We were more interested in talking than reading, although we did find some very instructive books about sex. Ms. Bennett kicked us out as soon as we pinged her noise meter."

"Huh," said Kat. "I never saw her do that. It's hard to imagine, actually."

"If she likes you so much, maybe you should be there the

first time the kids show up to work, just to make sure it goes smoothly."

"But I'm not—I don't have that kind of time."

"So you make time," said RJ with a shrug. "You would only need to stop by to make sure they get off on the right foot. Dora told Tessa that Jack Emerson would help to supervise the kids. Do you know him? He was in school the same time as Tessa, which would also have been the same time as you. He's a local cop now. He'll keep them out of Mary Evelyn's hair."

Pushing away from the doorframe, RJ took a step toward the back stairs leading up to his office. Before he disappeared, he caught the doorframe with his hand and ducked his head back into her office. "Think of the children."

He was gone before she could throw something at his head. Stupid RJ with his clichés and his knack for pushing her buttons. He knew the kids were her weakness, and now that he had planted the seed in her head, she couldn't squash it. She imagined Mary Evelyn fussing over the kids who came in to go to the bathroom and get a drink and cool off, because the next few weeks of September were bound to be warm and humid. They would inevitably track mud on the carpet, which would irritate her. She pictured Jack ordering them around. He had always seen the world in black and white, and might not have much patience for teenagers pushing boundaries. The two adults could easily—if unintentionally—suck all the fun out of an otherwise promising community service project. And then the kids would stop showing up, and then they would get in trouble for blowing off community service, and the whole thing would go off the rails.

The universe was nudging her to get involved in this project, and she wasn't sure how to refuse. She wasn't sure if she *wanted* to refuse, which surprised her more than anything else. Work had been overwhelming lately. She had taken on way too many cases. She had planned on devoting herself to work—and nothing else—until she had cleared the backlog and could set better boundaries. But a part of her was screaming for a break, for anything other than work. This must be what burnout felt like, and she had to admit she was not a fan.

Kat drank the last of her coffee and decided to follow her gut on this one, even if it wasn't the practical choice. As a concession to the reality of her caseload, Kat sternly warned herself that there would be no more Netflix until the backlog was cleared, and there might be times when work took priority over community service. As long as she was there for the first session or two, just to help get things rolling, she could play the mediator and make sure everyone started off on the right foot. Hoping she was making the right decision, Kat picked up the phone to call Mary Evelyn.

CHAPTER FOUR

After work, Rob stopped by the library to talk with Mary Evelyn again. He was a little cleaner today, so he didn't have to worry about dirty boots ruining the carpet. Mary Evelyn was busy checking out a giant stack of books for a kid who couldn't be more than eight.

"Back so soon?" she chirped when she finished with her small customer. "I can only hope this means you're ready to get started."

"Maybe," he said. "I have some questions for you first."

She planted her hands on the counter. "Fire away."

"Is it okay if I publicize my involvement in the project?" he asked.

"I assumed you would." She seemed surprised by the question.

He hadn't realized his shoulders were tense until they relaxed on hearing her answer. Was it really this easy?

"In fact," she continued, "I have some volunteers who are going to work on publicity for the whole project, and they're open to ideas. We need to build some buzz so that the unveiling can be a big event."

This was good. This was really good.

"I can definitely help with the garden design," he said. "I'm concerned about installation. Do you have enough volunteers to help with the hands-on work?"

"Maybe," answered Mary Evelyn, cocking her head as she thought about it. "I've just secured a group of teenagers who need to do community service. Not sure how many there will be. The garden club is on board, and a few individual volunteers. One way or another, we'll have a bunch of helping hands."

"It's a start." He'd prefer the garden club over a bunch of teenagers who didn't want to be there, but he'd take what he could get.

Before he could ask another question, the arrival of another person caught Mary Evelyn's attention. Rob turned to see a police officer approaching them. The familiar face had him searching his mind for a name. Jack something. They had been in high school at the same time, but Jack had been a few years older, maybe a junior or senior when Rob was a freshman.

"Jack, you know Rob Murray, don't you?" asked Mary Evelyn.

Jack shook his head, then offered a hand. "Don't think we've met. Jack Emerson."

Rob accepted the handshake, unsurprised that Jack didn't remember him. Seniors didn't pay much attention to the underclassmen, especially quiet kids like Rob. He remembered Jack as an athlete—maybe on the track team? Rob hadn't had much time for sports. Too many chores. Jack still had the wiry build of a runner. Rob squeezed his hand gently so as not to hurt him.

"Rob is going to do the landscape design for my mural project, and he'll need help from the community service crew. Any news on that front? Are you still their supervisor?"

"Haven't found a new area coordinator yet," he said, "but I don't mind doing it. They're not much trouble."

"If you say so," said Mary Evelyn. "I'm sure Rob can help."

Rob needed to squash that idea immediately. "Herding teenagers isn't exactly my specialty," he said. Jack laughed, but Rob wasn't kidding. There was a reason he spent most of his time with plants.

"I'm not sure it's part of my skill set either," said Jack, "but the uniform helps."

"I'm working on recruiting more adults," said Mary Evelyn. "The more experience you have to balance out the youthful exuberance, the better."

Rob almost asked if Kat was one of those adults, but he bit his tongue before the words could fall out. As far as he knew from his eavesdropping, Kat had held the line at making a few phone calls. Besides, he was not getting involved with this project as an excuse to maybe, possibly run into Kat. Well, that wasn't the only reason. This was first and foremost a business decision, a way to generate some free (except for his labor) publicity. Instead of asking about Kat, he asked about the kids.

"Do you think they'll be willing to get their hands dirty?" He had heard a lot of griping about "kids these days" and wasn't sure how much was true and how much was normal grumpy old people.

Jack shrugged. "It beats picking up litter, which is what they usually get stuck doing. They'll complain, but I think they'll actually prefer working on a project."

"I would," said Mary Evelyn. "Litter is like laundry. It never ends." She reached for her desk calendar, placing it up on the counter and angling it so Rob and Jack could see it, too. "Rob, what's the soonest you might need help?"

"We could get started clearing the lot anytime. It's a big lot and will take some time. While that's going on, I can get started on the design."

Mary Evelyn turned her attention to Jack. "How soon do you think we'll have our work crew?"

"Could be as early as next week. County usually likes to wait until the kids are settled into their fall class schedules before sending them out."

"That's sensible," said Mary Evelyn. "And how many hours a week should we plan on?"

"It varies," he answered with another shrug. "I've only supervised a handful of groups, but they usually meet two or three times a week for a couple of hours."

That was actually a decent amount of time. Even with a bunch of slackers, they could have the lot cleared in a matter of weeks.

"Rob, do you think you could be here for the first session or two, so you could tell us all what to do to clear the lot? That way we could continue the work when you're not available."

"With a little advance warning, I should be able to make it work." He mentally skimmed through his schedule for the next week or two. "We usually wrap up by four p.m. What time does the high school get out?"

Mary Evelyn looked to Jack for an answer. "They release just before three," he said.

"We could probably rearrange a few things so that I'm available by three on the day you start. I'll just need a heads-up."

"Done," said Mary Evelyn. "I can't tell you how much I appreciate your willingness to help."

"Happy to do it."

Rob ignored the twinge of hope, or possibly guilt. Yes, the project would be good for his business, but he would be lying if he didn't admit, at least in the privacy of his own mind, that Kat's possible involvement made it very easy to say yes.

Kat liked to drive fast, but she pushed her own limits trying to get to the library before closing as she had promised. The day had absolutely crushed her. Nothing had gone her way, which for Kat meant that things hadn't turned out well for her kids. In one particularly wrenching case, a child was returned to a placement that Kat knew in her gut wasn't safe, but she hadn't had enough evidence to persuade the judge. She couldn't stop ruminating on it, searching for the words that might have changed the judge's mind.

As she flew down the hill into town, only remembering to slow down at the last second, Kat acknowledged the need to calm down. Deep, mindful breathing was not cutting it today. Sure, it helped, but not enough. What she really needed was to smell the trees, something her mother had taught her when she was very small. Trees had calmed her tantrums as a child and provided much-needed comfort as a teenager. The technique worked best barefoot, but in a pinch she could do it with shoes on.

Kat parked more than a block away from the library, on one of the side streets lined with hundred-year-old oaks. She slid out from behind the wheel, grabbed her purse, and shut the car door. Glancing up and down the street, Kat confirmed that she was alone, or as alone as you can be in the middle of town. Nobody was out in their front yards or walking down the sidewalk. No cars in sight.

The deep shade beneath the oaks offered relief from the humid September heat. Closing her eyes, Kat inhaled deeply. She could smell the musty earth and the breeze from the lake, but not the trees. As she moved down the sidewalk toward the library, she stopped beside a sizable tree growing right next to the sidewalk, close enough for her to touch. She placed both hands on the bark, closed her eyes again, and breathed. Now she could smell it. Trees had their own scent, like dirt but older, and if you stood beneath the canopy of their leaves, their cool exhalations would float down over you.

Kat calmed herself beneath the trees for several more minutes, hoping that nobody was looking out their windows and thinking she was a weirdo. Kooky or not, this trick worked much better for her than regular old mindful breathing, and it offered the comfort of her mother's memory along with it.

After stepping back from the trunk, she headed toward the library. It was a good thing she wasn't meeting any of the kids today. Business suits and high heels created distance between teenagers and adults. They were also impractical for garden work. When the time came to meet the kids, she would be sure to change out of her work clothes.

Kat's heels clicked on the sidewalk as she approached the entrance. The all-weather carpet just inside the doors muffled her for a moment, but the clicking began again on the tile as she headed toward the circulation desk. Her view was blocked by two sets of male shoulders, one very broad and muscled, the other leaner and wearing a police uniform. Kat tensed at the sight of the uniform just as the floor beneath her feet changed from tile to carpet. One of her heels snagged in the pile, yanking her off balance. Before she fully realized what was happening, she was flying—or falling—heading directly toward the set of broad shoulders. She realized in a split second that she was going to tackle the poor man. Hoping he was steady on his feet, she grabbed those shoulders and hoped for the best.

To her surprise, he only stumbled a bit on impact, and miraculously neither of them ended up on the floor, although it took a bit of fumbling to sort themselves out. Her shoe had been left behind, well and truly stuck on the carpet, and her big toe hurt like hell from being yanked out of the shoe. She was unsteady on one bare foot and one high heel. He turned around and steadied her, strong hands gripping her by the shoulders until she could stand on her own.

For the millionth time, she thanked her lucky stars that she didn't blush. Then she took a small step back and looked up at her savior.

"Rob?"

"Kitty?"

They spoke at the same time, confusion on both of their faces. She shook her head and started over.

"It's Kat now. Nobody calls me Kitty anymore."

The Rob she remembered had changed in subtle ways. He had always been strong—farm chores will do that to a boy— but he had grown into those shoulders, his body solid where it had once been lanky. His face, too, had changed, the softness of youth replaced by harder angles and the five o'clock shadow of a grown man. His hair was still a sun-kissed brown, his skin tan from spending time outdoors, and his eyes a glowing chestnut with gold at the center. The shock of dissonance—past and present colliding in a single person—left her disoriented, like she had stumbled into an episode of *The Twilight Zone*.

Growing up, Rob had lived on a farm just outside of town. They had been neighbors, although the acres between their houses meant they didn't see each other very often. Later, when she had moved into town to live with stepfather number two, she and Rob had still ridden the same bus, still sat one behind the other. When things started to get bad, he was the only person who had noticed something was wrong.

"I heard you were back in town," he said. "Kept thinking I would run into you, but I never did."

He smiled slowly, and she could feel herself sliding backward into the morass of her past, so she let go of his shoulders and hobbled a few steps back on one shoe and one tiptoe. She needed the distance. Just seeing him made her feel twelve again, and powerless.

"I've been working a lot, getting my law practice up and running," she said in response to his comment. It was as much information for him as it was a reminder to herself that she wasn't that scared little girl anymore. "It does seem weird that we've never run into each other. I guess I don't get out much." The rote response, one she had used many times over the last few years, rolled off her tongue without revealing any of her inner unsteadiness.

"Me, either," he said ruefully. "Building a business takes a lot of time."

A distraction. Thank goodness. "What's your business?" She had always imagined he would take over the family farm.

"I'm a landscape architect," he answered. "I've converted the farm into a nursery."

"That's amazing." Kat shoved all her unsettled feelings into a mental closet and slammed the door, focusing on the man in front of her. She had changed, and so had he. The past was not relevant here.

He grinned and said, "It is pretty cool," but then his smile faded. "My parents still don't get it. Farming is all they know."

"Do they still live around here?"

"They retired to Arizona last year."

She had seen Rob with his parents at school functions, but she had never really met them. From the outside, his life had looked like a Norman Rockwell painting, and his parents had been two-dimensional representations of the perfect parents. They had never quite felt real to her.

"I'm not sure if their retirement is going to stick," he continued. "When you grow up farming, it can be really hard to sit around doing nothing. They do like the sunshine, though."

"Kat, I'm so glad you made it in time."

Kat nearly startled out of her skin. She had completely forgotten that they were standing in the middle of the library and that she was here to see Mary Evelyn.

"You know Jack Emerson, don't you?" asked Mary Evelyn, gesturing to the police officer beside her.

"Of course," murmured Kat. She smiled stiffly at Jack and didn't offer her hand.

"Kat," he said with a nod.

"You're working on the project, too?" asked Rob. She wasn't sure how to interpret his expression.

"I said I'd make sure the kids were off to a good start." Kat realized that she was still missing a shoe. She limped over to the edge of the carpet and yanked it free, slipping it on as gracefully as she could.

"We need all the help we can get," said Mary Evelyn. "I certainly can't be outside and inside at the same time."

"And I can't always control my work schedule," said Jack. "Kat, if you can cover when I can't make it, I'd really appreciate it."

"As would I," echoed Rob. He looked distinctly uncomfortable at the idea of managing teenagers.

"I'm sure I can be here for the first few sessions," said Kat. "We can figure out the schedule from there."

Mary Evelyn was needed at the checkout, so she shooed Rob, Jack, and Kat away from the circulation desk. "My goal today was to make sure the three of you connected in person. Now that's done, and I'm sure you all can take it from here."

Kat tilted her head to one side, considering Mary Evelyn's tactics and the fact that three very busy people had committed to help her out. "She's very effective at getting things done, isn't she?"

"I'm concerned that this is only the beginning," said Rob.

"One phone call," said Kat, shaking her head. "It's a very slippery slope."

"A little garden advice." Rob nodded in agreement. "Quick and easy."

Kat rubbed the crease on the middle of her forehead. "We'll have to—"

Jack's radio crackled, interrupting her train of thought.

"Sorry, guys, but I have to go. Thanks for your help with this. I'll let you know when I hear that the teenagers are ready to start."

"I should go, too," said Kat quickly. "Mountains of work to do."

Kat felt a twinge of guilt using Jack's exit as cover for her own. There really wasn't anywhere else she needed to be, but the thought of being alone with Rob sent her into a mild panic, so she made a run for it.

As she hurried out to her car, trying to shake the feeling of being twelve and terrified, she questioned how this could possibly work. She should back out now, before she was in too deep, but she was already halfway down the slippery slope and no remotely plausible excuses sprang to mind. Instead, it appeared she would have to enjoy the rest of the downward slide.

Rob walked slowly back to his truck. He still couldn't quite believe that he had just seen Kat in person. The whole episode felt too much like a dream. She had literally and figuratively knocked him off balance, and he would need a few minutes— maybe a few days—to find his equilibrium again.

It could have gone better. He had mentally rehearsed their first meeting an embarrassing number of times over the last couple of years, and in his head he had always sounded much more smooth. The imagined conversations had often ended with some kind of date. A coffee meeting. A lunch. Once or twice, he had imagined jumping straight to dinner. This was the kind of thing that came easily to other guys. He had watched them in action and wondered how they did it.

He headed home, acknowledging to himself that he couldn't blame work or chance for the fact that he and Kat hadn't crossed paths these past few years. Some part of him, buried deep, must have known he wasn't ready. He didn't want to screw up this second chance.

Their first meeting hadn't been a disaster, exactly, but she had certainly hustled out of there afterward and he wasn't sure why. Maybe she really did have a mountain of work to do. Maybe she had an appointment or a hot date. For all he knew, she hadn't thought about him from the moment she left town to the moment she'd almost tackled him. This was a mystery that would have to remain unsolved for the time being, because he sure as hell wasn't going to chase her down and ask her.

He also didn't plan on asking what had happened that long-ago night, or after she left town, or why she had never reached out—not once—to let him know she was okay.

As much as he wanted the answers, he suspected that asking the questions would only push her away. It would take time and patience to get to know the new Kat. Deep down, he felt like the same person that he'd always been, and yet he recognized that he wasn't the same dumb kid he'd been in high school. He had learned a lot over the years, and she probably had, too.

He could be patient.

The following evening, Kat toyed with her super-healthy, organic frozen dinner while she scanned the background information Joan had sent over. One of these years she needed to learn how to cook, but in the meantime, she would continue to alternate takeout with...whatever this was. She had called Joan in a panic earlier, after a sleepless night and a truckload of second thoughts, asking for more information about the group of community service kids.

Yesterday's run-in with Rob had sent her stumbling into the past, and she needed to get out of that headspace. It wasn't Rob's fault. The poor guy probably had no idea he had knocked her for an emotional loop just as much as she had nearly knocked him down physically. This was entirely her own problem. All it took was one look into those eyes and she was twelve again. He had always seen her, even when she tried to pretend everything was fine.

Years of therapy had gotten Kat to stable ground, and she had no intention of backsliding, which left her in a quandary. Was she better off working on this project, which meant dealing with Rob and her own reaction to him? Or was it smarter to step aside and avoid the problem completely?

Even as she laid out the alternatives in her mind, she knew the answer. If you go to enough therapy, you start to anticipate the questions, and you get to know the right answers. Sadly, avoidance is rarely the right answer, which was too bad, really, because she was really good at avoidance.

Still, she might have been able to talk herself into backing out, but she had made the mistake of reading through the background information. Now these kids had names and faces and stories. They were humans who needed someone in their corner. There was no way she was going to leave them to Mary Evelyn or Officer Jack or even Rob. If that made her a control freak, then so be it.

She looked through the pages from Joan again, committing their stories to memory. Nine kids. She could handle nine kids. It wasn't like there would be true casework involved, just supervision. A little gardening and a listening ear. Maybe a few phone calls to hook one of the kids up with a good after-school job or a babysitting gig. Something to keep them busy and out of trouble.

Mary Evelyn had tentatively scheduled them for Tuesdays and Thursdays after school and Saturday mornings. There would be additional volunteers from the community, mostly on the weekends, which would also be good for the kids. They could use all the social support they could get.

Henry and Charlie had both been suspended from the soccer team for the remainder of the season. Their idea of a prank had turned out to qualify as actual vandalism. She would bet that Henry, the junior, had talked freshman Charlie into it. What a way to start off the year.

Luna and Paola had been caught vaping in the bathroom and cutting class. In past years, this might have been a small-time offense, but the schools were cracking down hard on vaping, and the girls were repeat offenders from the previous year. She wondered what they needed to talk about so badly that they were willing to risk cutting class. Maybe they just needed to get away from the bullshit for a while.

Barb and Carolyn, angelic-looking identical twins, had been caught taking placement tests for each other. A note in their file said that the parents had requested community service, even though this was usually a school discipline issue. Bravo for the parents on that one, for asking for a real conse-quence rather than ranting at the principal that it was somehow the school's fault. Kat hoped the girls wouldn't be full of attitude. That would get annoying fast.

Elías, Alejandro, and Santiago made for an interesting trio. The budding hackers had circumvented the school's firewall in order to watch Netflix and YouTube during study halls. At least they hadn't been watching porn. She shook her head and laughed to herself. It wasn't all that different from her own high school experience. Pranks gone wrong. Smoking in the bath-room. Cutting class. Accessing forbidden (and therefore really interesting) materials. New tech, old tricks.

Despite her reservations about working with Rob, Kat was

looking forward to meeting the kids. It didn't look like there were any hard cases in the mix, just regular kids trying to figure things out. That didn't mean everything was fine—darker issues could lurk beneath the surface—but if nobody was torturing animals or threatening violence, she would count it as a win.

And Rob—well, he had exposed a weakness in her hard-won armor. Maybe the more she got to know grown-up Rob, the less she would feel like child-size Kitty around him. She had panicked and run away yesterday, but she was stronger than that. Next time she saw him, she wouldn't let the flashback feelings take her by surprise. She would acknowledge them, and then she would let them go, like a mature human being who had been to lots of therapy. No problem.

Kat took a hard look at her calendar for the next month and blocked out her Tuesday and Thursday afternoons and her Saturday mornings. She would need to reschedule only a couple of meetings to make it work. Her nights would include a little more work and a little less Netflix, but she didn't mind. For the first time in ages, she would be trying something new, and that alone made it worthwhile.

CHAPTER FIVE

MEL GOT BACK TO THE HOUSE AFTER A MUCH-NEEDED STAND-UP paddle-boarding session to find her mother on the front porch drinking coffee. A second cup sat on the table beside her.

"I saw you walking up the hill," said Dora. "Thought you might be ready for a cup."

"Thanks," said Mel. She sat down in a cushioned wicker chair and picked up the coffee cup, waiting for her mother to share what was really on her mind. She didn't typically ambush her daughters without an agenda.

"Are you still planning to be up here for all of the weekends in September?"

"That's the plan."

Was this going to be another critique of her current living situation? Her mother was not comfortable with the fact that she was couch-surfing down in Chicago between sublets and house-sitting gigs. Mel wouldn't really call it comfortable either, but her unorthodox approach to housing had allowed her to save up a boatload of cash.

"Great," said Dora. "I need to confirm your availability with Mary Evelyn."

Mel tried to put the puzzle pieces together. What did Mary Evelyn, the librarian, have to do with anything? She remembered being cornered at the barbecue last weekend, remembered telling her mother later that night that she didn't have time to volunteer. Apparently her mother had decided not to accept her daughter's first answer and was giving her a second chance to get it right. Since Mel really did not have another weekend housing option lined up, she acknowledged that her mother had indeed won this round. However, she knew better than to concede too quickly, or the assignment would quickly mushroom out of control. She needed to make her mother work for the victory.

"What kind of help do you need, exactly?" asked Mel. "I come up here to relax, after all. Is this going to interfere with my relaxation?"

Her mother pursed her lips, an expression calibrated to show admirable restraint in the face of her daughter's disappointing attitude. "I don't think so. It sounds like they're going to do the bulk of the work on Saturday mornings, which will leave the rest of your weekend free."

"And what will I be doing? Painting a mural?"

"Oh no. We have a professional for that."

Mel raised an eyebrow at the insult. Just because she had focused on photography in art school didn't mean she had forgotten how to paint. The irritation must have shown on her face, because her mother shifted to a more soothing tone.

"Of course you'll be a great help to the muralist. He won't be coming up until later in the month, though, and in the meantime, we'll need to get the ground cleared and the wall prepped."

"So I'll be weeding?" Her least favorite job on earth.

"I was thinking you could focus on prepping the wall."

"Mom, I know nothing about painting on brick. The library

is brick, right? And that side wall is really tall. How are we supposed to reach the top?"

"See! I knew you would be good at this. I don't know anything about painting on brick either, but the muralist has a tip sheet for wall preparation. We can use that as a starting point. I think Mary Evelyn also said something about scaffolding."

"Fine. I'll help."

"Great! Get dressed and then we'll run over and talk with Mary Evelyn."

"Wow," said Mel, rubbing her face and swallowing a yawn. She had been out late last night, and this was a lot to absorb at one time. "What's the rush? Can't we figure it out tomorrow?"

"The library is closed on Sundays, and only open until noon today. I don't want to bug Mary Evelyn on her day off."

"Mom, why do you want me to work on this so badly?" Usually her mother harped on her vagabond lifestyle or hinted that she should move up to the lake and start a "real" business here, but this project didn't seem to have anything to do with the usual complaints.

"I just think it would be fun."

Mel gave Dora her very best attempt at the evil eye. It wasn't as effective as her mother's version, but sometimes it worked.

"What? You need some fun in your life, and if you happen to make a few more friends up here, maybe some gentlemen friends, where's the harm in that? It's not like you have a boyfriend right now."

Now they were getting somewhere.

"So you're trying to set me up with someone. Who? The muralist?"

Now Dora was getting huffy and insulted.

"I know better than to set you up with anyone, especially after the last time."

"Mom, he was practically a child!"

"He was a good-looking CPA with a steady job and a nice apartment. If you would only open your mind to new possibilities—"

"Who are you *not* setting me up with?"

Dora sniffed and looked out at the lake. "I may have heard that Jack Emerson will be supervising a group of community service kids."

"Ugh, gross. He's like my brother. I can't date Jack."

Dora gave her the original evil eye, complete with raised eyebrow. "Open mind, darling. You need to open your mind."

Mel crossed her arms. "Anyone else?"

"I may also have heard that Rob Murray will be helping with the landscape design. He owns his own business now, you know."

"I did know, yes. However, I can never date him, either. Sister code. He was Tessa's big crush in high school, remember?"

"Oh, please. That was years ago, she never actually dated him, and Tessa is very happy now with RJ. You can't possibly keep Rob off limits just because of ancient history."

"Sister code."

Dora threw her hands up in the air. "Fine. He's off limits. You'll just have to make do with the muralist, then. He's a few years older than you, but not too old. He's an architect with one of the big firms in Chicago. He does murals as pro bono work in between projects."

"And...?"

"What?"

"There's something you're not telling me."

Dora fussed with her fingernails before answering. "He may also be extremely handsome and the son of a friend of mine."

"Ah-hah," crowed Mel. She pointed an accusatory finger at her mother. "You are totally trying to set me up again. I'm out. I am not going to cooperate."

"Stop it. There is no 'gotcha' here. I just want you to meet an interesting man in a low-stakes setting. If you like him, great. If not, no harm done. You're just helping out on a community project."

Mel crossed her arms again and tried to resist the guilt-logic combo.

"Besides," said her mother. "He won't even be up here until early October. That's three Saturdays that you could be helpful without worrying about whether or not you like the guy."

Mel felt her resolve crumble and wished that she could stomp her foot like a little girl and storm out of the room. How sad that she had outgrown tantrums.

"Fine. I will help for the next three weekends. After that, it all depends on Mr. Perfect Architect. If he's a tool, I'm out."

"Fair enough," said Dora. She stood. "Why don't you go get dressed and we'll run over to see Mary Evelyn?" It wasn't really a question, and she disappeared inside the house before Mel could answer.

Story time was in full swing when Dora and Mel entered the library. Mary Evelyn surveyed her domain from behind the circulation desk. A younger woman was doing an enthusiastic rendition of *The Monster at the End of This Book* for a group of small children, while parents watched from the side or wandered the stacks. Between the goofy narration and the giggling children, it was hard not to smile. When the story ended, mass chaos ensued as parents located their children and either herded them deeper into the children's section or out of the library altogether. Once the commotion subsided, Mel and Dora were able to talk to Mary Evelyn.

"She's in," said Dora without preamble.

"Of course she is," said Mary Evelyn. "Did you show her the picture of the muralist?"

Mel needed to nip this in the bud.

"I'm not in it for the man candy. I'm here to avoid a guilt trip and that's it."

Dora looked annoyed at that characterization, but held her tongue.

"You're only saying that because you haven't seen the picture yet," said Mary Evelyn. "I'll find it."

Before Mel could object, Mary Evelyn had disappeared into a back room. Dora wasn't doing a very good job of hiding her smirk, but at least she was smart enough to keep her mouth shut. Mary Evelyn came back a minute later with a thick file folder in her hand. She thunked it on the counter and opened it up, revealing a photo of this poor man taped inside the front of the folder. Mary Evelyn spun it around so that the picture would be right-side-up for Mel and her mother. Dora took one look at it and sighed in appreciation. Mel crossed her arms.

"I'm sure he's very nice," she said.

"And hot," said Mary Evelyn.

Mel couldn't help thinking that it was just plain wrong for a woman in her seventies (at least!) to be drooling over a guy in his thirties. She took a closer look at the picture. Early thirties, she'd guess, but he liked spending time outside. He had that windblown look to his hair, and a few extra creases around his eyes and his smile.

Damn it, he *was* hot, and she was drooling over him, too.

"We are going to stop objectifying this poor man right now," said Mel sternly, mostly to herself. "He could be a total jerk for all we know. My God, he wears khakis and polos. He could be a dull and boring conformist."

"Who paints innovative and compelling murals in his spare time," added Dora helpfully.

Mel rolled her eyes. "I'm just saying..."

Her words trailed off when Mary Evelyn flipped over some pages and revealed a photograph of a gorgeous mural done on the outside of a building in the city somewhere. It was clever. He had worked with the surroundings and the features of the building itself to create an integrated work of art. In it, a giant was trying to hide (unsuccessfully) behind a tree—a real live tree that was growing next to the building. It made her smile, and it probably made the people in the neighborhood smile every time they walked by. She loved it.

As Mary Evelyn flipped page after page, Mel fell more and more in love with this man's work. The chances of him being a conformist tool dropped with each new work revealed. Finally she covered her eyes.

"Enough! He's amazing. I admit it. There is no chance that he's dull and boring. However—" At this point she uncovered her eyes and gave both her mother and Mary Evelyn another very stern look. "Just because I admit that he has talent and may not be a turd, this does not give you permission to do any matchmaking. Are we clear? I will be making my own matches."

"Crystal," said Dora.

"Clear as a bell."

She might have believed them, until Mary Evelyn high-fived Dora. Time to change the subject before she strangled her mother.

"So what do we need to do to prep the wall?"

Mary Evelyn flipped through the folder and found an instruction packet of some kind.

"Read this. Go ahead and buy any supplies you need. I can reimburse you. The scaffolding will be here sometime this week, so I was thinking we could get started on the wall next Saturday."

"Sounds good," said Mel. She was distracted, skimming through the sheet. It was very clear, and even had a handy supply list at the end. This guy was super organized in addition to being talented. Tessa would love him. Mel might decide to hate him just to be contrary. "Will I have any helpers?"

"I think so," said Mary Evelyn. "We don't have a final tally yet on the volunteers, but there are several community members who have said they could come on Saturdays. The teenagers will be helping clear the garden. You'll get the adults."

"Smart move," said Mel, "given that there's scaffolding involved."

"My thoughts exactly."

"Who do you have so far?" asked Dora.

Mary Evelyn rattled off a few names that were vaguely familiar to Mel, but the one that jumped out at her was Kat.

"Kat Rodriguez?" she interrupted.

"Yes, dear," said Mary Evelyn, and then she continued talking with Dora about the other volunteers, and Dora's ideas for more potential recruits.

Mel hadn't run into Kat since the Labor Day weekend barbecue, but it sounded like "a few phone calls" had morphed into a larger commitment. Big shocker. At least Mel would have someone to talk to that wasn't handpicked dating material.

A year ago Mel never would have predicted that she and Kat would be on speaking terms, and yet here they were, practically hanging out. A couple of conversations didn't absolve Mel of the lingering guilt. She would probably carry that around forever, but knowing that Kat didn't blame her made it an easier load to bear.

Karma was a bitch, though. Just as she lightened one load of guilt, she picked up another. Mel still hadn't found the right time to tell her family that she was leaving at the end of October. The days were ticking by, and she couldn't avoid the subject forever.

Mel tuned back in to her mother's conversation with Mary Evelyn to find that she had switched from volunteer recruiting to another of her favorite subjects—Dora's Grand Plan for Mel's Life.

Her mother had decided early in the summer that it was time to get Mel "settled." She didn't mean it in a 1950s "settle down and get married" kind of way, although that would be a welcome development from her mother's perspective. No, it was much worse. Dora had decided that Mel's career in photojournalism was too unpredictable, and that she needed something steadier. That "something" was a wedding photography business here in Hidden Springs. She had hinted at this plan for years, but now that Callie and Tessa were, in their own ways, "settled," Mel had her mother's full and undivided attention.

Mel had tried several times over the years to make her mother understand her own future plans, but so far nothing had worked. Dora never wanted to hear about life in the city, or the work Mel was doing in some of Chicago's toughest neighborhoods, or her daughter's plans to travel the world. At some point, Mel had stopped talking about it.

Only a month ago, Mel had realized that she had shared exactly none of her big plans with her mother or her sisters. Everything had come together so quickly, and there hadn't been a great time to ease her family into the idea. Besides, there was so much going on with everyone else right now—Tessa and her new romance with RJ, Callie's unexpected reunion with ex-boyfriend Adam, her father's decision to spend time in Nashville—that it didn't seem like the right time to pile on with even more change.

Mostly Mel worried about her mother. Everyone had something new going on in their lives except Dora, and it didn't seem fair to leave right when her mother needed her. Fair or not, though, Mel would be heading for the other side of the world in October, and she needed to find a way to tell them before she got on the airplane.

Callie would understand, but Tessa would freak out because Mel had kept her plans secret, and in her sweet therapist way would analyze the hell out of Mel's secrecy. It wasn't that complicated. She had been nurturing this dream for a long time, and she didn't want anyone to crush it.

Before her mother could get too involved in describing her vision of "Mel the Wedding Photographer" with Mary Evelyn, Mel interrupted.

"Mom, I can't sell romance for a living."

"Of course not, dear. Your style is totally unique. You'll be something new entirely."

Rather than fight with her mother in the middle of the library, Mel made some vague excuses about needing to get work done and made her escape.

She was a coward, plain and simple.

CHAPTER SIX

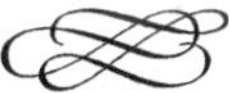

ROB ARRIVED AT THE LIBRARY EARLY ON SATURDAY MORNING, long before the library itself would open or the volunteers would arrive. He had cleared his schedule, needing this quiet time to make sketches of the exterior and get the exact dimensions down on paper. The final design would depend on the mural, of course, and the concepts for that wouldn't be ready until early to mid-October. In the meantime, however, he needed to understand his blank canvas, capture his initial ideas, and get them on paper.

Truth be told, he had also come early so that he could calm the hell down. He hadn't seen Kat since Wednesday afternoon at the library, but she might as well have been his sidekick all week because he hadn't stopped thinking about her. Even the guys on the crew had noticed and started giving him shit about being distracted. They recognized the signs.

He had spent most of the last few days comparing his first impression of all-grown-up Kat with his memories of teenage Kitty. He wasn't an idiot. He knew that ten years was a long time, and he hadn't expected to see the seventeen-year-old girl she had once been. Still, her confidence had taken him by surprise. The old vulnerability had disappeared, replaced by a strength and directness that he hadn't seen in her since she was much younger. But he had glimpsed no more than a glimmer of the girl within the woman, her confidence functioning like a shield.

He kept himself busy for more than an hour, pacing out the space between the library and the back of the church and calculating the square footage and the slope of the land. The area was fairly level, though completely overgrown. At the very back it took a sudden steep turn uphill, so that the property bordering to the back would overlook the park from above. It would be beautiful, but he would need to swing by next time it rained, see what the water management situation looked like, maybe talk to the uphill neighbors. They were used to having a lot of privacy with all the scrub trees, and they might not take kindly to a big change in their backyards.

At about quarter to nine, Mary Evelyn arrived. She gave him a wave but didn't stop to talk. Instead she unlocked the library and, he assumed, got things ready inside. He climbed out of the truck and started to unload tools and equipment. Kat and Jack arrived shortly after that. He watched them say their hellos over the roof of Kat's little Fiat. She looked stiff as she talked with him, which was odd. She was wearing casual clothes and should have been relaxed. Yeah, it had been years, but he had made something of a study of Kitty and her body language in high school. He knew when something was off and wondered what it was. Maybe something to do with work. It would make sense that the two of them would cross paths, professionally speaking. Or maybe they had dated and broken up. Not his favorite theory, but to his relief he didn't sense any chemistry between them now. He was going to have a hard enough time getting out of his own way when it came to Kat. The last thing he needed was competition.

·   ·   ·

Kat had hoped to have a few minutes of peace before all the volunteers arrived, but she had missed her chance, rolling in at exactly the same time as Jack, which led to a few minutes of stilted conversation before she could escape.

Sighing as she walked over to the work area where Rob had already stacked some tools, she gave herself a mental kick in the pants. Jack wasn't a bad guy, and technically he had done nothing wrong. Besides, it was all ancient history, right? She should be far beyond this, able to interact with him without it bothering her. And yet it did.

She caught Rob's eye and waved in greeting, but didn't immediately go over to talk to him. Rob's presence wasn't helping. Instead of feeling strong and capable, she was feeling unsteady, as if the ground beneath her feet were no longer solid and she couldn't trust it to stay still. Maybe this was how people felt after surviving an earthquake. She didn't like it.

Rob was standing at the downhill end of the lot by the church, watching the volunteers as they arrived in the Hidden Springs version of morning traffic. When she didn't head his way, he started up the hill toward her.

"Hey," he said as he drew close. The deep rumble of his voice didn't help her equilibrium at all. He didn't look or sound like a teenager anymore.

"Hey," she replied automatically. They surveyed the arrivals together, standing shoulder to shoulder.

It took a moment for the realization to sink in. This was how they had greeted each other hundreds of times on the bus. Not a lot of chatter, just one word each as she took her seat in front of him. She would sit with her back to the window, her feet on the seat, and look at him through the narrow opening between the window and the seat. Right now those memories were so strong that she could smell the dark green vinyl.

When they were small they had talked. She remembered him being a very patient listener as she explained unicorns and how magic worked and her favorite book, *The Secret Garden*. He had brought her little gifts, tiny plants that he had grown himself, or sometimes a cool rock he had found in the fields. She had kept the rocks in a small box beneath her bed and tried to keep the plants alive until she could find them a home in her garden.

As they got older, there were fewer gifts and less talking, but every now and then, he would still bring her something special. It had made her feel a part of something when she had never felt a part of any clique at the high school—not enough in common with the pretty blond cheerleaders or the pale Goths or the FFA girls or even the other Latina girls, chattering away in Spanish too quickly for her to understand. Boyfriends helped a little. They offered an umbrella of protection from teenage cruelty and thoughtlessness, but they never really knew her. The only real comfort to be found, as things got dark, was in her shared silence with Rob on the bus, solidarity in the fact that he made sure the seat in front of him was always open for her.

The rock box had been left behind that night. It was part of her life *before*. She hadn't thought of it in years, and the sudden rush of memory made it hard to breathe. She forced herself to draw air into her lungs, slowly, in and out. The memories she banished for now, needing to pull herself together or she would make a horrible first impression on the kids.

After a few deep breaths, she left the past behind and settled back into the present. The smell of trees and dirt. The murmur of conversation. The chatter of birds. The confused girl of ten years ago had long since given way to the strong and capable person she had become. She had left that girl behind and was stronger for it.

·   ·   ·

Rob didn't say much as the volunteers arrived. He was having enough trouble processing the fact that he was standing beside Kitty Rodriguez as if it were totally normal—as if he hadn't spent most of his adolescence in love with her, most of college in denial and doomed relationships, and the last few years avoiding the dating scene altogether. She had knocked him completely sideways with that near-tackle the other day, and he still hadn't quite caught his balance.

He wasn't sure what to make of the grown-up version of Kitty. Her mother had been beautiful in a fragile sort of way. Not Kat, though. As a kid, she had always been strong and wild like a weed. After she moved into town, things had changed. She had never talked about home anymore, and she had seemed angry and afraid—not that she would admit it, but he could tell. When her home life finally blew up, it had all become clear. Something toxic had been going on in that house. But by then, of course, it had been too late. She was gone.

Grown-up Kat had reclaimed her wild strength, but she held it inside, contained, in a way that she hadn't before. Maybe she would relax as they got to know each other again, or maybe she was just wired that way now.

At nine o'clock on the dot, Mary Evelyn came out of the library and called the group together for a meeting. He and Kitty—Kat, he corrected himself—walked over to join the fringes of the group. Rob mentally thanked Mary Evelyn for taking charge. He had never been the type to seek the spotlight, and even now he'd rather do backbreaking labor than speak in front of a crowd. At some point, though, he would need to give everyone their marching orders. He would keep it short.

Mary Evelyn, after giving a brief history and overview of the project, explained that they would be split into two teams this morning. The first team would work with Mel James on prepping the wall for the muralist. The second team, including the teenagers as well as some garden club volunteers, would work with Rob on clearing the area for the park. This news triggered groans from the teens, who had been eyeing the scaffolding with interest. They quieted down pretty quickly after a stern look from Officer Jack.

Mary Evelyn wrapped up her remarks, and Kat helpfully began herding the teenagers away from the library building so that they wouldn't be distracted by the scaffolding anymore. She walked backward down the sidewalk, leading the group toward the pile of tools and equipment. Rob, in the middle of the pack, watched the teens with curiosity. Apparently, Kat's impact on teen male hormones remained as strong as ever. The boys hung on her every word. The girls not so much.

When had he gotten old enough to read teen behavior? Half the time he still felt like a teenager himself, albeit one who could fake adulthood.

As the group gathered around Kat and the tools, Rob psyched himself up to speak, but Kat took the pressure off by doing the introductions.

"My name is Kat Rodriguez. You can call me Kat. I work as a guardian *ad litem* for the county, and I've agreed to help supervise your community service work." She focused on one boy in particular who was already starting to goof around. "Don't make me regret that decision." He straightened up pretty quick once he realized he was the focus of her attention.

She was pretty good at taking charge. Definitely more confident than she had been in high school and not one to put up with nonsense from teenagers.

"This is Rob Murray," she continued, gesturing for him to step up, which he did. "You can call him Rob. He's the gardening expert. He'll be telling us all what we need to do."

Rob raised a hand in greeting, happy to follow her lead.

"So what about you guys?" she continued. "Do you all go to the same high school?"

There was some mumbling, and one or two kids shook their heads.

"Sounds like we need to do a full round of introductions. Why don't each of you say your name and which high school you go to?" She studied the group for a minute. They were looking anywhere but at her. "Let's start with you," she said, pointing to the kid who had been screwing around earlier. He pinked up around the ears and stood taller.

"I'm Charlie," he said. "I go to Springwood." Rob would bet that Charlie was a freshman. His voice hadn't quite changed yet, and he was on the short side. Brown hair. Fading summer tan. His buddy went next.

"Henry. Springwood." Henry was older than Charlie by a few years, but they had a similar athletic build.

The introductions continued on down the line. The group had self-segregated into smaller clumps, and Rob realized that some of them must have been partners in crime. Trouble didn't seem to discriminate based on gender or ethnicity, because they had an equivalent number of boys and girls, and it also looked like an even split of white and Hispanic kids. The kids all went to either Springwood or Little Creek, a nearby high school. It made sense, transportation-wise, that they had been assigned to a project close to home. He'd have to keep an eye on the loner, Hannah. She looked like she needed somebody on her side.

Curious about what had landed each of these kids in community service, Rob made a mental note to ask Kat later. It would be handy to know what kind of trouble to watch out for.

"Any questions before we get started?" asked Kat once the introductions were over.

Henry's hand went up.

"What's the mural going to be? And what's the garden going to look like?"

"The short answer is, 'We don't know yet,'" answered Kat.

"The muralist will need to see the space and talk with community members, including all of you, before designing the mural. Rob, I'm guessing you'll need to know more about the mural before designing the garden."

He nodded. "It would definitely help."

"Rob is a landscape architect, so he knows a lot about designing outdoor spaces. Do you all know what a landscape architect does?"

They answered the question with mostly shrugs, so Rob found himself drawn into a discussion of landscape architecture and how that was different from garden design or being an architect who designs buildings. Kat let that discussion meander for a good five minutes before she brought it back to the project at hand. Funny thing was that by the time he had answered all their questions, he wasn't nervous anymore.

"Rob, why don't you tell us what needs to be done here?"

He gave them the overview. First priority was to clear the lot. The mature oak tree in the center of the lot would stay, of course. The other trees and shrubs were invasive species that needed to be pulled out. After removing the bigger stuff, there would be a lot of weeding. Some landscapers might skip the weeding and just plow the plants under, but those tough plants would be back with a vengeance in the spring. Far better to clear them out now and start with a clean slate, particularly since they had time and free labor. There might be some interesting native plants hiding back there, but so far he hadn't seen any. Stump grinding and earth moving might be needed at some point, which would involve bigger equipment. Maybe some water management. Then they would implement the new design, still to be determined. A lot would depend on the budget for new trees, shrubs, and perennials. He was thinking of talking to the garden club to see if they could help out with the perennials.

As the teenagers groaned about the amount of work that needed to be done, Kat pulled Rob to the side.

"Do you think you can keep them busy for a little while?"

"Sure," he said. "And Jack is here for backup. Why? Do you need to head out?"

"I'm thinking they'll be happier if they have work gloves. Why don't I run to the hardware store? I'll only be gone half an hour."

"Sounds like a plan."

As she slipped away, it dawned on him that he was going to be seeing Kat on a regular basis, without having to ask her out or manufacture reasons to run into her. He felt a goofy sense of happiness and caught himself before he started grinning like an idiot. He needed to rein in these good feelings before he got ahead of himself. She might not be married (yes, he had checked for a ring), but for all he knew, she had a serious boyfriend. Or girlfriend. Sheesh. You couldn't assume anything these days. Best to take it slow, try not to scare her away. It had been a long time, and people changed. He needed to get to know Kat all over again, and maybe, just maybe, he would have a second chance.

CHAPTER SEVEN

KAT KEPT HER WALK CALM AND UNHURRIED AS SHE RETURNED TO the car, her movements smooth as she opened the door and slid into the driver's seat. Rob Murray. She shook her head as she shifted into reverse. After all this time. They hadn't crossed paths in all the years she'd been back, and yet now she would be seeing him every week? The flutters of panic chasing through her stomach were more appropriate for a preteen than a grown woman.

Given the size of Hidden Springs, it was almost ridiculous that she hadn't run into him sooner. Most of the time this town felt so small. It *was* small—only 1,517 people according to the "Welcome to Hidden Springs" sign. But she was starting to realize that she had made it even smaller. She saw a wide range of people up at county, sure, but once she was off the clock, she kept to a very small orbit. Instead of making frequent trips to the tiny local grocery store, she stocked up once a month or so at the superstore. She rarely went out. She never made the effort to try new things. She was acting like someone who didn't want to meet people, and—looking at her life with fresh eyes— it was all very disheartening.

Maybe Lucy (and literally everyone else in her life) was right. Maybe it was time for a change.

Kat made it in and out of the hardware store quickly and returned to the library less than half an hour after she had left. As she handed out the new gloves, she checked in with each of the kids. Despite their initial grumbling, they brought a lot of energy to the work. She would bet money that Rob had let them choose their own work groups, because they had broken into the same cliques she had observed during introductions. Barb and Carolyn, the twin con artists; Luna and Paola, the vapers; Alé, Yago, and Elías, the hackers; Henry and Charlie, the jocks; and the lone girl Hannah, trailing behind Rob.

Hannah had been a last-minute addition to the group, her case file not included with the others. She was awfully good at fading into the background, which made Kat wonder exactly what she might have done. She was also wearing long sleeves and long pants on what would likely be a warm and humid morning, which made Kat all the more grateful to be old enough to choose comfort over style without stressing about it. Innocence long lost, Kat couldn't help pointing out—if only inside her own head—that long sleeves and pants could also hide signs of abuse or self-harm, but she quickly quashed those negative thoughts. Not all children lived with trauma. Not all stepfathers were evil. Not all stories ended in tragedy. *Get a grip, Kat.*

Rob was the only person using a power tool, and he seemed to be enjoying the chainsaw a bit too much as he attacked the scraggly shrubs, cutting them off at the base. As each one toppled over, Hannah would grab it and drag it over to the growing pile of debris at the downhill corner of the property. The other groups were tackling the invasive trees. One person would take a turn sawing while the others stabilized the trunk, ready to catch the tree as it fell. Luckily, none of the invasive trees were all that big, so each one would be easy for a group of teenagers to handle.

As Hannah struggled to move a larger shrub on her own, Kat saw her opportunity to dive in. She walked over and grabbed a branch down low by the base and helped Hannah drag it over to the pile. Hannah didn't look all that excited about having help, but she didn't object, either. When Rob realized Kat was back, he gave her a nod but didn't stop the chainsaw. They continued their work in this rhythm for the remainder of the morning. Mary Evelyn had set up a table with water and lemonade, and as the volunteer shift drew to a close, she brought out two trays of cookies. The kids swarmed over them like locusts.

"Nice work today, everyone." Rob was visibly happy with their progress. "It should only take one or two more sessions to clear the trees and shrubs, and then we can dive into the weeding and stump grinding."

One of the twins gave a sarcastic "hooray" at the news.

Kat collected the gloves. She could have sent them home with the kids, but that would lead to forgotten gloves, whining, and possibly even refusal to participate. Keeping the gloves eliminated excuses. This also allowed for a quick run through the washer between sessions. Kat wouldn't put it past the blond twins to get fussy about wearing dirty gloves.

Parents started to pull up in their cars. It looked like Henry had his own set of wheels and would be driving Charlie home. When she looked around for Hannah, she saw her halfway down the block rounding the corner by the church. She must live nearby. Kat made a mental note to follow up with Joan to get Hannah's file.

In a matter of minutes, she and Rob were the only ones left from the landscape crew.

· · ·

As the volunteers drifted away, Rob surreptitiously studied Kat. She looked different now, more like herself than the other day when she had been all dressed up in her lawyer clothes. Today, she wore no makeup and had her long, dark hair in a ponytail. The outdoor work had left her face glowing and smudged with dirt. She looked good, a hell of a lot better than he did. He'd been working hard this morning and probably smelled like it. He eased back a step, hoping he was downwind.

"They're good kids," he said. "Worked harder than I thought they would."

"I know," she said on a laugh. "I was surprised, expected a lot more complaining."

"There was some of that, especially at the beginning, but less once they got going."

He almost asked if she wanted to go grab lunch or something, but realized that not only did he stink, he also had a mountain of work to do when he got home. If he didn't do the estimates and the billing, he wouldn't get any new business, and he wouldn't get paid, and that would bring a quick end to the business.

Maybe next Saturday he would make sure he had all that done ahead of time.

"Can you make it on Tuesday?" she asked.

He nodded. "You?"

"I should be good."

He could feel warmth uncurl in his gut at the thought of seeing her again so soon.

"Until Tuesday, then," he said.

She smiled. "Looking forward to it."

He watched her walk away, a thousand memories racing through his mind. He had so many questions about her life over the last ten years. Where had she been living? Had she stayed with family? Friends? Where had she gone to school? A full-on inquisition would scare her off, but they had time. He smiled at the thought. They had time to get to know each other all over again.

Mel sipped her lemonade while her mother and Mary Evelyn talked through the progress made this morning and basically patted each other on the back for recruiting so many volunteers and making the whole thing a huge success. She hid her smile in her lemonade and filched a third cookie. This might be a good time to pull a fade.

She had made it only a few steps away when Kat caught her.

"How did it go on the wall this morning?" asked Kat.

"Not bad," said Mel. "We made more progress on the bottom of the wall than the top. We can only have a few people up on the scaffolding at one time, so I think the wall prep may take more time than anticipated."

"If you need teen volunteers, they were all itching to climb the scaffolding."

Mel laughed. "Why am I not surprised?"

At that moment, Kat's stomach growled. Mel looked over at her, raised an eyebrow. "Need a cookie?" There were still a few left on the table, sad castoffs on the edges of the large crumb-strewn trays.

"What I need is lunch, I think. Too much sugar and I'll fall asleep instead of getting any work done this afternoon."

Mel nodded. "Me, too. About the lunch, I mean. I don't actually have any plans for the afternoon. Want to grab a burger at The Beach?" The words tumbled out of her mouth before she could stop them, but once spoken, Mel realized she found the idea of stilted conversation over lunch with Kat weirdly appealing. Maybe she had been spending too much time with her mother lately. Maybe she was missing her sisters. Mel didn't begrudge her sisters their newfound happiness and the thrill of being IN LOVE, but she did wish they were a little more available for hanging out.

Kat smiled that mysterious half-smile that drove Mel up a wall. It was like Kat knew exactly what Mel was thinking and yet was willing to take her immature self under Kat's oh-so-mature wing.

"The Beach sounds great," said Kat. "Let's go."

Kat wasn't sure what had prompted her to accept Mel's impulsive invitation. She had a mountain of work waiting for her back at home. She was hungry, yes, and she would have to eat at some point, but taking another hour out of her day wasn't something she would normally do. She would have to blame it on the weirdness of the day, the shakiness of her foundations, or the fact that none of her girlfriends lived close enough to make a get-together practical. She must be freaking out more than she realized, because all it took was one beer and a curious question from Mel to get her talking about personal stuff.

"Did you and Rob ever date in high school?" asked Mel as she dipped a fry into the puddle of ketchup in her basket.

"No, nothing like that." Kat wasn't sure how she would characterize her relationship with Rob, but it had never involved dating or kissing or "benefits" of any kind. That said, while it may never have been physical, it had definitely been intimate. Kat clued in to the fact that Mel looked suddenly—inexplicably—uncomfortable. "Why do you ask?"

Mel stared into her nearly empty beer bottle and shrugged. "There's an interesting energy between the two of you, and it reminded me of high school." Mel looked up at that point and actually made eye contact. "My sister Tessa crushed on him pretty hard back then. She wanted to know if you two were a thing, even though you were officially dating someone else. That's how I got the bright idea to..."

"Steal my English journal?" Kat completed the sentence for her. They had skated around this topic before, but never really broken through the ice. At Mel's surprised look, Kat smiled wryly. "I knew you must have been the one to take it. You were always the boldest of the trio."

Mel winced. "Bold seems to equate to 'the one who doesn't think before she speaks or acts.'"

"Action was needed." Kat understood Mel's skeptical expression, but what she had said was true. "Let's call the journal-stealing a useful mistake. I was stuck, and you got me unstuck."

"I got your mother killed."

The guilt in Mel's voice was crushing and made Kat even more determined to convince her that what had happened was in no way her fault. She could not allow Mel to carry that kind of guilt around any longer.

"You did not kill anyone. Those dominoes were going to fall sooner or later. You helped them fall sooner, and you may have saved my life in the process."

"But—"

"No buts. Did you read the whole journal?"

Mel rubbed her face with her hands, mumbling, "Pretty much." Dropping her hands, she said, "If it helps, I was the only one who read it."

"There was one thing I couldn't bring myself to put down in writing."

"Something bad?"

"I was pregnant."

"Fuck."

"Exactly. Sooner or later the dominoes were going to fall. I had a ticking time bomb inside me, and I wasn't going to be able to hide it forever. Once people found out, the shit was going to hit the fan. You just blew things up a little early."

"Still, things should not have gone down that way."

"And that's not on you. Lots of blame to go around, but none of it on you."

It was very important to Kat that Mel understand this. Yes, it sucked that her mother was dead, but the person to blame was the one who had pulled the trigger, not the person who had brought the truth into the light.

"How can you not hate me anyway?" asked Mel, sounding completely bewildered.

"Lots and lots of therapy."

Their server chose that moment to stop by the table to ask, "Another round, ladies?"

Kat met Mel's eyes, raised an eyebrow. They answered in unison.

"Definitely."

CHAPTER EIGHT

MEL HEADED UPSTAIRS TO TAKE A MUCH-NEEDED SHOWER. THE wall prep had left her sweaty and a little sunburned, and the combination of beer and the intense conversation at lunch with Kat had left her fuzzy headed. She didn't normally drink in the middle of the day, and she certainly didn't have deep conversations. It had left her feeling raw and exposed.

She was distracted by the sound of voices in her mother's bedroom and discovered both of her sisters there with Dora. Callie sat crisscross on the bed, leaning back on the padded headboard. Tessa stood beside the bed, folding clothes and placing them in an open suitcase. Dora was elbow-deep in her closet, pulling out clothes, putting them back, muttering to herself, and occasionally tossing a selection on the bed, which Tessa would then shake out, fold, and place in the suitcase.

"Someone going on a trip?"

Dora stuck her head out of the closet. "New York. It's time." Then she disappeared again.

"I thought we were all going to go together." Mel didn't mean for it to come out sounding whiny, but it did.

Tessa smoothed out the top layer of folded clothes. "Mom's

decided to go alone." She was using her therapist voice—never a good sign.

This time, when Dora emerged from the closet, she stayed out, looking a little fidgety and more than a little guilty. "It doesn't seem fair to drag you girls with me when I'll spend most of my time hanging out at the hospital with Lauren. I'm not even sure how long I'll stay. Maybe a day. Maybe a week. It makes more sense for me to go alone."

Mel wasn't sure how to respond. Growing up, her parents had never talked about their lives before they met each other, never even hinted that they had family still alive. But then Callie had stumbled across some old letters this past spring, revealing the existence of an old friend named Lauren, and over the last few months, secrets from the past had continued to bubble up. Mel and her sisters were trying to be patient, but if their parents didn't start offering real explanations soon, they would need to stage an intervention.

She leaned against the doorframe and crossed her arms. "Are you sure you don't want some moral support?"

Callie or Tessa may have asked the question already, but Mel wanted to see her mother's face when she answered. Both Callie and Tessa had been away a lot over the last ten years. Mel had picked up the slack, making sure her parents were okay, trying to make sure they didn't miss the girls too much, just trying to be available so that they wouldn't notice they had only one daughter hanging around instead of three. The news that Lauren was dying had knocked her mother for a loop, perhaps more than her sisters realized.

Dora stopped fidgeting and walked right over to Mel, enfolding her in a hug. "Oh, sweetheart, I can tell you're worried. You need to stop that right now. I will be just fine."

"But you never travel, and now you're going to tackle New York City all by yourself?"

Her mother laughed. Not a giggle, or a chuckle. It was a great big belly laugh. She even had to wipe her eyes.

"Oh, honey, that's very sweet, but you need to remember that I grew up on Long Island, and then I lived in New York City. Sure, it's been a while, but I know how to get a cab, and I know where I'm going. I don't think they moved Central Park in the years that I've been away."

She patted Mel on the shoulder and then turned back to her packing. Mel just folded her arms more tightly and scowled. All was not right with the world, and she was not comfortable with this plan.

While Mel stewed, Dora and Tessa ran through the end-of-season checklist for the sailing school. This made Mel even grumpier, because it sounded like her mother would be gone for a lot longer than a week. Sure, Tessa had talked about taking over the sailing school one day, but "one day" suddenly sounded like tomorrow.

"I'm going to take a shower," Mel announced. "Are you leaving in the next ten minutes?"

Dora looked up, startled, and shook her head no.

"Good," said Mel, and went to wash away her discombobulation.

Kat sat on the couch later that night, feet up, with a mountain of paperwork next to her. She had lost another hour earlier in the afternoon, falling asleep and drooling on one of her case files. Note to self: Day-drinking is not conducive to productivity.

Some were cases that she needed to close out, and others were reports she needed to file in a timely manner. All of it urgent, but only a handful were really important. Obligations could not be avoided forever, though, so she was methodically working her way through the pile.

On a normal night she would have trouble focusing because she was tired, but tonight she had the opposite problem. The physical labor in the morning, followed by the beers and the nap, had unexpectedly energized her and left her fidgety. She kept flashing back to her interactions with Rob, particularly the tackle, her face warming even if the blush didn't show on her skin.

Rob. After all this time.

He had been her one true friend growing up, no matter how unlikely the pairing. Maybe their shared isolation on farms outside of town helped to strengthen the bond between them. That isolation was one of the reasons she chose to live in town now. In town, she didn't feel quite so alone, even if she lived like a hermit.

Rob had been kind from the first day of kindergarten. He hadn't seemed to care that Kitty was a girl, or that her mother spoke accented English, or that her skin was a few shades darker than his. It had only occurred to her years later that Rob had grown up working side by side with immigrant farmhands. The differences that to her seemed vast might have seemed perfectly normal to him.

Mexican immigrants, drawn north by the promise of steady agricultural work, had established a strong local community. Rob's family farm had depended on their help, though most worked for the big corporate producers. Not that Kat or her mother had ever been a part of the immigrant community. Her mother, anxious to be accepted by her stepfather's family, had stopped speaking Spanish. She insisted that they communicate only in English, as Kitty's new papa preferred, so he wouldn't feel excluded. It hadn't taken long for the words to fade from memory. Her mother's obsession with acceptance had shut her off from the local people most likely to welcome and support her. Growing up, Kitty had only heard Spanish spoken at home when her mother was very, very angry.

Misplaced pride probably also played a role. Her mother had been tall and strikingly beautiful, her grandfather the mayor of their small town in Colombia, and her family wealthy. No matter that her grandparents were dead, the family shattered—her mother had still considered herself to be a step above the Mexican farmhands, even if they had lived here far longer and spoke better English.

In the absence of other friendships, Kat's daily conversations with Rob on the bus became her lifeline. At first, they talked at school, too, until the boys stopped talking to the girls and it would have been weird. The long bus route gave them plenty of time to catch up at the end of the day.

It had all gone to shit when her first stepfather died unexpectedly. Kat still had no idea what exactly had killed him. Her mother had been too distraught to understand what the paramedics told her, so all Kat knew was that it had something to do with his heart. Kat's mother had met her second stepfather not long after, and before she knew it, they were moving into town. She and Rob still rode the same bus, but things were different. They didn't have nearly enough time to talk. He still checked in, though. Still seemed to care. And later, when things had gotten really bad, he had stuck by her. Despite the inevitable rumors, he had even started sitting with her at lunch. She hadn't cared about the rumors. She had been too happy to be spending time with him again.

Kat wondered about his story, what had happened after she left. He had always planned to study up at UW-Madison, go to the Ag school, take over the family farm. Even back then he had dreamed big dreams. He hadn't wanted to keep doing what they had been doing for so long, working harder and earning less money every year. He had talked about going organic, or branching out into different crops. Anything, as long as it was different.

The only class they ever had together was art. She had

needed a break from the core classes, but wasn't looking for something social like music. He had simply loved art. They had worked their way through the art curriculum together. No matter how many times she had encouraged him to look at careers that would use his art, he had always shaken his head and laughed. He didn't want to let his family down. She knew that he loved growing things, even if it was a little dorky to say that you dreamed of growing up to be a farmer, but she had hated thinking that art would no longer be part of his life after high school.

Her one regret, looking back, was that she hadn't reached out to him after it all fell apart. It wouldn't have been that hard to track him down—to let him know that she was okay, even if she was never coming back. She had stalked him online a few times over the years, confirmed that he had indeed gone to UW-Madison, although she couldn't know for sure what he was studying. She had come so close so many times, but in the end always chickened out, her life neatly clipped into two parts. Before that night. After that night.

It had taken years before she was ready to revisit her old life, and by then it was too late. He had graduated and moved on. She had done the same, and it seemed easier to start fresh. Her close college friends, the ones who knew her story, thought she was crazy to come back here, crazy to build a life on the ruins of her old one. Sometimes she wondered if they might be right. It didn't make a lot of logical sense, but in her heart, she still believed it was the right choice. Dark things had happened here, and someone needed to shine a light into that darkness. Kids everywhere needed help. The system didn't always work perfectly—it certainly hadn't worked for her—but it worked sometimes. Kat figured that if she was involved, she could improve the odds, and she intended to do that here in Hidden Springs.

Rob was driving out to pick up a load of rocks when he saw it. A sculptor had transformed a dead tree stump into a whimsical sculpture of a young bear trying to catch an eagle. He had driven by a thousand times without really seeing it, but this time all it took was once glimpse to launch his imagination into overdrive. Toward the back of the project lot, there was a dead tree that would need to be removed. Until now, he had been thinking they would rip it out completely and then grind down the stump. Now he had a new plan.

On the way back, he stopped at the farmhouse to ask who had done the sculpture, and he came away with not just a business card but also a small bag stuffed with freshly baked muffins. It turned out that the owner of the farm had done the artistic handiwork himself with a chainsaw, and his wife was his biggest promoter. She liked the idea of an income stream that didn't depend on the weather, and she was willing to cut his usual fee in half if he got a lot of publicity out of the deal. Rob had shaken his head at that offer. Apparently PR was the grease that made the business world go 'round.

Later that evening, he started googling "chainsaw art" and went down a rabbit hole. There were a lot of creative people out there in the world. Some were maybe a little too out there, but he got about a hundred ideas in the space of ten minutes. He also realized that free publicity could help him rope in other key players as well. There was the guy who owned the nursery specializing in native plants. He knew how to make structures like domes and tunnels out of living willow trees. Then there was the couple who sold concrete lawn sculptures. They had lived in the area forever and would probably donate something small to the project. Maybe, if he were lucky, they could turn a water management problem into a water feature, getting rid of the swampy area in the back corner and creating something beautiful at the same time.

He scribbled a list of phone calls to make the next day, hoping that everyone would be as excited about free publicity as the stump-carver's wife.

What did Kat do on weeknights? Did she work late the way he did, or did she go out with friends? He still hadn't figured out if she was dating someone, or how to casually work the question into conversation. He had debated asking Mary Evelyn, but didn't want to telegraph his intentions to the entire town. He wasn't quite that desperate—yet.

CHAPTER NINE

KAT HADN'T SPENT THIS MUCH TIME OUTSIDE SINCE HER EARLY years on the farm. Sunday morning she had woken up sore all over, hearing loud complaints from muscles she hadn't used in years. It took half an hour of stretching and some ibuprofen before she started to feel normal again. And here she was, only a few days later, ready to do it all over again. She had cleared her Tuesday afternoon so that she had plenty of time to go home, change into gardening clothes, wash off most of her makeup, and still make it back to the library with time to spare. She didn't kid herself that this was only about the kids. Yes, she wanted to help them, and yes, she would give them the time and attention they needed, but she hadn't come early for their sake. She had come early hoping to catch a couple of extra minutes with Rob.

She didn't go into the library. Instead, she leaned against the big old oak and sipped iced tea from her thermos, waiting. This would be the best spot in the future park. She could feel the strength of the oak rising behind her and sinking deep into the ground beneath her feet. She could smell the cool air drifting down from its canopy of leaves above. There was nothing like a tree to help you feel connected to the world around you. Rob had better not fence off this tree or trap it within a circular bench. She would have a word with him about it. Trees needed to be free.

As if she had conjured him with her thoughts, Rob's work truck turned onto the street and parked next to her car. Instead of feeling off balance this time, she felt a little leap in her chest. He had come early, too. Not that she assumed he had come early just for her. That would be crazy. Even so, his quick, shy smile as he climbed out of the truck made her lips perk up at the corners. She strolled over to say hello, feeling more natural in her muck boots than she would ever feel in high heels. He closed the door to the driver's side and leaned against it.

"Hey," she said.

"Hey."

The greeting felt natural, when she would have expected awkward or uncomfortable.

"How was your day?"

He made a face. "Quiet. Work is a little slow right now."

"You can have some of mine," she offered.

He laughed. "I wish." The smile faded too quickly. "What about you?"

"It could have been better," she answered, looking down at her tea instead of meeting his eyes. Sometimes it felt like he could see too much. "I couldn't help one of my kids today, and it sucked."

He nodded and didn't try to make her feel better, which did more to make her feel better than all the platitudes in the world.

He reached into the open window of the truck and grabbed his own thermos from the cupholder. They walked over to the bench in front of the library and sat in companionable silence, waiting for the kids to arrive. She would have been content to sit there for the rest of the day, oddly at ease in his presence, but the kids started to trickle in and their brief quiet time came to an end.

Rob gave each kid an assignment, leaving Kat's for last. She caught herself hoping that they would work together and squashed that immediately. This was not a date. Besides, something about the slump of Hannah's shoulders caught her eye and pinged her radar. That was where she needed to be today. She said a quiet word to Rob, who immediately agreed, and she tromped though the weeds toward the girl. Hannah had chosen to work on the section of the garden closest to the church—and farthest away from all the people. Kat was grateful that she had worn muck boots with her shorts. It wasn't all that wet, but the tall boots would protect her lower legs from scratches and bugs. She picked her way across the lot, which had really opened up after Saturday's hard work, and made it over to Hannah without tripping on any of the shrub stumps.

"How can I help?"

Hannah gave Kat a once-over that almost made Kat laugh. She dealt with a lot of teen skepticism in her work, but this girl could teach a master class.

"You'll want to grab a tool from the pile," said Hannah. "We're supposed to rip out all this crap. I guess it's invasive, or something. They'll plant something nice once it's all clear."

"Sounds good." Kat found herself a clawlike tool and started working alongside Hannah. After a little while they fell into a rhythm, yanking out the weeds and tossing them into a big rubber trash can. Kat had always considered her workouts to be comprehensive, catching all the major muscle groups. Now, she wasn't so sure.

Kat and Hannah had been weeding side by side for about ten minutes when Kat decided she had had enough of the muttering and the grumpy face.

"You have something to say, go ahead and say it."

Hannah looked surprised, then smiled as she shook her

head. "It took me a little while to figure out why you're here. You're not doing this out of the goodness of your heart, and you're not retired and bored. You just want to sleep with Rob." She shrugged. "It's okay. I get it. He's hot."

Kat studied the girl, wondering yet again what her deal was, and why she was trying so hard to distance herself from everyone around her. Joan hadn't replied to her email yet, so Kat was flying blind here. Instead of arguing with Hannah's conclusion, she decided it would be more fun to run with it.

"How do you know we're not already sleeping together?"

The girl snorted. "It's obvious. Too much unresolved tension."

"Huh." Awkward, if it was obvious to everyone, but good to know.

"Am I right?"

It was Kat's turn to snort. "As if I would tell you. Not your business, missy."

"My name is Hannah."

"Not your business, Hannah."

After that, they worked in silence. Kat didn't attempt any further conversation. Hannah had made her communication preferences clear.

They had been working for what seemed like forever (but was probably more like an hour) when Hannah stopped. She poked the dirt with the toe of her sneaker, then reached down to dig with her hands.

"Problem?"

"There's a rock or something here. I'm just trying to figure out how big it is."

She ripped out some more vegetation. The roots came up as one big clump, revealing the rock. Only it wasn't a rock. It was a small, neat rectangle of gray stone with markings on it.

Hannah brushed the remaining dirt off the surface of the rock. Kat bent down to get a closer look.

Rose.
Kat stood slowly.
"I think we need to talk to Mary Evelyn about this."
Hannah rose more slowly, nodding.
"Is it a grave?"
"Yep."

CHAPTER TEN

THE COOL INTERIOR OF THE LIBRARY WAS A WELCOME RELIEF
after the humidity outside, but Mary Evelyn was nowhere to be
seen. Kat was about to ring the bell on the circulation desk
when the librarian emerged from between two bookcases on
the far side of the room.

"Ladies, how can I help you?"

Kat had never felt less like a lady. Both she and Hannah
were sweaty and bedraggled and smelled like dirt.

"We wanted to ask you about the gravestone in the garden,"
said Kat.

"The what?" Mary Evelyn clearly had no idea what they
were talking about.

Hannah jumped in. "I found a grave when I was weeding.
We thought you would know more about it."

"Show me." Mary Evelyn did not look happy about the
discovery of dead bodies in her backyard.

They led her to the spot, and the unexpected activity
attracted the attention of the entire work crew. Rob told the
kids to keep working, then came over to see what was going on.
Mary Evelyn knelt slowly beside Hannah and traced the letters

on the stone. Her expression changed from skeptical to thoughtful.

"Are there more?" she asked.

Kat and Hannah looked at each other and shrugged. It hadn't occurred to Kat to check. Mary Evelyn grimaced with impatience and struggled back to her feet.

"Well, let's find out, shall we?" She looked at Rob, who motioned for the rest of the crew to come over. Mary Evelyn quickly explained the situation and what she wanted to do. "Everyone line up side by side." She nudged them into a line perpendicular to the sidewalk starting at the existing grave and the search began. "Each of you move forward slowly, clearing as you go, and let me know if you find another gravestone."

Her words transformed the boring, sweaty work into an archaeological dig, and each person wanted to be the first to find something. Kat stepped out of the way and let the suddenly eager volunteers do their thing. Rob had gone back to his truck, and now he returned with a large rolled-up paper. They walked together down to the far end of the lot and watched the volunteers slowly work their way downhill toward them. Rob unrolled the paper, and she realized he held a copy of the plat of survey, one that was covered with handwritten notes and sketches in pencil. He laid it out on the sidewalk and marked the approximate location of the grave.

"Anything on the plat?" she asked.

"Nothing," he answered, "although this lot used to be owned by the church. I guess stranger things have been forgotten."

The hum of activity was punctuated from time to time by a call to Mary Evelyn, signaling that yet another marker had been found. It took over an hour, but by the time the group had reached the edge of the lot, they had uncovered more than twenty graves, and a mystery much larger than anyone had expected.

During the search, Rob had sketched out a grid on the plat and marked the location of each grave, including the name on the grave. None of the stones had any other information on them. No last names. No dates. No scrollwork or decorative markings. A few simply said *Infant, Born Asleep.*

Mary Evelyn had disappeared inside the library only to emerge moments later with a measuring tape and her own copy of the plat of survey. She soon had the teenagers measuring the open space and the grave locations, while she noted the measurements on her survey. Between Rob's rough locations and her detailed measurements, they had a pretty good read on the boundaries of the graveyard. Mary Evelyn had the crew double-check the boundary areas to make sure they hadn't missed any gravestones along the edges. Rob got some caution tape out of the truck and staked it around the area, so that nobody could accidentally disturb the graves.

It was close to wrap-up time when everyone gathered around Mary Evelyn, looking at her as if she had all the answers. She did not.

"It may take some research to find out more about these graves," she began, "and what we learn will certainly affect the project. Would any of you like to help me?"

There was a lot of fidgeting and ground-staring, but over the sound of shuffling feet, Hannah's voice came through clearly.

"I'll help," she said.

It took Mary Evelyn a moment to locate her, but once she had, she nodded sharply. "Excellent. Thank you, everyone, for your help in clearing and mapping the area. You all can continue to work on the rest of the lot, but let's take it easy around the graves. Basic weeding only, and hold off on removing any more trees and shrubs, or grinding down any stumps. I don't want to disturb anything that shouldn't be disturbed, if you know what I mean."

This earned her a few snickers from the teenagers and a few scandalized looks from the handful of older volunteers. To Kat, it sounded like a practical solution, at least for now.

A phone alert caught her attention, the device vibrating briefly in her back pocket. She pulled it out and was surprised to see that Joan had replied to her email with a text. Someone was working late today.

No last-minute add-ons to the group, just the original nine. If you have another teenager, she must be a volunteer. Keep up the good work!

Kat studied Hannah as the girl followed Mary Evelyn into the library. If she wasn't here for community service, then she was here by choice. The question was, why? Thinking back, Kat realized that nothing about the initial introductions had made it obvious that the rest of the teens were not here by choice. Maybe Hannah was just a good kid trying to help out? While it might not be typical teen behavior, that didn't mean it never happened. She would have to get to know the girl better in order to figure it out.

So. Two mysteries to solve.

Rob worked like a maniac on Thursday so that he could arrive early at the library again. The guys gave him a hard time, but it's not like they minded getting a full day's pay with a couple of extra hours off. He ignored their bullshit and even made sure to swing by home and change into a fresh T-shirt before showing up at the library.

He kicked himself for the stab of disappointment when he didn't see Kat's little red Fiat. A busy woman, building a business just like he was doing, might have important stuff to do up at the courthouse or a meeting with a client. It wasn't as if they had scheduled a date or anything. She didn't owe him a phone call or a text to explain why she wasn't here early. He should be grateful she was here at all.

Taking his time unloading the tools from the back of the truck, Rob set them out for the kids and then grabbed his thermos and notebook. He was heading toward the bench in front of the library to sketch out some ideas when he heard the vroom of a tiny car engine. He fought the grin, even while telling himself he was being an idiot, and gave Kat a little wave as he sat down. He needed to play it cool, give her lots of space.

He liked the bounce in her step as she walked over to sit beside him, the little smile playing around the edges of her mouth as she leaned back and took a sip of her iced tea.

"Hey," he said.

Her lips twitched. "Hey."

He liked that they were falling into a rhythm again, that their communication had the feel of a secret code. There were very few people in this world that he felt comfortable with. His parents. A few friends from college. Otherwise, he mostly talked to plants, and he was fine with that. But this was something special. Something fun. Something he wanted to keep private between himself and Kat.

They sat side by side, their shoulders almost but not quite touching. He could feel her body heat, and he wondered if maybe next time—but that would be rushing things, and he had already made himself a pledge not to rush things.

He was about to ask about her day when a squad car rolled up. Officer Jack put the vehicle in park and leaned out the window to talk to them.

"Sorry I haven't been able to make it this week. Shifts didn't work out. You guys doing okay with the kiddos?"

"They've been great," answered Kat. "No trouble at all."

"Heard you found some grave markers?"

Kat nodded. "It's a bit of a mystery. Mary Evelyn and

Hannah are going to investigate. Do you know anything about it?"

"Nope. I asked the zoning department, but they didn't have anything in their records to explain it. The oldest surveys haven't been scanned yet. They're still on paper up at the county. Good thing you uncovered them before going in with diggers. That could have gotten weird fast."

Rob hadn't even thought about that possibility. It would have been a PR disaster, to say nothing of traumatizing the kids. Bullet dodged.

"Hey, I have a question for you," said Kat.

"Shoot."

"What's the story with Hannah? I asked Joan for more background, but she said Hannah's not a part of the community service group. Do you know her?"

"Sure," said Jack. "I told Mary Evelyn, but in all the excitement she must have forgotten to tell you. Hannah is the stepdaughter of one of the other police officers. She had stopped by the station for something when we were talking about the community service kids and who might be available to supervise them. She asked if she could help with the project, and I didn't see any harm in having an extra volunteer. She seems pretty shy, so I figured if she had the guts to ask, I shouldn't say no."

"Huh," said Kat. "Did her stepdad have any concerns about her hanging out with the other kids?"

Rob frowned, surprised that Kat would characterize the kids as a bad influence. Jack didn't seem to notice anything odd about her question.

"Now that you mention it, he did seem a little annoyed, but I had already welcomed her aboard, so he probably felt like it was too late to object." Jack paused, considering the issue. "Was that a bad move? Do you have concerns, too?"

"Not at all," said Kat. "I've just seen some parents freak out when their little angels have to do community service. They never see their own kids as troublemakers. It's always the other kids who are likely to do the corrupting." She smiled. "Hannah is going to be fine. They're great kids."

"Glad to hear it," said Jack. His radio crackled, and he turned away to check in. "Gotta run. Call me if you need me."

They waved him off, then Rob turned to Kat. "You have any idea why Hannah volunteered for this?"

She tilted her head to one side, and his attention was caught by the line of her neck and chin. He wished that he could freeze this moment just long enough to sketch her without making her think he was some kind of freak stalker. He committed the image to memory instead.

"I have a few theories, but I'll need to get to know her better to figure it out." She flashed him a smile. "Who knew that we would end up with two mysteries?"

"I'll let you know if I find any clues," he said. "Maybe I should paint my truck like the Mystery Machine."

"You absolutely should! I will add Scooby Snacks to my grocery list."

He laughed. "You know they make those for real, don't you?"

"You're kidding."

He shook his head.

"Well, then I'm definitely getting some. Can't solve a mystery without Scooby Snacks."

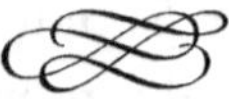

CHAPTER ELEVEN

MEL DIDN'T INTENTIONALLY SNEAK UP ON KAT AND ROB, BUT they were so cozy on the bench that they didn't even notice her until she was almost on top of them.

"Hey, guys." Mel kept her voice cheery and hid a laugh when both of them jumped. The role of "parent catching teen in the act" was new to her.

"Mel." Kat spoke first. She was the one who would have seen Mel coming, if she hadn't been staring so dreamily into Rob's eyes. "It's Thursday. I thought you were working in the city."

Mel gave a one-shoulder shrug. "Didn't have any gigs lined up for today or tomorrow, and I can do my photo editing anywhere." Also, she hadn't heard a peep from her mother since Dora had left for New York, and she was feeling the need for sister time. Maybe one of them had talked with her. "Might as well do it here, staring out at the lake. It's a hell of a view."

They both made noises of agreement, but Mel didn't need her sister's psych degree to read the signs here. She had stumbled onto a little date. Rob was sipping something out of a thermos, so he wasn't looking at Mel, which gave her the opportunity to raise an eyebrow at Kat and signal that she was happy to duck into the library to give them some more time alone. Kat gave a quick head shake in response, clearly embarrassed.

"Well, it's great that you could come today. 'Many hands' and all that," said Rob.

"I figured a little fresh air and movement might help the headache from staring at the computer screen all day, and the crick in my neck from bad posture."

"It definitely will," said Rob.

"What's with the caution tape?" asked Mel. "Toxic chemical spill? Quicksand?"

"Dead bodies," answered Kat.

Mel laughed, then realized Kat was serious. "What? You're punking me, right?"

"Not kidding," said Kat. "We literally stumbled onto some graves on Tuesday, and now we need to figure out what to do about it. Nobody had any idea."

"Are we even going to be able to work today? It looks like half the site is blocked off."

"Oh, sure," said Rob. "Plenty to do on the first half of the lot, and of course this doesn't really affect what you're doing with the wall. We can even move forward with weeding around the gravestones, as long as we're careful."

"That's good." Mel looked back and forth between Rob and the taped-off area. More than anything, she wanted to go play Nancy Drew and check out the graves.

"You can go look," he said, answering her unasked question. She grinned. "Thanks."

It was easy enough to step over the tape, but small shrubs and trees still blocked her way. Pale gray rectangles contrasted with freshly disturbed soil, marking neat rows in an otherwise messy landscape. Each bore an inscription. Mel did a quick count, and found it impossible to believe that nearly forty graves had lain hidden for so long. How could an entire grave-yard have been forgotten? And, based on the names she'd seen so far, why were most of its residents female?

Mel walked each of the rows before returning to Kat and Rob's bench, where she found them once again absorbed in conversation. This time, though, Kat noticed her approach.

"So?" she asked.

Mel shook her head. "It's strange. Beautiful, but strange. I'd love to take some photos before we clear the site anymore. Would it be weird if I ran home to get my camera?" It wasn't far. She could be there and back in twenty minutes.

Kat and Rob glanced at each other before Kat responded. "That would be amazing. I was actually thinking on Tuesday that we should be doing a better job of documenting the project. Mary Evelyn is taking snapshots, but it's not the same thing as quality photography."

Mel's tough professional heart melted a little at Kat's words. "I would love to do it."

Mary Evelyn poked her head out of the side door of the library just then, and Henry and Charlie pulled up in Henry's ancient Crown Vic. Rob stood and stretched, then extended a hand to Kat to pull her to a stand as well.

"You grab your camera," he said to Mel. "We'll get things rolling here."

Mel gave him a quick salute and jogged off in the direction of home.

After wrapping up for the day, Kat ventured into the dim cool-ness of the library in search of Mary Evelyn and Hannah. She found the two of them in the conference room, sitting at the large table with clippings and photos spread all around them. From their wardrobe choices, you would think winter had already arrived. Mary Evelyn wore a wrap that looked suspiciously like a blanket, and Hannah once again sported long pants and a long-sleeved shirt, this time with a short-sleeved T-shirt layered over the top.

"Wow. It looks like you two have been very busy," said Kat from the doorway.

Mary Evelyn smiled. "This is my 'war room.' I've been collecting all sorts of historical tidbits for the muralist. I didn't realize they would be needed for another purpose, but it certainly provided a head start."

"Any luck?" asked Kat.

Hannah shook her head.

"Nothing so far," said Mary Evelyn. "I even called the county offices to check the early property records, the ones that haven't been scanned, but there's no mention of a cemetery. They're going to send me copies anyway, but it looks like a dead end."

At Kat's raised eyebrow, Mary Evelyn laughed.

"Pun intended, I suppose. It's strange. You would think a cemetery would be a hard thing to forget."

"What about the death records up at county?" asked Kat. "Do we have enough information to check those?"

"I thought about that," said Mary Evelyn. "There are two problems with that approach. One is that we have only first names. Without a date or a last name, we won't be able to narrow down our search results."

"And the second?"

"They only have death records going back to 1939, and the land was sold to the village in 1935."

Kat pondered that for a minute. "I'm no genealogist, but don't churches usually keep those records, too? Maybe we should ask them."

Mary Evelyn stiffened. "That may be the next logical step, but unfortunately I can't step away from my duties here at the library to do research off-site. It would be better if you or one of the other volunteers could look into it."

Given Mary Evelyn's known passion for historical research, this was the last thing she expected the librarian to say. Something about her answer, and her attitude, felt off. Another mystery to add to the list.

"Okay, then," said Kat cautiously.

"So who's going to figure this out?" asked Hannah. She sounded irritated.

Mary Evelyn looked from Kat to Hannah and back again. "I'm sure you two can handle it." She stood abruptly. "I really should get back to work. Let me know if I can help you find anything else."

Before Kat or Hannah could protest, she had fled the conference room. Hannah and Kat were left staring at each other. For a brief moment, Hannah's annoyance leaked onto her face. Then it was gone, her impassive mask firmly back in place.

"Guess we're stuck with each other." Kat raised an eyebrow, turning the statement into a challenge.

Hannah shrugged one shoulder. "Whatever."

"Want to go over there now?" asked Kat.

"Fine."

They walked over to the church only to find it closed, which left Kat feeling deflated. She was impatient for answers, but it's hard to argue with an empty building. Looking down at her filthy clothes and hands, she said, "What do you say we stop by the church on Sunday, when we know somebody will be here?"

"Do we have to actually go to the service?"

Kat had been pondering the same question.

"I don't think so. We can stop by afterward and see if anyone can help us."

Hannah was silent, and Kat wondered if she was nervous

about showing up at a church all by herself. "Do you want to meet in front of the library and walk over together?"

Hannah nodded, looking relieved.

"Great. Let me check the church's website to see what time the service might start and end."

Before Kat could pull out her phone, Hannah spoke. "They're usually done just before eleven." At Kat's inquiring look, she continued, "We used to go here."

"Eleven o'clock on Sunday, then," said Kat, holding back the many questions this small clue had sent tumbling through her mind. "We have a plan. And now I think it's time to head home. You good to go from here?"

Hannah nodded.

"Cool. I'll see you Saturday—and Sunday."

The girl nodded again before walking away toward what Kat assumed was home. If only Hannah were one of the community service kids, with a file full of background information, Kat would have had some idea of where to begin. Without that starting point, Kat and Hannah were going to have to do this the hard way.

On that thought, Kat turned and headed back to the library and her car. Time for a shower and an evening of catch-up work.

Mel wandered downstairs on Saturday morning to find both of her sisters in the kitchen, working on breakfast. It was awfully sweet of them to keep her company, given that they were each sleeping somewhere else, but Mel wasn't going to comment on it. She didn't want them to stop.

"Omelets?" she asked.

Tessa nodded. She had taken on the job of prep cook and was chopping her way through a small pile of veggies. Callie was buttering some toast. Mel grabbed another cutting board and started slicing up some fruit for the side. This was a much nicer breakfast than she would ever make for herself. Her usual was Cheerios and milk.

"Either of you heard from Mom?"

"Nothing yet," said Callie, "other than the call to say that she got there safely."

"It's been a week," said Mel. "This is bullshit. Why aren't you guys worried about her?"

"I talked to Dad in Nashville last night. He's not worried about her either."

Tessa gave Mel "the look." "She's a grown woman. Perfectly capable of looking after herself for a week. Let's give her the time and space she needs to deal with this."

"With what?" demanded Mel, fruit forgotten on the counter in front of her. "She won't even tell us what's going on, or why it's so damn important that she reconnect with this old friend." She stalked over to the cupboard to grab a coffee cup. "Some friend, disappearing from her life entirely for almost thirty years, and then poof, poor me, I'm so sick, come sit at my bedside and keep me company." She poured coffee into the cup too fast, and some sloshed onto her hand. She hissed, and Callie handed her a paper towel to wipe it up. It didn't stop her rant, though. "I call bullshit. There's something bigger going on that Mom isn't telling us."

"And you think we should, what, torture her until she tells us?" Tessa wasn't pulling any punches this morning.

"I think we should go to New York."

Both of her sisters stopped what they were doing and looked at Mel. Callie walked over and gave her a big hug. It wasn't—she didn't need to.... Damn it, she was not going to cry.

"Mom's going to be fine," said Tessa firmly. "She'll tell us when it's time."

Mel gave Callie a squeeze and then pushed her away.

"I know. I just don't like it."

"Duly noted," said Tessa wryly.

Mel scraped the sand out of her eyes with the paper towel, then took a sip of the still-scalding coffee.

"So how come you guys don't have to help with this garden and mural project?" asked Mel. New topic. No crying.

"Because Mom is not trying to set us up with the hot muralist from the city." Callie said it so matter-of-factly that it took Mel an extra second to process what she had said.

"That's so not fair."

"True," said Tessa, "but there it is."

Mel shook her head. "It's never going to work. The setup, I mean."

"Why not?" asked Tessa. Mel didn't like the mischievous smile that came along with the question. "He's hot and super-talented. You're hot—"

Mel raised an eyebrow at that. They were, after all, identical triplets. Tessa grinned in response.

"And super-talented. You could have an epic end-of-summer affair and then ride off into the sunset. Separately, of course."

"So now we live in a solar system with two suns?"

Callie snickered but wisely kept her eyes on the toast she was buttering.

"We do," said Tessa. "Learn to love it."

Mel picked up an apple core and aimed at Tessa's head. "Enough about the hot muralist."

"Fine," said Tessa.

Mel knew this wasn't the last time he would come up, but no matter how hot he was, it didn't make sense to bite. He had distraction written all over him, and no hot muralist was going to derail her plans.

"How are you and Kat getting along?" asked Callie. "Is it weird?"

"Weirdly, no," said Mel. "We actually grabbed lunch last Saturday after the work session."

"And...?" asked Tessa.

Mel shot her a look. Yes, she was using her therapist tricks to get more details out of Mel, but she also appeared to be genuinely curious.

"We talked about it, a little. I apologized for stealing the journal. She told me that it had actually helped by bringing everything out into the open. I'll probably feel guilty about her mom forever, but she seemed to have a really healthy perspective about it all."

Both her sisters were staring at her.

"What? I told you it was weird."

"That's super-weird," said Callie.

"She must have had lots and lots of therapy," said Tessa.

"She did," answered Mel.

Tessa nodded, as if everything now made sense.

"So are you really going to open a wedding photography business up here?" asked Callie.

Mel choked on her coffee.

"What?" she asked, once her throat was clear.

"Mom has been talking about it like it's a done deal," offered Tessa helpfully.

"No chance in hell."

"You might want to let Mom know when she gets back. I heard the other day that she went to check out some commercial space to see if it would work for your office and studio."

Mel set down her coffee and put her face in her hands.

"Somebody shoot me now."

"You just need to tell her," said Tessa. "Firmly."

Mel dropped her hands. "Oh, I will," she said. "I definitely will."

CHAPTER TWELVE

R OB PULLED UP IN FRONT OF THE DESERTED LIBRARY MORE THAN an hour early on Saturday morning. He had his cover story ready—getting in some work on design ideas—but didn't try to fool himself. He was here because he was hoping Kat would be here early again, too.

A braver man would just ask her to meet him for coffee, like regular people do when they date. A smarter man would have slept in for a few extra hours, instead of popping awake at six in the morning and staring at the ceiling, and then seriously over-caffeinating as he waited impatiently for it not to be too early to head to the library. A cooler man would have rolled in at five after nine, taking it as his due that Kat—and everyone else—would be waiting for him.

Rob was none of those things, and he didn't really want to be any of those things. So what if he wasn't a big risk-taker when it came to relationships? If you don't put yourself out there, you won't get hurt. It had always seemed like a sensible plan, and so far it had worked well. In this case, though, he was losing sleep over an amazing woman that he was too scared to officially ask out. It was a lot like being back in high school, without the convenient excuse of being in high school.

Rob paced the lot and pretended to take some notes, but really he was realizing that those two and a half cups of coffee had caught up to him and he needed to use the restroom. He could (a) go back home for a bit, missing out on the chance to see Kat, (b) run over to the gas station, use their restroom, grab a fresh cup of coffee, and come back as quickly as possible, or (c) try to do a stealthy public urination. Waiting for the library to open was not an option.

He wandered casually toward the back corner of the library to evaluate option c, but they had done too good a job at clearing this section of the property. There was no decent cover, and the steep hillside meant that several houses overlooked the lot. Who knew how many people were watching him right now over their breakfast toast?

Abandoning that plan, he turned back toward his car and, just in case, tried the back door of the library. To his surprise, he found that the handle was a bit loose and the door opened easily. Without overthinking it, he slipped inside. There were just enough windows back here to light his way through the dim hallway toward the bathroom. When he entered, those lights switched on automatically, and he took care of business. He was midstream when he realized that he might have tripped an alarm system. That would be an awkward start to the day.

He finished up as quickly as he could. Emerging from the dim hallway back into the sunlight, he was relieved to find that he was still alone. No police cars. No early volunteers. Just Kat's car pulling into the parking spot next to his truck.

She had come early. Very early.

After walking back over to his truck, he pulled out his half-full coffee mug. Then he went around the back of the truck to greet her as she stepped out of her car.

"Good morning," he said. Was it his imagination or did she look a little flustered?

"Morning," she replied.

Her voice was a little rough, and he wondered if it was like that every morning. Now there was a goal—to wake up next to Kat. All that long, dark hair would be messy instead of styled, and her eyes would be soft and unfocused. He filed the thought away for later, when he didn't have to worry about his body's enthusiastic response to the idea.

They wandered over to the bench and sat in silence for a bit. So few people in this world knew how to simply be still. They needed to fill up every second with words or music or games on their phones. To be able to sit quietly with someone, without the pressure of conversation, was a gift. Kat finally broke the silence when his coffee was nearly gone.

"What did you end up doing after high school?" she asked. "I saw bits and pieces on your public profile on Facebook, but not the whole picture."

He wondered what that meant, the fact that she had kept tabs on him. "I used to search for you sometimes, but you never came up, at least not on Facebook."

She looked down at her coffee. "I had my privacy settings locked up pretty tight, so I wouldn't show up in searches. I didn't want to keep in touch with anybody from 'before.'"

Before. The word had more weight than it should. When she didn't say more, he answered her question. "I followed the plan, mostly. Graduated high school. Worked on the farm in the summers. Studied at the Ag school up in Madison."

"How did you end up doing landscape architecture instead of agribusiness? That wasn't part of the plan, at least not the last time you told me about it."

"Well, I did promise to keep taking art classes."

She laughed. "Yes, you did." She had imagined, during her

more optimistic moments, that they might both end up in Madison and take a few art classes together. It had been a silly daydream, not one that she had ever expected to come true. Still, a part of her ached at the thought of him keeping that promise even after she had disappeared from his life. "So the art classes were a slippery slope for you?"

"It didn't take long to figure out that landscape architecture was a cool way to combine everything I loved into one career."

The wind whipped the first few fallen leaves of the season in a swirl around their feet. Rob debated asking Kat about her years away. They couldn't avoid the subject forever, not if he hoped to rebuild a relationship, and a better opportunity was not going to come along anytime soon.

"What about you?" asked Rob. "Where did you go...after?"

There it was again, a word that carried too much weight. She didn't answer right away, and he began to wonder if she would answer at all, but finally she spoke.

"I ended up in foster care and finished out the school year. It took some time for me to get...sorted out, I guess, but I graduated from high school on time. Luckily, there was some life insurance money that I could use for college. I ended up at UW-Milwaukee. Kept busy. Eventually everything settled into a new normal. I worked hard, took summer courses, finished college and law school in five years."

She took a long sip of her coffee. He wondered how much of the story she had left out, and reminded himself that it would take time to earn her trust again. Still, he wanted to know more. He wanted to know *her*.

"And then?"

"I got a job at a big law firm, the kind where you work eighty hours a week and have no life. It should have been awful, but it was so much fun. There was a whole group of us that went straight from school to this big firm. We worked like crazy and let loose on the weekends and had an amazing time."

She sounded wistful. Did she regret leaving?

"And you never reached out to anybody from home?"

She shook her head.

"So why come back here at all? Why not keep building that new life in Milwaukee?"

"It wasn't me." She smiled wryly. "I could play the game, and it was fun, but it was always a role. We were doing work for giant companies, and I wanted to work with real people. Make a difference in a tangible way. The only place I could imagine doing that was back here. Not that many lawyers go to the rural areas, so I figured there would be room for me to build a practice."

"Doesn't it bother you, though, to be reminded of the past all the time?"

"The past doesn't matter. It can't be changed. I focus on the things I *can* change, and making a difference now."

Rob nodded, but he didn't really know what to say. Sure, the past was in the past, but it could screw you up for a long time after it was gone. Hell, there was an entire profession dedicated to unraveling the messes left behind.

He was just forming something to say when a car pulled up, parked, and Jack climbed out. Beside him, Kat stiffened, then relaxed, as if it were a conscious choice. He wondered what would make Kat react that way, and whether it was recent—work-related—or something far older.

Kat caught herself tensing when Jack stepped out of the car so she took a deep breath, held it, and then released both her breath and the tension from her shoulders. The coping technique had become habit, but it couldn't eliminate the trigger. Maybe her reaction would never fully go away. She hated it—hated feeling like a hostage to her past. So, as she had with the rest of the hurdles life had placed in her path, she stiffened her resolve and calmly walked around it.

Without the squad car and the uniform, Jack looked like any other guy. Maybe his posture was a little better, his demeanor more self-assured. Most women would find him attractive. Instead, he made Kat tense. She understood, intellectually, that the job of a police officer was to serve and protect. Most of them were wonderful, loyal, dedicated people. She knew from personal experience, however, that not every cop was one of the good guys. Her instinctive response was still one of fear.

"Am I early?" asked Jack as he strolled up. He wore faded jeans and a T-shirt, and had a pair of work gloves stuffed in his back pocket.

Rob checked his watch. "A little. Why don't I show you around the site?"

Kat stayed on the bench while the two of them walked the lot. It didn't take long. When they returned, she stood. The three of them couldn't fit comfortably on the bench, and it was too awkward to stay seated while the two of them loomed over her.

"How are the kids doing?" asked Jack.

Rob filled him in, with Kat adding the occasional comment. Jack seemed pleased that nobody was causing any trouble.

"What can you tell me about Hannah?" asked Kat. "I'd like to understand her better."

Jack shrugged. "I don't know that there's much to tell. She seems like a sweet kid."

"No cute family stories you've heard from her dad?"

"He doesn't talk much about his family on the job. He's her stepdad. Married Jennifer—her mom—a couple of years ago. There's a little sister, too. Fiona, I think. They call her Fee."

"Do you know what happened to her biological father?"

"I think he died."

"Everything okay at home?" At Jack's sharp look, she back-tracked. "I'm just trying to figure out why Hannah would volunteer for the project when she doesn't seem all that excited about gardening. Girls her age are usually all about their friends, but she's doing this on her own. I can't ask her directly until I know her better. She's not all that big on conversation."

The explanation seemed to appease Jack.

"As far as I know, everything is okay. I'm not exactly best buds with Carl, but I see him fairly often. He does seem to worry about Jenn a lot. Always checking in with her, making sure she's okay. I figured that was a married people thing."

"I wouldn't know." Kat laughed it off, dismissing the twinge of paranoia. Keeping in constant contact with your spouse could be creepy, sure, but it could also be a sign of love and care. Her past had a tendency to color her perception, leaving her predisposed to jump at shadows and see threats when none were there. Given her known bias, she had learned that unless and until she had evidence of a problem, she needed to keep an open mind. There was no way she could trust her instincts.

The rest of the volunteers started trickling in not long after Jack's arrival. The Saturday crowd was substantially bigger than the weekday crowd, with the volunteers skewing older.

Hannah pulled her usual loner routine, choosing to work as far as possible from the other kids. Kat adapted, making sure she was always within about ten feet of Hannah, so that the girl had her space but was never isolated. She also made the occasional offhand comment, giving Hannah an open door for conversation if she wanted it.

She didn't. It was a quiet, sweaty three hours. The late September sunshine and humidity meant that Kat's T-shirt was sticking to her back by the time they finished for the day.

"Meet you here tomorrow at ten forty-five?" Kat couldn't let Hannah leave without at least a brief exchange of words.

Hannah nodded, then spun on her heel and headed home, throwing a half-hearted wave over her shoulder. Kat just nodded to herself as she watched Hannah head off down the road. Well played, teenager. Well played.

The volunteer crew cleared out pretty quickly. Kat helped Rob move a pile of brush away from the base of the scaffolding, closer to the side of the road. They were walking back toward the building when the back door opened and Mary Evelyn poked her head out.

"You all wrapped up for the day?"

"Yep," answered Rob. "You closing up?"

She nodded. "Anybody want a drink from the bubbler before I lock up?"

"I'm good," said Rob. He turned to Kat, who shook her head. "We're all set. Before you lock up, though, we should check the back door. It was unlocked when I got here this morning."

"Not again," groaned Mary Evelyn.

"Problem?" asked Rob.

"We need to get the door handle replaced, or at least the lock. It's not urgent, I suppose, but I'm getting a little sick of the daily calls from the police station saying that the night shift found the door unlocked and had to do a walk-through of the building." She released a long-suffering sigh. "It's not like we live in a high-crime area. I'll try to remember to call the locksmith on Monday. While we're here, can you test it for me?"

"Sure."

Mary Evelyn locked the door, then yelled, "Okay, try it now."

Rob tried the handle, and with a strong jiggle, it was easy to open.

"Damn door," said Mary Evelyn.

Both Kat and Rob laughed.

"Don't tell anybody about the flaw in our security," said Mary Evelyn. "I'll see you two on Tuesday afternoon."

She shut the door, and Kat realized that they were alone. She turned toward Rob and discovered that they were standing awfully close together. So close that she had to tilt her head back to meet his eyes. Neither of them took a step back.

"So." She couldn't help smiling a little.

"So," he echoed. "I was thinking...."

She raised an eyebrow when his voice trailed off.

He cleared his throat. "I was wondering if you have any plans this coming Thursday. Apart from being here, I mean. After that."

Her smile widened. He was flustered and adorable, and she was pretty sure he was asking her out on a date. She shook her head slowly.

"Nope. No plans. You?"

"Just work," he said glumly.

So, he wasn't asking her out? Now Kat was just confused. Some of her confusion must have shown on her face, because he started explaining.

"I mean, all I would normally do is work, but I was thinking that maybe, you and me, I mean, you and I could grab dinner or something—after we shower and change. Separately. I mean we should eat together but shower separately." He closed his eyes in defeat. "I'll shut up now."

"I'd like that," said Kat softly.

Rob opened his eyes cautiously, as if he wasn't sure he had heard her correctly. "You'd like me to shut up?"

She shook her head, fighting a smile. "Dinner."

"Oh. Great."

She waited, just to see what he would do. It would be so easy to rise up on her toes and kiss him. Too easy, almost. The anticipation was excruciating and wonderful at the same time.

She could wallow in it for hours. She wanted to imprint it on her brain so that she could come back to it any time she wanted. She wished—

"Hi, guys."

Not so alone, after all.

CHAPTER THIRTEEN

MEL MADE SURE HER CHEERY GREETING WAS OVERLY LOUD AND accompanied by the creaks and groans of the scaffolding as she made her way down the remaining rungs of the ladder. The last thing she wanted to do was to witness a makeout session between Kat and Rob. They were standing suspiciously close together, and she could practically feel the electricity zinging between them.

"Hey, Mel," said Rob. His voice sounded a little hoarse.

Kat took a small step back and turned around. "I didn't realize you were still working up there. We almost left you on your own."

"Just wanted to finish up a section. Feels good to make progress."

Mel pretended to be oblivious to the sexual tension in the general vicinity. Maybe she should feel guilty about breaking up the moment, but every romance needed a few obstacles to overcome, right?

Rob nodded, and it took her a second to realize that he was agreeing with her earlier out-loud statement, not answering the question in her head.

"I'm going to head out," he said. "Need to get ahead on some work so I can go out on Thursday night."

This last bit made Kat duck her head. It was cute to watch. Kids. They grow up so fast.

"Will we see you Tuesday?" Rob asked Mel.

She thought about it for a second. "Unlikely," she said, "but if my calendar is open later in the week I may show up on Thursday again. We'll see."

"Cool," said Rob. He turned back to Kat and brushed his fingers across her cheek. "See you soon."

"Soon," she repeated. She kept staring at him as he walked away.

"Hello, earth to Kat." Mel waved her hand in front of Kat's face.

"What?"

Kat sounded a little grumpy.

"Sorry I interrupted your little moment, there. I didn't realize I was crashing until it was too late."

"It's fine."

"Yeah, I can tell it's not fine, but whatever. You two are pretty adorable, what with all the unresolved sexual tension and all."

"It's not...we're not..."

"Sure you are, and that's okay. Really. No law against it." Mel thought about that for a second. "As long as you're not planning anything too kinky, you should be in the clear."

Kat just stared blankly at Mel.

"Not even a chuckle?" asked Mel. She shook her head. "I give up."

"He just asked me out." Kat looked sick after saying it, like it was actual word vomit.

"And that's a problem?"

"I haven't been on a real date in so long...."

Mel patted her on the shoulder. "You'll be fine."

"No, you don't understand. Rob is...confusing. I lose track of who I am with him. Sometimes I feel like myself, and sometimes I feel like before. I don't like it."

Kat seemed genuinely distressed, even if Mel couldn't quite figure out what the problem was.

"So don't go out with him. If you don't like how it feels to be with him, you don't need to be with him. Simple."

"My life is never simple," Kat wailed. She started pacing, out into the sunshine and then back into the shade under the scaffolding. "I've done such a good job of building a new life, and then I see Rob, and it's like the old me comes popping back out again, saying, 'Here I am! You never really got rid of me. I've just been hiding!'"

"What's wrong with the old you?"

Kat whipped around at that, pinning Mel with one hell of an evil glare.

"Do you not remember the old me? Clinging to any guy who would prop me up? Too scared to report what was going on at home? Closing my eyes and covering my ears and pretending that if I just waited long enough it would all go away?"

Kat stood there, breathing too fast, waiting for an answer. And what did Mel really have to say? She remembered it all too well—all the cruel things she had thought and said about Kat before making the boneheaded decision to steal her English journal. Before she understood what was really going on. There was no way to undo the past, no way to reset all those dominoes.

"I remember," said Mel. "It sounds like you're the one who doesn't remember."

That provoked a sharp look from Kat.

"You were going through some awful shit, both at home and at school, and you didn't let it destroy you."

"It did destroy me."

"Don't be ridiculous. You're here, aren't you? You made it

through. So what if you tried a few different coping strategies along the way? Denial. Totally valid strategy in your situation. Or 'ignore the bitches'—myself included. That mostly worked, until I stole the diary. You were seventeen, for Pete's sake. What would you expect a seventeen-year-old to do?"

"Ask for help." Kat looked like she was going to cry.

"My sisters and I tried that on your behalf, and it blew up in all our faces. I think you knew, deep down, that if you tried to go through channels—to trust the system—that something horrible would happen."

Kat just stared at her. The tears never fell.

"Why am I telling you all this stuff?"

Mel shrugged. "No clue."

Kat was silent. She looked lost. Mel couldn't bring herself to just walk away. Kat needed to talk to someone, and she didn't seem to have a lot of friends. She and Kat might not be BFFs, but they were at least heading toward friends, and Mel could imitate her therapist sister when necessary. Seemed like it might be necessary this afternoon.

"Want to grab lunch again?" Her words seemed to break through the confusion. Kat blinked a few times, and her eyes cleared.

"That sounds great." She turned toward the sidewalk, then whipped right back around. "No beer this time."

Mel lifted both hands in surrender. "You make the rules."

Rob spent Saturday afternoon and evening catching up on quotes and billing, and most of Sunday morning cleaning mower blades and other random maintenance. After lunch, he walked the fields and the greenhouse, checking the health of the plants. The biggest risks to his stock were weather and disease. Weather had been cooperative so far this year, but he still needed to keep an eye out for disease or pests.

By midafternoon, he had run out of things to do and was getting antsy. His body might be ready to kick back and relax and watch the game, but his mind was running in circles. Why had he suggested Thursday to Kat? Why not tonight? Then they could get this first date over with and maybe he could finally calm down.

He needed to get out, go do something. Maybe the crowd down at The Beach could provide the distraction he needed. They would definitely have the game up on the big screen.

The Beach was packed. Nothing like a Bears-Packers game to bring out a crowd. This close to the border with Illinois, you could count on a good mix of fans in the room, and plenty of heckling. He got lucky, found an empty stool at the end of the bar by the kitchen. Within minutes he was set up with a beer, some wings, and plenty of distraction.

After the game, the crowd thinned, but Rob didn't head home. He could hear his mother's voice in the back of his mind. *You're lonely, honey. You need to get out more.* Possibly true, but there was no reason to admit that to his mother, either in real life or in his imagination.

Someone came up to the bar next to him to order, and it took him a second to realize it was Jack. It wasn't like the guy was in disguise or anything. He just looked different without the uniform.

"You come down to watch the game?" asked Jack.

Rob nodded.

"Bears or Packers?" At Rob's raised eyebrow, he clarified, "Have to ask. You never know."

"Packers."

Jack nodded in satisfaction. "Good game to watch on the big screen."

"No kidding. It's like you can see every blade of grass on the field."

They talked about the game for a few minutes, but it had been a total blowout. Not that much to talk about, really, except that the Bears weren't even worth playing this year.

"So you and Kat, huh?" Jack's question took Rob by surprise.

"Heading that way," he answered cautiously. He didn't want to jinx it, but he wanted to make his intentions clear, just in case Jack was thinking—

"Not planning to get in your way," said Jack, clearly following Rob's train of thought. "Just glad to see her happy. After everything with her mom and stepdad went down, I wasn't sure she'd come out the other side okay."

Something about Jack's tone of voice pinged Rob's radar.

"You were there?" It wasn't a completely ridiculous idea. Jack had been just a few years older, in college, but home a lot. And his dad had been a cop at the time.

Jack grimaced. "Not exactly." He looked as if he regretted saying anything. "Mel kind of put me in the middle of it."

"That makes no sense."

"Mel and her sisters had somehow...acquired Kat's journal, and she had written some serious stuff in there about her stepdad and the things going on at home. No reason not to believe it. Private diary and all. But he was a cop, and that made things really complicated." Jack paused to take a swig of his beer. "They brought it to me, asked me what to do."

Rob could see where this was going, and it wasn't good.

"What did you tell them?"

"I told them you gotta do the right thing, even when it's hard. After all, that's what dear old Dad always said. We took the journal to him, figuring he was a cop and would know what to do." Jack took another long pull on his beer, then shook his head. "My dad did not do the right thing. He ignored protocol and confronted Kat's stepdad directly. Guy was a cop, asked for professional courtesy. A chance to pack up his things, say goodbye to his wife."

"Shit."

"Yeah," echoed Jack. "Pure luck Kat was still at school."

Rob nodded without bothering to correct Jack. That's where she should have been. They had planned to work on their art projects after school, but she had been freaking out about something all day—the journal, probably—and had gone home after school instead. He had been so mad at her for blowing him off.

And he had never seen her again.

"I still think about it sometimes," said Jack. "Still pissed at my dad, even though he's gone. Wonder what I should have done differently."

"Not your fault, man. You were just a kid trying to do the right thing."

"Doesn't matter. I still wonder."

CHAPTER FOURTEEN

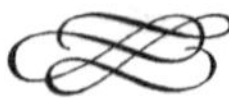

ON SUNDAY MORNING, HANNAH WAS WAITING ON THE BENCH IN front of the library when Kat pulled up. The leaves had begun to change color, and for the first time Kat caught a hint of fall in the air. Hannah's unnatural stillness put Kat in mind of a deer hoping not to be seen. She had the same mix of strength and fragility. One strong gust of wind and she might blow away.

Kat smiled when she saw that Hannah had dressed up for the occasion, choosing a sundress and a light sweater with her signature long sleeves. These were so long that they almost covered her hands, reminding Kat of that girl in the Twilight movies. Maybe it was a self-conscious teen fashion choice. Maybe it was just the "in" fashion and Kat was out of touch. Either way, at this point she would be startled to catch sight of Hannah's bare arms, like a Victorian getting a glimpse of someone's ankle.

Kat had dressed up as well, unsure of the protocol, but the day was supposed to warm up so she had skipped a sweater. Instead, she had channeled Jackie Kennedy in capris, a dressy T-shirt, flats, big sunglasses, and a scarf tied around her throat. Dora had assured her that the little church was casual, but Kat had grown up with a Catholic mother. They might not have gone to church except for weddings and funerals, but in her mother's mind, and therefore in Kat's as well, you dressed up for church—Sunday Best and all that. This little church might be casual, but Kat couldn't imagine stepping through the doors wearing jeans.

As she approached the bench where Hannah waited, Kat surveyed the empty lot and realized that their scrappy little group of volunteers had made substantial progress. They had met a total of, what, four times now? Saturday, Tuesday, Thursday, and yesterday, which added up to maybe ten hours of work time. The lot was nearly clear, except for the cemetery. Rob was already strategizing about how to remove the scrub trees and shrubs without disturbing the graves.

"Morning," said Kat.

"Hi."

"How's it going?"

Hannah answered with a one-shouldered shrug.

Okay, then.

"Shall we walk over?"

Hannah nodded and stood up. Kat wondered briefly why Hannah hadn't suggested meeting at the church or her house, which couldn't be more than a few blocks away. She had probably walked past the church to get here.

They walked in silence around the block to the main entrance of the church, and it looked like they had timed their arrival perfectly. Most of the parishioners had left, but there were still a handful of cars in the parking lot. Kat followed the sign pointing toward the office. She felt a little odd just wandering in, but the church was supposed to be open to everyone, right? Sanctuary in times of trouble? They found an efficient-looking woman sitting at the desk in the office.

"Can I help you?" the woman asked, before she spied the

teenager trailing behind Kat. "Hannah! We haven't seen you in a while. How are you?"

The warm welcome startled Kat, whose limited experience with church had been quite anonymous. She stepped to the side, leaving Hannah with no cover. The girl ducked her head.

"I'm good."

"We've missed you." The lady seemed nice, but she was also clearly fishing for information. Kat felt awkward on Hannah's behalf.

"Yeah, well, my stepdad isn't really into church."

"I had heard that your mom got remarried. Please tell her that I say 'hi,' okay?"

Hannah nodded, still staring at the floor.

Looking up at Kat, the lady said smiled warmly and said, "I'm Irene, by the way, the church secretary."

"Kat Rodriguez." Kat offered her hand, hoping to make a good impression.

"What can I help you ladies with today?"

It was clear that Hannah didn't plan to say anything further, so Kat stepped up.

"We're helping with the mural project at the library, and we've been clearing the underbrush in the area between the church and the library. We found some grave markers, and we were hoping someone here at church might be able to tell us about them. Mary Evelyn at the library didn't have any information in her files, and we haven't had any luck with the property records."

"We have a cemetery? I had no idea. Pastor?" She called over her shoulder toward an inner office.

Kat hoped her surprise didn't show on her face when a middle-aged woman stepped out. Apparently not all ministers looked like Santa Claus. This one looked like a mom, without even a fancy collar to give her away.

"Hannah, is that really you? I can't believe how you've

grown. You'll be, what, a junior this year?" The minister came around the desk, and although she looked like she wanted to enfold the girl in a hug, she held back, squeezing Hannah's shoulders and then patting her on the cheek.

"That's right," said Hannah. She still had her head down, but she did meet the woman's eyes briefly.

The minister sighed. "Time goes too fast. If you're a junior, that means Fiona must be starting high school."

Hannah nodded.

"Well, it's wonderful to see you. Please send my love to your mother and Fiona. And introduce me to your friend."

Kat quirked an eyebrow at Hannah, who narrowed her eyes right back. Apparently she would not be doing any introducing.

"I'm Kat Rodriguez," she said, offering her hand again. "I'm an attorney here in town, and I'm supervising a group of kids doing community service on the mural project."

Hannah stiffened at the mention of community service. Maybe she would finally admit that she was volunteering, not making amends. The minister had glanced at Hannah when Kat mentioned community service, but the girl didn't offer any explanations.

"It's a pleasure to meet you, Kat. I'm Reverend Russo, but please call me Pastor Rachel. Everyone does. Now what's this I overheard about a cemetery?"

"We found gravestones behind the church," said Hannah. "Small and plain, with no dates on them."

"That's odd," said Pastor Rachel. "I've never heard anything about a cemetery on the property, and I've been here for almost ten years now. Could you show me?"

Hannah nodded. Irene seemed pretty excited about seeing the graves as well, so in the end all four of them walked around the block to the back side of the church to survey the rediscovered cemetery. After scrutinizing how the layout of the graves related to the church building, Pastor Rachel nodded to herself.

"It's clearly part of the original church grounds. Pity that they didn't put dates on any of the markers. That would really help us to find the related death records. Now that I think about it, I'm not even sure where the oldest church records are kept. Irene, do you know?"

Irene shook her head. "I haven't been here all that much longer than you, and I've never needed to go looking for older records."

"Hmm. We'll have to ask the Ladies Aid, then."

"The Ladies Aid?" asked Kat, wondering if that was a local historical society.

"The Ladies Aid Society founded our church in the 1800s," said Pastor Rachel. "The group still exists today, although membership has dwindled. They run our secondhand shop. We can ask them about it on Monday. I'm sure they'll know where the records are kept."

Hannah didn't say anything, but the expression on her face said it for her.

"Would you like to come with me when I talk to them?" asked Pastor Rachel.

Hannah nodded.

"What time does school get out?"

"Just before three," said Hannah.

"Perfect timing. That's right about the time they close up the shop. Why don't you meet me in the church office and we'll go talk to them together?" She turned to Kat. "Will you be able to join us as well?"

Kat was already mentally scrambling to rearrange her Monday calendar. She wanted to learn more about the mystery of the graves—and the mystery of Hannah. She nodded. "I can be here by three."

～

Mel parked at the library on Sunday afternoon, wishing she had time for a quick nap before the meeting. The day had started out cool enough, but it must be over eighty and humid by now, a combination guaranteed to put Mel to sleep. Even her curiosity about meeting Hot Muralist in the flesh wasn't enough to shake the afternoon drowsiness.

Mary Evelyn had some kind of family thing, so Mel was filling in. It was the muralist's second visit to the site, but the first time he would get a close look at the wall. She wondered if he would be as hot in person as he was in the publicity photo. Probably not. Nobody ever looked as good in real life as they did in their publicity photos.

She got out of the car and wandered over to lie down on the bench in the shade. Even a mini-nap might help her make it through the afternoon. She would probably be both sweaty and sunburned by the time they were done here today.

She must have dozed off, because the sound of a deep male voice woke her up.

"You are definitely not Mary Evelyn."

Mel opened her eyes and stretched, taking her time to check out Hot Muralist. It was tricky because his face was in shadow, but the silhouette of his body did not disappoint. Broad shoulders. Narrow hips. She was lying down, but he seemed to be pretty tall. She sat up, then stood slowly, grateful that her sunglasses shielded her eyes from view. The more she saw, the more she liked.

"I'm Mel. Mary Evelyn asked me to meet you here. She has a family thing today."

"You're the one who's been prepping the wall?"

"That's me," she answered.

He held out a hand. "Fitz."

"First name or last?" asked Mel as they shook hands. She knew he had a long name, but she couldn't remember it right now. She had dubbed him "Hot Muralist" in her head and not bothered to remember his actual name.

"Just Fitz," he said cryptically.

"Oooh, one name only, like Sting or Beyoncé," she replied. "Me, too."

The twitch at the corner of his mouth suggested a sense of humor and ruined the serious vibe he was trying to put off. She had expected him to be older, but he couldn't be more than thirty. And he *was* hot in person. It was almost unfair for a guy to be that good-looking without trying. Even more intriguing was the hint of a tattoo in the shadow of his collar. Khakis and a button-down, with a hidden bad boy side. She wouldn't let her resentment of his insane good looks get in the way of a hookup, if things moved in that direction. He was too interesting to pass up.

"Shall we?" he asked, looking over at the scaffolding hiding the side of the building.

"Follow me," said Mel. She put an extra sway in her step as she led the way to the ladder, glad that she had chosen her sexier pair of ratty jeans.

"Mary Evelyn said you wanted to see how the wall prep was progressing."

"That's right."

"Let's start at the top, then. We're almost done with that level."

Fitz followed her easily up the ladders until they both emerged on the top of the scaffolding. Under the hot sun, the metal framework threatened to burn her skin, so she kept to the wooden planking, which seemed narrower now that she shared the space with him. His presence was intense.

"We finished all the tuck pointing and sealing yesterday. Next step is to paint with primer, if it looks good to you."

He took his time looking over their handiwork, running his hands over the bricks in a way that bordered on sensual. She had never heard of a guy with a building fetish, but there's always a first. He checked the entire stretch of the wall, paying particular attention to the edges. She let him take the lead and followed along, right to the end of the scaffolding. Finally, after what seemed like forever, he delivered his verdict.

"Nice work."

"Thanks," she said, unable to suppress the little snap in her voice. She and a few of the adult volunteers had worked their asses off to create this perfect little stretch of wall. She had not realized their work would be graded.

"It's really important to prep the wall," he explained, as if he could sense her simmering temper. "Nothing worse than pouring your heart into a mural that starts cracking and peeling after the first week, or the first frost."

"I could see where that would be annoying," she said, somewhat mollified.

He flashed a grin as he turned away from the wall to check out the view. At this height, they could see over the tops of the trees to the lake beyond. Resting his forearms on the metal railing, he didn't say anything for a few minutes. She would have copied his pose, but she didn't have long sleeves to protect her arms from the hot metal, so she leaned her back against the expertly prepared wall instead. They admired the view for a few minutes before her curiosity got the better of her.

"So how did you get into this line of work?" she asked.

"It's like anything else," he said with a shrug. "You stumble into something and discover that it suits you."

"What did your stumble look like?"

He laughed. "I was in school to become an architect, but I had a lot of friends who were art majors. One of them volunteered to do a community mural project, and I got roped in to help. That's all it took. I was hooked."

This explained the weird combination of tattoo with khaki

pants. He was a man who moved between the art world and the business world. Just the kind of man she liked.

"So you're an architect when you're not doing murals?"

"Yep."

"Where do you work?"

He mentioned the name of a big firm based in downtown Chicago, the kind of place that designs huge skyscrapers in exotic locations around the world.

"The nice thing about working for a big firm is that they'll let me take on pro bono projects from time to time. It helps to take a break in between the big projects."

"So you're in between projects right now?"

"Yep."

"What about you?"

"Me?"

"What do you do? Mary Evelyn said that you were an artist, but that could mean a million different things."

Mel laughed. "Mary Evelyn is friends with my mother, which means she subscribes to my mother's version of my life."

"Which is not the same as yours?"

Mel shook her head.

"So tell me about it. Both versions, please."

"I'm a photographer. I'd like to take those skills on the road —internationally."

"Sounds very cool. What are you doing now?"

"Freelance work, mostly. Weddings and events when they want a photojournalistic style. Some newspaper work covering city life. I sell stock photos to make a little money on the side. At this point, I'll take pretty much any gig if it helps me build the travel fund."

"Why didn't Mary Evelyn just say you were a photographer, then?"

Sighing, Mel shook her head. "My mother is an artist,

acrylics mostly. I've done some watercolor work, and my mom is obsessed by the idea that I'm going to follow in her footsteps. Move up here to the lake. Build up a business as a wedding photographer. Paint watercolors on the weekends. Marry a nice, stable boy and pop out a few grandchildren. Her idea of heaven, having all three girls settled and living right here in town."

"You have sisters?"

Mel burst out laughing. When he looked confused, she just shook her head. Nobody believed her about the triplet thing until they actually saw her sisters. "Never mind. I'll introduce you to them. Callie's in town for the moment, and Tessa has moved up here permanently."

He looked suspicious, but simply said, "Okay."

"What about you? Siblings? Spouse? Offspring?"

At the suggestion of offspring he looked mildly alarmed. "Sister, yes. Wife, no. Kids, definitely not, although it would certainly make my mother happy."

"Which, the spouse or the kids?"

"Grandchildren, of course, preferably with a spouse, although it's not an absolute requirement."

Mel snorted. "It's a disease, I tell you, this obsession with grandchildren."

"Exactly."

"What about your sister? Is she likely to produce any grandchildren soon?"

"She has already provided three, and I suspect that's her limit."

"But that didn't take the pressure off you?" asked Mel.

"Sadly, no. If anything, it made things worse."

"I'm sorry," said Mel. From the expression on his face, Fitz did not seem to think her sympathy was genuine.

"Any news on the graves?" he asked.

"Not yet, but one of the high school kids is researching the old files at the church." She gestured vaguely in that direction. "Hopefully she'll find something soon."

He contemplated the small cemetery below and the church beyond it. "I really don't think we'll be able to move forward with the design until we know the history here."

"I figured."

Fitz looked over at her. "Thanks." At her raised eyebrow, he said, "It's really important to me that the mural be connected to the local context. That includes the cemetery, and whatever history goes along with it. Not everyone thinks context is important."

"Preaching to the choir, my friend."

He smiled, and she forgot to breathe for a moment. "I knew I liked you."

Later that night, Mel tossed and turned in her bed, Fitz's smile haunting her half-dreams. The man was beyond tempting. The idea of a late-summer fling—one with a clearly defined end date—suddenly seemed like a very good idea.

CHAPTER FIFTEEN

Monday afternoon came all too quickly. Kat pulled into the church parking lot still trying to shake off the stress of the workday. The bright blue sky and balmy temperature went a long way toward helping as she walked over to the entrance. Give it a month or two and they would all be longing for perfect late-summer days like this.

She saw Hannah approaching from the far side of the church and waited so that they could walk inside together.

"Hi, Hannah."

"Hey," mumbled Hannah.

Pastor Rachel had seen them coming and met them in the entryway.

"Good afternoon, ladies. Please, follow me."

She ushered them down a hallway and into the second-hand shop, which took up a large room at the newer end of the building. The room was packed with racks and racks of clothing, all neatly organized and labeled. Three older ladies sat around a table at the side of the room drinking tea, while a fourth stood at a counter nearby folding clothes. The folding lady was quite tall and thin, while the seated ladies appeared to be smaller. One had fluffy hair and wore an equally fluffy sweater, making her look soft around the edges. She was knitting something even softer. Looking up from her work, her clacking needles paused as she examined the visitors curiously through little round glasses. The second lady was refilling the teacups on the table. She smiled in welcome. The last one was small and self-contained. She didn't smile at all. No blue hair here, although they did sport various shades of gray.

The minister presented Mel and Hannah as if they were exhibits. "You all remember Hannah. She went through confirmation here at church a few years ago. This is her friend, Kat Rodriguez. They have a mystery for us to solve."

The ladies perked up.

"A mystery?" said the knitting lady.

"Hannah, you may remember some of these ladies." She gestured to the tall lady folding clothes. "This is Florence."

"Welcome back, Hannah," said Florence, nodding briskly at Kat.

"Agatha," continued Pastor Rachel, indicating the knitter. Agatha smiled at them both before her needles resumed their clacking.

"This is Letty." The one with the teapot.

"Welcome," said Letty. "Would you like some tea?"

Hannah and Mel murmured their no-thank-yous as Pastor Rachel finished the introductions.

"And this is Mary Catharine."

In contrast to the other ladies, Mary Catharine's brief nod was not all that welcoming. Kat stiffened, reflexively assuming that the chill was due to her skin color. It took her a moment to realize that the chill extended to Pastor Rachel and Hannah as well. Mary Catharine was just a grump.

"So what's the mystery?" asked the knitting lady. Agatha? Kat tried to get the names to stick in her mind.

"It appears we have a cemetery in the backyard. I was hoping one of you might remember something about that."

"It's been an overgrown thicket back there for as long as I can remember," said the folding lady. Florence.

Mary Catharine and Letty nodded their agreement, but Agatha frowned and tilted her head to the side.

"Maybe not when I was a girl," she said.

The others quieted.

"You all wouldn't remember," she continued. "I was very small, but I remember a garden in back. Now that you mention graves, I wonder if that's why the flowers were planted in such neat rows."

She paused in both her speaking and her knitting as she considered. Kat began to wonder exactly how old she was.

"This was back when the church owned the property on High Street, the one that backs up to the garden. The house was the parsonage, and there was a garden shed at the back of the lot. I remember helping once with the yard work. They found me a small rake in that shed. Later, that shed was knocked down, but the house is still the same house."

"When was this, Agatha?" asked the minister.

"During the war. I couldn't have been more than ten."

"I wonder if we have records that go that far back," Pastor Rachel mused.

"We do," said Florence. She finished folding a shirt. "The really old records are in the hidden closet."

"We have a hidden closet?" asked Pastor Rachel. "I've been here for ten years and you're only just telling me now?"

Florence gave them a small smile. "It never came up."

Agatha shook her head. "The reason you haven't seen the closet is because nobody has been in there for years. One of our members went on a housecleaning blitz about twenty years ago, and we cleared out a lot of junk. He sorted through all the oldest records and stashed them in the closet. We all figured that they would be safely out of the way, and we could go get them if we needed them. I haven't thought about them since." She paused to sip her tea. "We haven't needed them until now."

"Would it be okay if we took a look?" asked Kat.

"I don't see why not," said the minister. "Florence, could you show us this hidden closet?"

"Of course."

She set aside her folding and led the way from the resale shop to the main sanctuary of the church. The minister followed on her heels while Kat and Hannah trailed behind.

Kat had never been inside this particular church. It was beautiful, and far older than she had realized. The section of the building that housed the church office and the resale shop was clearly a newer addition—from the '70s, if the decor was any indication. The sanctuary was another matter entirely. Kat had taken an art history class in college, and she remembered this style of architecture. It had been one of her favorites, called Carpenter Gothic. She had loved the idea of hardworking people in rural areas building their version of a gothic cathedral out of wood and other local materials. In this case, ancient beams held up the vaulted ceiling. Wooden pews sat in neat rows facing the altar. Stucco walls contrasted with the dark woodwork, while patterns of colored light played on the creamy walls where the sun streamed through the stained glass windows.

Florence led them to a door at the back of the sanctuary and opened it to reveal a closet. Inside, they found a bookshelf lined with old hymnals, and a few boxes of candles on the floor. The closet was otherwise empty and appeared to be little used. Kat had the sinking feeling that the old records had been lost or moved. Then Florence slid a freestanding candelabra out of the way, lifted a simple lever from its latch, and opened a panel set into the back wall of the closet. Peering inside, they could see stacks of file boxes under a low, sloped ceiling. Kat couldn't help but think of Harry Potter and his bedroom in the cupboard beneath the stairs.

"This closet uses the space under the balcony stairs," said Florence. Then she sneezed.

"How long has it been since anybody looked in here?" asked the minister.

Florence stood back up, the stooped posture required to see inside the closet clearly bothering her back. "Not sure," she said with a shrug. "Probably fifteen, maybe twenty years."

"That explains the dust." Kat rubbed her own nose to keep from sneezing.

Pastor Rachel looked inside the door, then pulled out a plastic sleeve that must have been hanging on the inside wall. "Someone was thinking ahead." She brushed the dust off the sleeve. "They left us a guide to what's in each box."

She carefully pulled the document out of the sleeve, and they all crowded around to get a better look. The list started with newer files and worked its way back through time, detailing the contents of each numbered box. Sadly, nothing was labeled "Cemetery."

Florence put her hands on her hips. "Well, I suppose there's nothing to do but pull out all the boxes. Pastor, where do you suppose we could put them?"

Pastor Rachel considered for a moment. "We don't have any big meetings scheduled for the next few weeks. Let's use the big table in the meeting room. Between the table and the floor we should have plenty of room for all the boxes, and they'll be out of the way on Sunday."

"Let's get to work then." Florence brushed off her hands in anticipation and looked like she was ready to contort her tall frame to fit in the small space.

"I'll do it," said Kat, kneeling in front of the closet opening before Florence could object. The older woman might be young and spry compared to her friends at the secondhand shop, but Kat still didn't want her to try to move boxes while bent in half. She'd rather risk her own back.

As it turned out, the only thing she truly risked were her work clothes, which snagged on the edges of the opening as she reached through. Had she known about this in advance, she would have stopped at home to change into jeans and a T-shirt.

There wasn't a lot of extra room inside the closet, and Kat took shallow breaths to avoid choking on the dust. She scanned the first row of boxes, realizing that they had been numbered and stored in order.

"You ladies ready?" After getting the go-ahead, Kat held her breath, pulled the first box off the stack, and pulled it through the small doorway. Hannah grabbed it and handed it off to the next set of hands. As Kat passed boxes out to Hannah, they were handed person to person and stacked outside the door of the main closet, in the back of the sanctuary. Pastor Rachel had gone in search of a cart to help move the files into the meeting room.

Kat climbed inside the closet once she had pulled out the first layer of boxes. Dust swirled around her, coating her skin and dredging up memories that should be safely buried. The confined space didn't help. Unwilling to freak out in front of an audience, Kat gritted her teeth and began hauling boxes out to Hannah. The sooner they finished, the sooner she could get out of this hellhole.

At one point, when Kat paused to rest, she could swear she heard the skittering of tiny feet—mouse feet?—somewhere in the closet. She sucked in a startled breath and immediately began coughing. By the time she had her breathing back to normal, there were no more scrabbling sounds, just concerned questions from the outside.

"You okay?" Florence poked her head through the low door to check on Kat.

"I'm good," she answered, wiping tears from her eyes. "Let's get this done. You ready?" she asked as Florence backed up to clear the door.

"Keep 'em coming," responded Hannah.

Kat could hear Florence directing the stacking of the boxes outside the main closet, to keep them in order. It wasn't clear if the other ladies were still helping or were just talking about how to move the boxes to the other room. Finally, Kat handed the last box out to Hannah and then ducked out of the closet, taking a very welcome deep breath.

The ladies took one look at Kat and burst out laughing.

"What?"

"We need to clean you up," said Florence matter-of-factly.

Kat reached up to brush off her hair and her hand came away covered in cobwebs. "Ugh. Point me to the bathroom."

The bathroom was back in the direction of the second-hand shop. Pastor Rachel closed up the inner and outer closet doors while Hannah pushed the first cartload of file boxes. Kat and Florence stopped in the bathroom, while Hannah and the rest of the ladies worked on shuttling file boxes into the meeting room. It took more than a few minutes to get all the dust and cobwebs off Kat, but she was grateful for the help. She would never have been able to reach all the spots on her back, and just thinking of all the spiders that may or may not have crawled on her was creeping her out.

When they were finished with the cleanup, Kat and Florence returned to the sanctuary to help move file boxes. There were more than thirty in total, far more than anyone had expected. While they worked, Kat watched Hannah curiously. The girl actually smiled a few times, which made her look younger.

"Hannah, honey, how's your mom doing?" asked Florence. "I remember when she was just your age. You look a lot like her."

"She's good, I guess." Hannah didn't meet Florence's eyes when she answered. "Same as always."

"Well, you tell her that we miss her here at church. If your great-grandmother were still alive, I bet.... Never mind. You just tell her that we miss her."

"Okay."

Hannah clearly wanted nothing to do with this conversation, making Kat wonder what things were like at home, after losing a father and gaining a stepfather. She knew from experience that some stepfathers were wonderful and others were not. These days she tended to start from a place of skepticism.

Luckily, they were on their final load, which provided the distraction Hannah needed. She helped to push the cart and unload the last few boxes. The group surveyed the mountain of files to be reviewed. The table in the center of the meeting room was barely visible beneath the file boxes, and there were more stacked in each corner of the room and along the walls. Digging through all this old stuff was going to take time—time Kat didn't have. And yet....

Pastor Rachel asked, "Hannah, do you have any time after school tomorrow to help sort through all this?"

Hannah visibly perked up at the idea of diving into the files, then shot a glance at Kat, who nodded in approval, not that Hannah needed her approval to change her volunteer duties. She wasn't technically doing community service.

"I can be here," she said.

"Florence, the shop will be closed by the time Hannah arrives. Do you have time to stay late and help her get this project organized?"

"I'd be happy to help, Pastor."

"Excellent." The minister glanced over at Kat and she nodded.

"I'll be at the library with the other volunteers, but I'll stop by here afterward to see how it went," said Kat.

"Until tomorrow, then."

Kat couldn't make it early on Tuesday. As much as she wanted to find a way, her schedule just didn't cooperate. The last few days had been intense as she tried to clear her backlog so that she could enjoy a night out on Thursday without worrying about work. A first date with Rob. She could hardly believe that it was happening. Oh, first dates were nothing new. In fact, they had become something of a specialty over the last few years. Friends had tried to set her up with all sorts of eligible bachelors, but none had ever made it past that first date. Joan said she was too picky. Kevin Archer, the school psych, said that she kept people at arm's length so that they couldn't get close, couldn't hurt her. Kat preferred to think that she had high standards.

This thing with Rob, though—it was different. No matter what face she showed the world, he had always seen through to the heart of her. There was something truly terrifying about losing the protection of the mask. Kat had learned to be strong by hiding her vulnerability. Rob threatened that strength with nothing more than his presence.

Her late arrival on the project site meant that she could dive into the work without too much thought or conversation. Floating among the work groups, she lent a hand and listened in on the conversations without saying much. The flash of regret when she couldn't understand the rapid, slangy Spanish of the fledgling hackers was nothing new. She had wrestled with that demon her whole life. A part of her was still angry with her mother, whose desperation to fit in had denied Kat her heritage. Kat had been only three when her mother stopped speaking with her in Spanish. It was important to fit in with her new family, she had explained years later. By then the damage had been done. The words had faded from Kitty's memory, and even Spanish classes in high school couldn't bring it all back. Kat had never truly fit in, not with the white girls, and not with the Spanish-speaking girls. She had studied enough Spanish to be competent—fluent, even—but she would never be a native speaker.

Shaking off the old ache, Kat checked her watch and realized it was after four. Time to head up to the church and check on Hannah. She put away her tools and walked over to let Rob know what she was doing.

"Are we still on for Thursday?" he asked.

She nodded, smiling slowly.

"Why don't I pick you up at your place at seven?"

"That would be great."

"Do you think maybe you could tell me where you live?" His expression was sheepish, but Kat felt equally foolish.

"Right," she said with a laugh. "I guess that would be useful information."

They exchanged both phone numbers and addresses, and then she headed over to the church to meet Hannah.

The secretary, Irene, was on the phone when Kat arrived but waved her toward the meeting room where they had put all the files. The boxes were no longer stacked neatly on the table. Instead, most were stacked against one wall. Hannah sat in a large upholstered chair in the corner, her feet tucked up beneath her, with a box next to her on the floor, a stack of folders beside her on the table, and a folder open on her lap. Kat watched her for a moment from the doorway, noting that she once again wore long sleeves and leggings despite the late summer heat. There was no reason to jump to the worst-case scenario. Maybe the girl was anemic. Maybe the sun gave her a rash.

Hannah blinked when she realized someone else was in the

room. She tensed, briefly, but then relaxed again when she recognized Kat.

"Oh, it's you."

"Yep, just me. How's it going?"

"Nothing so far, but these old records are way more interesting than I thought they'd be."

"How so?"

"I don't know how to explain, exactly."

Following her instincts, Kat waited for the girl to continue rather than jumping in to fill the silence. Her patience was rewarded a moment later, when Hannah said more words in a row than Kat had ever heard from her before.

"It's just strange to imagine all the people who have been in this church over the years, putting on bake sales and quilting bees. It seems a lot more real when I see the notes written in a person's actual handwriting."

Kat wandered over to take a closer look.

"May I see?" she asked.

Hannah handed her the folder, labeled "Bake Sales," and she paged through it. Hannah was right. There was something oddly fascinating about the careful records of bake sales starting in the 1930s and continuing through the 1970s. Over the years, the handwriting grew more fragile, until it abruptly changed to a stronger, younger hand. Kat swallowed, finding the change unaccountably upsetting, and handed the folder back to Hannah.

"Any hints about our graveyard yet?"

Hannah shook her head. "Florence and I decided that we needed to be methodical, or we might miss something important."

"Makes sense."

"I'm also supposed to talk to Irene about making copies of some of the older documents, so that we don't hurt the originals, but she's been on the phone a lot today."

"She was still on the phone when I walked in," said Kat. "Is there anything I can do to help?"

"Do you want to see if she's off the phone and ask about the copies?"

Kat smiled. "I'll do that right now."

Hannah actually smiled back. It was a small smile, but real. Kat counted it as a major milestone.

Stepping back into the hallway, Kat found that Irene was indeed off the phone and available to talk.

"Got a sec?" asked Kat. "Hannah and I have a question."

"Sure. What do you need?"

"Would it be okay if we made copies of the oldest documents? The originals are pretty fragile."

"Of course," said Irene. "I'll also do a little research and see if we need to store the originals in special sleeves or boxes."

"Thanks."

Irene nodded. "No problem."

Kat returned to the meeting room to give Hannah the news. Although Kat hadn't intended to stay for very long, she found herself drawn into the historical materials as Hannah was. Taking the next folder from the pile, she sat down at the table to page through it.

The folder she had selected contained the church membership roster from the late 1800s. The same flowing script filled page after page, and she wondered if the same person had kept the church records for more than twenty years, or if he or she had simply recopied old records. The list for each year had not been annotated, and so did not reflect any deaths, or departures, or marriages. Each presented the membership as of that date, with no further details. Nothing here spoke to the existence of a cemetery. Kat set the folder in the "completed" pile.

The next folder contained old sermons, at least a hundred of them. Pastor Rachel would probably want to see those, so Kat set the folder aside to hand off to Irene. The folder after that contained accounting records from the mid-1950s, beyond their time window of interest. Kat added it to the completed pile.

Irene knocked softly at the door. "I'm heading out for the day. If you ladies could please be sure to turn off the lights and pull the door firmly shut when you leave, I would appreciate it. Everything is all locked up, and you're the last ones here."

"Will do," said Kat. "Thanks, Irene."

Checking her watch, Kat realized it was after five, and she had been there for more than an hour. Hannah abruptly started cleaning up her work area.

"Everything okay?" asked Kat.

"I just need to get home," said Hannah. "I didn't realize how late it was."

"Were you planning to come again tomorrow after school?" asked Kat.

Hannah nodded.

"Maybe you could stop by the project site on Thursday and give the team an update on what you've found so far. I know we don't have answers yet, but they'll have questions, and some of them might want to help."

An interesting expression flickered across Hannah's face. The girl didn't want to share, Kat realized. In a way, she couldn't blame her for being protective of the records, and the stories that went along with them. On the other hand, this project was going to take a lot of time and effort. It was a lot for one girl to tackle on her own.

"You would still be in charge, of course, but helpers could come in handy. There are a lot of boxes to review."

Hannah sighed as she looked at the wall of boxes, then nodded slowly. "I guess help would be good."

They were putting the last of the files back into the third box, when Hannah's sleeve caught on the corner of the box, revealing the inside of her forearm. A series of ugly red scars laddered up her pale skin, starting at her wrist. Before Kat could get a good look, Hannah had pulled her arm back out, and her long sleeve slid back into place, hiding her arm again.

Oblivious to Kat's shock, Hannah put the top on the file box and stacked it with the other two boxes that had already been reviewed. Kat pushed in her chair and straightened the ones next to it, trying to act as if she hadn't seen what she thought she had just seen, all while scrambling to make sense of it. The glimpse had been so fast that she couldn't be sure if the injury had happened all at once—maybe a bad scrape, or a burn on some kind of hot, ridged metal—or if it was a series of injuries. But that only raised more questions. Were the injuries self-inflicted? Accidental? Was someone harming Hannah?

Kat gave herself a stern mental order to calm down. In order to answer those questions, Kat would need to gain Hannah's trust, and she would need another look at that arm. Until then, speculation was not helpful.

CHAPTER SIXTEEN

On Thursday, Rob stood back and watched Hannah talking with the volunteer team, both adults and community service kids. She had left her work at the church early to give everyone an update on the historical files before they left for the day. He also watched Kat hover over her baby chick as that chick grew increasingly self-confident. He loved that about Kat, the way she watched out for each of the kids. Some of them needed tough love. Some needed a friend. Some needed a coach. Hannah was so quiet that it was hard to tell what she needed, but Kat seemed to have figured it out. The girl would probably always be shy, but she was learning that she could step into the spotlight once in a while and not get burned.

Eventually, Kat faded into the background and came to stand beside Rob.

"She's doing great," he said.

She made a face. "I know. I just can't help worrying that one of the boys will make a boneheaded remark, or one of the girls will get snarky, and Hannah will go right back into her shell."

"She's tougher than she looks," said Rob. At Kat's questioning look, he continued. "She didn't complain once during the hard work of clearing the site, and she's taken on some big responsibility with those files. She might be quiet, but she's willing to step up. That takes guts."

"You're right. I shouldn't worry so much."

"It's part of who you are," said Rob philosophically. "There is no 'should.' Besides, it helps the kids. They can tell that you care."

She smiled slowly. "I do."

"So go ahead and worry."

"I will."

They watched Hannah finish her update. Mary Evelyn was full of questions, to the point that she and Hannah were basically having a one-on-one discussion.

"If she has so many questions, I wonder why she doesn't go over to the church and help with the research," said Rob.

"She says she's too busy."

Rob snorted. "Busy, my ass. She's got help in the library. She wouldn't be out here now if she were too busy to do special stuff. I don't know what her issue is with the church, but she's certainly not too busy."

Kat pondered that while they watched the discussion wind down. Mary Evelyn was full of questions, not just about the research but also about the church and the people Hannah had met. She had lots of advice about how to handle and store historical documents. The discussion was getting a bit technical for the rest of the crowd, so Kat headed over to intervene, giving Rob an opening to ask the work crew to help put everything away for the day.

"Mary Evelyn," she interrupted, "you have so many great ideas. Maybe you could stop over at the church one day to give Hannah a hand, and to see all these documents in person."

"Oh, no, I couldn't possibly take the time."

Kat wasn't going to let her off the hook that easily. "Oh, I'm sure they could spare you for an hour. You'll want to meet all the ladies who are helping Hannah. There's even another Mary. It's Mary Catharine, right, Hannah?"

Hannah nodded.

"That's a very common practice, especially in Catholic families, giving their daughters a double first name that starts with 'Mary,'" said Mary Evelyn. "Very common. Nothing strange about having that in common with someone."

"Of course not," said Kat, not really sure why she was soothing Mary Evelyn's ruffled feathers. "Think about stopping by. I think you would really enjoy working personally with all these historical documents."

"I'm sure you'll do a fine job, Hannah," said Mary Evelyn. "I should really get back inside."

Kat stared after her as she hurried toward the back door of the library, wondering what in the world was going on, while Hannah mostly seemed relieved.

"That was strange," said Kat.

"It's fine," answered Hannah. "She had some good suggestions, but it's okay if she doesn't come help."

Kat glanced down at Hannah's arms, covered as usual by a long-sleeved shirt, but before Kat could think of a way to ask Hannah about the injury, the girl mumbled something about needing to get home and promptly left. Any more of this and Kat was going to start thinking she was doing something to scare people off.

Rob walked over a minute later, as nearly everyone else had gone, and said, "Are we still on for dinner?"

All the butterflies in her stomach woke up.

That night, to her surprise and despite the butterflies, Kat found she was able to relax and enjoy herself. Ken's Pub was wonderful—all wooden booths, dim lighting, and miraculously healthy comfort food. The restaurant was in the town on the far end of the lake, and though they saw a few familiar faces, for the most part she had had Rob to herself for the whole evening.

The absence of a problem might not be an issue for most people, but Kat was a professional problem-solver. In the absence of a problem, she didn't quite know what to do with herself.

"What are you thinking?"

Kat shook her head slowly. "I'm amazed that so many people are out to dinner on a Thursday night."

He laughed.

"What?"

"I was thinking exactly the same thing."

She had worried that they would run out of things to talk about, the way she sometimes did on dates. It had been months since her last attempt, but she remembered all too well the panicky feeling of flipping through her mental list of date-appropriate topics of conversation, searching for one they hadn't tried yet. So far that hadn't happened with Rob. Even when she had zoned out on him, he had laughed it off. The merlot—or maybe it was Rob—had given the evening a contented glow that she didn't want to let go.

"All these people, with all this free time. What do they do for a living?" she mused.

"I have no idea," said Rob. "Whatever they do, it seems they can leave their work behind and do fun stuff in the evenings."

"Every night?"

"I think we might work too much," said Rob.

This time she was the one who burst out laughing. "You think? I feel guilty that I'm not working right now. It feels selfish to take a night for myself."

"Don't feel guilty. I'm told that it's okay to have a life."

"By who?"

He actually flushed. "My mom."

"And are you planning to take her advice?" she asked. "From what I understand, you're just as bad as I am."

"Hey, I went down to The Beach just last weekend to watch the game."

She gave him a skeptical look. "Did you go with friends?"

"I hung out with Jack for a little while."

"Hmmm..."

The waitress stopped by to ask about dessert. Kat was torn. She really didn't need anything else, but she had walked past the dessert display as they walked in, and it all looked so good. One look at Rob's face answered her question. She had seen that look on the faces of hungry teenage boys and knew what it meant.

"We should at least look at the dessert menu, don't you think?" asked Kat. Rob's boyish grin was all the answer she needed.

In the end, they decided to split something very large and full of chocolate. Rob ate most of it, and Kat ate just enough to satisfy her chocolate craving. It worked out very well.

The dreaded check arrived, along with all the baggage about who would be paying. "Split?" asked Kat, reaching for her purse and making no assumptions.

Rob shook his head. "You can treat next time."

She melted inside a little more. Gallant without being chauvinistic. He was pushing all the right buttons. She knew she was overthinking this date with Rob, but she couldn't help it. It wasn't just that it had been a long, long time since a first date had gone well. This was Rob. He mattered. This date mattered more than any of her earlier half-hearted attempts.

When Rob pulled up in front of her town house, she wasn't sure what to do. She didn't want the evening to end, but she also didn't think she would be able to forget the stack of work waiting for her on the kitchen table. Despite her best efforts, a small pile remained to be done. She stewed about it until they were at her front door. The porch light off, they stood in the shadows.

"I want to invite you inside, but…"

"Work, right?"

She nodded.

"I have the same problem," said Rob. "I'd love to come in, but I'm not sure I'd be able to stop thinking about all the stuff I need to do when I get back home."

It was both amazing and awful to have found someone who was as much a workaholic as she was.

"I had a wonderful time," she said, wondering if she would need to make the first move.

"Maybe it should be our Thursday night thing," he suggested.

She smiled slowly. "I'd like that."

"Is it too soon to kiss you?" he asked.

"Definitely not too soon."

He placed his hands on her hips and leaned in slowly, his face highlighted only by the streetlight halfway down the block. She slid her hands up the front of his shirt and leaned in to meet him, letting thoughts of work fade into the background. If they had only a few minutes here by the door, she was going to make the most of it.

She melted into the kiss, winding her arms up around his neck. He pulled her closer. She got lost in Rob, in the kiss, barely registering that he had pressed her up against her front door, except for the fact that the cool against her back, in contrast with the heat of his body in her arms, set all her senses tingling. One of his hands slid up to clasp the nape of her neck and adjust the angle of her head, deepening the kiss even farther. She whimpered, and he paused, pressing his forehead against hers.

"Too much?" he asked.

"Not enough," she breathed in answer.

He chuckled under his breath but didn't resume this kiss.

"Glad to know we're on the same page here."

"I'm thinking you should come inside," she said, all thoughts of work chased from her head.

He stroked her cheek and kissed her one more time, briefly, on her swollen lips.

"I would like nothing better, but it's a school night, and I think we'll both regret it if we're not on our game tomorrow."

She nodded reluctantly.

"Saturday night, however, would be a completely different proposition," he said. "You free?"

"I am most definitely free on Saturday."

They laughed together, not wanting the moment to end. Finally, he disentangled himself from Kat's arms and walked back to his car. She watched him until he was out of sight, then turned, unlocked her front door, and floated inside. Now *that* was a first date.

CHAPTER SEVENTEEN

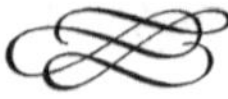

KAT HAD DECIDED TO SPEND SATURDAY MORNING WORKING WITH Hannah at the church. This had *nothing* to do with the unusually hot and sticky weather for early October, nor was she avoiding Rob. Not at all. Their still-to-be-determined plans for tonight did *not* have her in a panicky mix of anxiety and excitement, with a little lust thrown in for good measure. She was as levelheaded as always, just very interested in air-conditioning and historical files.

Hannah had beat her there, and Kat found the girl once again curled up in her favorite wingback chair, halfway through a new box. Comparing the size of the "to be reviewed" wall with the "completed" wall, Kat guessed that they were about a third of the way through the boxes. They might make it to the halfway mark today, if they didn't get distracted.

Kat really hoped today was the day for a discovery. Hannah had dedicated herself to the project and seemed fascinated by the stories of real people from long ago.

When Hannah looked up from what she was reading, her face was definitely splotchy and she wiped away fresh tears.

"Hannah, honey, are you okay?"

"I found it," she said, closing a small book nestled within the folder and handing it to Kat.

Kat took a seat at the table and carefully opened the yellowed pages. It appeared to be a journal written in the same graceful handwriting that Kat had seen on the membership lists.

December 14, 1897: Rose arrived at the parsonage late last night. Sixteen years old. With child, about six months along. Family will not have her. Young man has denied responsibility. Of course we sheltered her for the night, and while she slept, we discussed the proper course of action. I understood God's call quite clearly, but Lucas required my help to open his heart to her plight. She may use the spare room while she awaits the arrival of the babe. God has given us three months to make a plan for her new life once the babe is born.

January 6, 1898: Rose conceals herself from family and friends during Sunday services. She watches from the loft, as if she were a ghost. Several of the busybodies have expressed deep concern to Lucas about the situation, as if loose morals in a houseguest were contagious. He handled them quite well. I do wonder sometimes if those ladies listen to the sermons or simply daydream about new gowns.

January 22, 1898: Gerta arrived in the morning after walking most of the night. Thank the Lord the weather was unusually mild. No frostbite. Fifteen years old. Fleeing her family. Father has incestuous intentions. Thankfully she is not with child. She will share the room with Rose.

February 9, 1898: Placed Gerta with the Hubbles in Milwaukee. They will train her as a cook and foster her until she can find employment. I am so grateful to my good friend for offering this lifeline to a young girl in need of a fresh start. Rose hopes to follow after the babe is born, if we can place the babe with an adoptive family.

February 13, 1898: Fanny stayed after church today asking for sanctuary. I could not refuse her. She is barely fourteen years old. One of the farmhands has taken her virtue and her own mother would not believe her. Lucas spoke with the parents, but they have washed their hands of the matter, and of their daughter as well. She will stay with us for now and be a welcome companion to Rose, who is already missing Gerta.

February 27, 1898: Martha the midwife came to help with the birth of Rose's child, but the baby boy was born asleep. We grieve his loss.

March 3, 1898: We lost Rose to fever today, but also I suspect to a broken heart. I pray that she has at last found peace, but my own soul is heavy with grief. I must write to Gerta...

April 19, 1898: Fanny's courses have still not appeared, and we fear she may be with child. These months have been difficult as her family still comes to church every Sunday but will not speak to her, and her friends are not permitted to visit.

May 1, 1898: Praise the Lord that Fanny's courses finally arrived. This will ease her heart and allow her to move forward with a new life.

May 14, 1898: I have sent Fanny to the Hubbles as well. She is a sweet girl, and I know that Gerta will help her find her feet. It is my hope that they will offer support to one another in the years ahead.

Kat found she couldn't continue to the next page. Instead she closed the thin volume, her movements slow. She needed a moment to compose herself and understood exactly why Hannah had been crying.

"Have you had a chance to show this to Pastor Rachel yet?"

Hannah shook her head. "I just found it a little while ago and have been reading ever since." She took a deep breath. "There are so many."

"I'm glad that the girls had a place to go," said Kat, thinking about what that could have meant for her, to know that there was a safe place to go.

"I've never heard stories like that before." Hannah sounded lost, almost forlorn. "I guess I thought—I don't know, that everything in the past was like the books. You know, *Anne of Green Gables* or the Little House books or American Girl." She rubbed her forearm. Kat was starting to get a really bad feeling about those marks.

Reaching out, Kat gave Hannah's hand a gentle squeeze. "These girls found help when they needed it. They were not alone."

Hannah nodded, but Kat wasn't sure she really understood. What she really needed was time to process what she had just read, and Kat needed time to catch up with her.

"If it's okay with you and Pastor Rachel," said Kat, "I'd like to take the journal home and read it for myself."

"Can I see it again when you're done? I didn't make it all the way through." Hannah's eyes looked bruised, but her expression was determined.

"Of course. Do you want to read more now?"

"I don't think I can handle any more today."

Kat smiled weakly. "I completely understand."

"What time is it? Am I supposed to give another update to the volunteers?" Hannah looked ready to run for the hills.

"We don't need to do that today." Kat kept her tone calm

and reassuring. "Why don't we sort through more file boxes? We can give them an update this week, or maybe next Saturday."

Hannah nodded slowly. "I think I'll be okay by then."

"Do you want to wash your face?" asked Kat. If anybody stopped by, they would definitely start asking questions.

While Hannah was in the washroom, Kat stopped by the church office to see if either the secretary or Pastor Rachel was available, but she found the office closed. The sound of voices from down the hall led Kat to the secondhand shop, where Florence and Mary Catharine were folding T-shirts. Kat asked their opinion on her plan to take the journal home with her, without actually mentioning what was in it. Both ladies thought it was perfectly fine for Kat to take it home with her, as long as she brought it back Sunday afternoon or Monday morning. Kat agreed and met Hannah back down in the workroom.

They worked silently together through the morning, sorting through five more boxes of records. The new boxes contained everyday records of church life. Nothing to do with the cemetery, or the girls, or the writer of the journal.

Rob was finishing up with the volunteers on Saturday morning when a squad car rolled up. Jack must be stopping by to check in on their progress. He could wait while Rob thanked everyone again for their hard work and let them know what the next steps would be.

His head hadn't really been in the game today. Luckily, at this stage of the project there wasn't much thinking to do, leaving him free to relive that kiss and ponder where things might go tonight. He and Kat hadn't actually talked since

Thursday night—not that he knew the right thing to say anyway—but he'd thought of little else.

As he approached the squad car, he realized it wasn't Jack behind the wheel, but an older officer who looked awfully serious for a sunny Saturday morning.

"Morning," said Rob. "Something I can help you with?"

"And you are...?"

Rob was not a fan of the man's tone, but he tried not to let the irritation show.

"Rob Murray. I'm supervising the volunteers today."

"I can see that my stepdaughter, Hannah, is conspicuously absent this morning. Has she been here at all?"

Everything about the question struck Rob as wrong. Hannah was the only kid here of her own volition. She had been volunteering every day this week, not just Tuesday and Thursday like the rest. She had committed to researching the old church files, and she had kept going even after five days without success. As far as Rob was concerned, she was the most committed volunteer in the bunch. Regardless of her motivation, he found it hard to keep from pointing out that she could simply be inside at the moment taking a bathroom break. Her stepfather had assumed the worst before finding out the facts. Rob could only hope that his bad attitude did not extend to his law enforcement work.

"Actually," said Rob, choosing his words carefully, "she's been one of our most reliable volunteers. This morning she's over at the church with one of our other supervisors—" instinct prompted Rob to avoid naming Kat as the supervisor, although he would be hard-pressed to explain why "—helping to sort through some old records. As you can see, we've uncovered a cemetery, and we need to learn more about it."

The stepfather, who still hadn't provided his own name, made a dissatisfied noise in the back of his throat, as if he didn't like having his conclusions challenged.

"You're welcome to stop by the church if you need to speak with her."

The officer looked like he was going to say one thing but changed his mind. Instead, he said, "Just let her know that she should come straight home when she's finished."

"Will do," said Rob. He didn't bother to say farewell, just turned and walked back to the volunteer crew. The itchy feeling of being watched didn't fade until the squad car drove away. Honestly, if that was Hannah's stepdad, he could totally understand why she was spending so much time volunteering on the project. Rob wouldn't want to spend time with the man either.

Mel was just coming out the back door of the library as the squad car drove away. She jiggled the handle after it closed, then walked over to Rob.

"That door handle is really screwed up."

"I know. Mary Evelyn says she's going to fix it one of these days."

"Everything okay? The police officer looked kind of cranky."

"It's fine. He's Hannah's stepdad, and he was looking for her. Got kind of bent out of shape when she wasn't here."

"Huh," said Mel. "Hope she's not in too much trouble."

"As I recall, you were no stranger to trouble yourself in high school."

"Let's just say I'm better at it than my sisters."

"How's it going on the wall?" asked Rob. "Did it pass inspection by the big city muralist?"

"It did," she answered, looking very pleased with herself. "We should finish the second level today."

"Cool," said Rob. "I'm supposed to meet with him tomorrow."

At that moment, Mary Evelyn slipped out the back door of the library, giving the door handle a rattle, and marched over to Rob.

"Is everything okay? A couple of the tiny tots said that you were getting arrested."

Rob laughed at that. This was exactly how small town gossip started.

"I'm fine. Everything's fine. That was just Hannah's stepdad stopping by to check on her."

"Oh," said Mary Evelyn, glancing around but not seeing Hannah. "Isn't she still working up at the church?"

"Yes, with Kat. I'm hoping that they'll swing by here to give us an update soon." And so that Rob could finalize his plans with Kat for tonight, but that was not something he planned to share with either Mel or Mary Evelyn.

"Wonderful, wonderful," said Mary Evelyn. "Did you two have a nice dinner out the other night?"

"That's right," echoed Mel, grinning, "I heard you had a hot date."

He closed his eyes. Small towns sucked. He was going to have to move.

"No comment."

"That's code for hot sex, I think," said Mel, ignoring Rob's glare.

"Oh, good," said Mary Evelyn. "The world needs more of that."

"We are not discussing this," said Rob.

"What about you, dear?" Mary Evelyn turned her attention to Mel. "How was the meeting with the muralist last weekend? I never had a chance to ask. Isn't he a hottie?"

Rob turned to Mel, his expression innocent. Not so funny when the tables are turned, is it?

"He seems very nice," said Mel mildly.

"And attractive?"

Mary Evelyn needed to find her own (preferably age-appropriate) love interest, if only to spare Mel the torment of featuring in the Hidden Springs edition of *The Bachelor*.

"Yes, very nice looking," she conceded.

Mary Evelyn seemed satisfied despite Mel's lukewarm response. "I knew you'd like him," she said. "Let me know if you ever get a look at that tattoo."

Mel blushed a fiery red at that, and Rob suppressed a laugh. Mary Evelyn clearly had Mel's number, and he now knew exactly what buttons to press if Mel gave him any shit about Kat in the future.

"I'm meeting him here tomorrow afternoon," said Rob. "I'll let you know if I get a glimpse of it."

"Excellent," said Mary Evelyn. "I'm dying of curiosity."

Mel opened and closed her mouth before finally asking, "Is he around all weekend or just tomorrow?"

Apparently the fish was hooked.

"I'll find out," said Rob.

"No need," said Mel. "I was just curious."

"It's not a problem," said Rob.

"I'm going back to work now."

Mel turned on her heel and walked away. Mary Evelyn's smile was quite smug.

"I knew she would like him."

Rob figured the smart move was to stay silent, but Mary Evelyn looked up at him anyway and said, "Keep up the good work with Kat. That girl needs to get out more. And have hot sex, of course."

"Yes, ma'am." Rob honestly couldn't think of anything else to say, and he was truly grateful when Mary Evelyn returned to the library.

When the time came to wrap up for the day, Hannah showed Kat the detailed notes that she had created for each box, to supplement the file guide. In the future, anyone looking for historical records would have a much more robust starting point in their search. Together, they cleaned up the work area, said farewell to the ladies in the secondhand shop, and walked outside into the sunshine and unseasonable humidity.

Kat debated asking about the marks. She and Hannah had connected today in a way that made the question possible, but Hannah already looked so vulnerable, Kat couldn't bring herself to say the words. Her own emotions were all over the place after learning the story behind the graves, and if she fumbled the ask, she could jeopardize their fragile relationship. Her emotional baggage weighed more than usual today, making her all the more aware that she could easily be misreading the signs. Just because Hannah's stepdad was a police officer didn't mean that history would repeat itself. Lots of police officers were fathers and stepfathers, and they didn't hurt their children. Kat needed a second opinion from someone who could look at the evidence and be impartial. She needed to talk to Joan.

Kat and Hannah agreed to meet at the church the following day, so that Kat could return the journal and the two of them could talk with Pastor Rachel about what to do next.

Hannah wandered off in the direction of home, while Kat walked slowly toward the library. Only a few hours ago, the second-date jitters had threatened to overwhelm her. She had hoped that working with Hannah would provide the distraction she needed to calm down. Instead, their discovery had scraped open old wounds, leaving Kat feeling raw and exposed.

She didn't want to explain her strange mood to Rob. He might not understand, and that would be worse than anything. Their connection felt too new—too fragile—to be tested in that way. Frankly, she didn't want to go digging around in all those old feelings at all. She had processed her experience and moved on years ago. No need for a stroll down that particular block of memory lane.

Pausing beside a sturdy maple, she leaned back against it, pretending to check her phone. Really she just needed a moment to breathe. The solidity of the trunk at her back steadied her. The depth of the roots supported her. Even the air in the shade of the tree felt cleaner as it filled her lungs. But even with that lifeline, Kat could feel herself starting to fray around the edges. She needed to get home.

When she reached the library, she found Rob's truck still there, as was Mel's car. Mel waved from her perch up on the scaffolding, where she was in the process of collecting all the tools and supplies. Rob, loading the garden tools and equipment back into his truck, stopped as she approached, a welcoming smile on his face. She hated herself for wanting to turn and run the other way.

As she got close enough for him to see her face, his smile faded.

"You okay?"

She shrugged. "I'm not feeling all that great, actually. But I do have some good news. Hannah found old records that seem to tie in with the cemetery. We'll cross-check the names tomorrow, but I'm pretty sure we're on the right track."

"That's great," said Rob, but there wasn't much enthusiasm behind the words. She understood his disappointment. Only a few short hours ago, she had been daydreaming about date number two. Now she felt heavy, as if all her baggage had suddenly found her again after years of searching. More than anything, she wanted to go home and crawl into bed.

Under the weight of all that baggage, though, anger started to bubble up. Her stupid past was screwing up her present and possibly her future. She needed to dump this baggage once and for all, then she would get back on track with Rob.

"Can we do a rain check on our date?" she asked, and his face brightened. "Maybe later this week. I can call you tomorrow and fill you in on the details of what Hannah and I have found so far."

"That would be great," he said. "And if you're still feeling under the weather I can bring you some chicken soup."

She smiled. He was such a good guy. He deserved so much better than her own battered and broken heart.

"Thanks." She could feel the rumbles of an emotional storm brewing and needed to get out of here before it hit. "Talk to you tomorrow," she mumbled, then escaped to her car.

Mel had descended from the scaffolding and was about to climb into her own car as Kat rounded the back of Rob's truck, heading to the driver's side door of the Fiat. All it took was one look at Kat's face and Mel could tell that something was very, very wrong.

"You look like shit," she said, pitching her voice so that Rob wouldn't hear.

"Thanks." Kat barely reacted, which ratcheted up Mel's level of concern. They might not be all that close, but if Kat were okay, she would have snapped out a sassy comeback.

"What happened?"

"I can't talk about it. Not here," said Kat. Mel heard the waver in her voice, and her gaze sharpened. At lunch last week, Kat had admitted that she didn't have a lot of close friends around here, just work friends. Nobody to call in a crisis—and this looked a lot like a crisis. Kat could phone a friend later. For now, she would have to make do with Mel.

"So let's go someplace else."

"Okay." Kat stared at Mel as if she had no idea what to do next. Mel had seen sisters and other friends in this state and knew she would have to keep the instructions simple.

"Follow me home," she said gently. "Nobody else is there.

You can freak out as much as you need to and fill me in when you're ready."

Kat still didn't move, and Mel recognized the wounded animal response. Kat probably wanted to crawl into her bed and hide, but that would only make her feel worse.

"Follow me," she repeated, more firmly this time.

"Okay." The robotic response reinforced Mel's belief that this was the right thing to do. Kat was crumbling.

Mel climbed into her car, and Kat did the same. Mel watched her rearview mirror carefully to make sure Kat actually followed, which she did, dutifully trailing Mel's car all the way home. The house Mel had grown up in, one of the houses in The Gardens, was not all that far from the church and the library. Mel probably could have walked over, but she had been feeling lazy this morning. Thankfully, the summer people had all gone back to work and school, leaving the subdivision, for all practical purposes, deserted. Nobody would be stopping by to chat.

Mel exited her car first and walked over to open Kat's door. Kat grabbed her purse from the passenger seat and followed Mel into the house.

"This way," said Mel, heading down a hallway that led to the front of the house, which faced the lake. They passed through a storm door and onto a screened porch that wrapped around most of the house.

Mel guided Kat into a cushioned wicker chair facing the water. "Freak out all you want. I'm going to make some tea."

Kat looked at Mel blankly. "Tea?"

"Supposedly it makes everything better. Mostly it gives us something to do."

Kat nodded, and Mel disappeared back into the house. When she returned about ten minutes later with an honest-to-God tea tray, Kat was still in the same chair, only this time her face was wet with tears. Mel set the tea tray down on the wicker coffee table. Luckily, she had thought to put a box of tissues on the tray. These she silently handed to Kat, who blew her nose and dried her face and took a very deep breath.

"Thank you."

"Anytime," answered Mel. "You want to pick your flavor of tea or shall I?"

Kat looked completely flummoxed by the question, so Mel chose a peppermint herbal tea to wake her up a bit without the jolt of caffeine. At some point the emotional crash would hit and she would need to sleep. Mel handed her the steaming mug, made herself a hibiscus infusion, and took a seat on the wicker sofa. They drank their tea in silence for a few minutes before Kat spoke again.

"You do this often?"

Mel cracked a wry smile. "I have two sisters and a bunch of girlfriends. So, yes, I seem to do this a lot."

"I don't have very many friends," said Kat, "and none of them live around here."

"Sounds like you need to make some more friends."

Kat nodded.

"You ready to tell me what happened?"

"It's stupid."

"It always is, or at least that's what everyone says. You may as well tell me anyway."

Kat sighed. "I realized the other day that very few people know my real story. The abuse never made the papers, at least not that I saw."

"We didn't tell anyone," said Mel, "and I never saw anything about it in the papers either. Everyone thought it was a murder-suicide, and that his reason died with him. For sure nobody knew about the pregnancy."

"I don't even think Rob knows, and I knew him better than anyone."

"He doesn't," said Mel firmly. At Kat's questioning look, she continued, "There were things he said after it all happened, questions he asked, that made it clear he had no idea. I thought maybe it was better that way."

"I'll have to tell him at some point."

Mel nodded. "Maybe not today, though."

Kat gave a choked laugh. "Definitely not today."

"You said before, when we had lunch, that you were totally over this. I hate to break it to you, but this does not look like 'totally over it.'"

"Apparently not," said Kat wearily.

"What set you off?"

"Hannah found the story—stories, actually—behind the cemetery, and it's beyond sad. From what we can tell, those are all teen moms who died in childbirth, or from complications afterward, and the babies are theirs. Some were stillborn. Others didn't survive very long. Their stories are...hard to read."

"I can imagine."

Kat stood suddenly, her teacup abruptly landing in its saucer, and strode over to the screen separating them from the outside world. The tension rolled off her body in waves.

"I was beyond this, damn it. I worked so hard, for so long, to get past it, and now this. All it takes is some sad stories and I fall to pieces." She whipped around. "I deal with these stories every single fucking day, and it doesn't break me. Why is it breaking me now?"

"Something must be different about these old stories. What is it?" Mel wished she could take a time-out and call her sister Tessa, the therapist, for advice, but Tessa was away at a regatta this weekend and very likely on the water right now. Mel would just have to wing it.

"I don't know!" cried Kat. "Maybe...maybe I just can't stomach the idea that this kind of thing has been going on for more than a hundred fucking years, probably for all of human history. Humanity sucks. We never learn. What's the point?"

The wicker chair creaked in protest when Kat flopped back down into it, looking at Mel defiantly. "There will always be more. It never ends."

Mel was quiet for a minute, scrambling for something to say that would help. Kat thunked her head back on the chair in defeat and stared at the ceiling. It took a minute for Mel's brain to dig something up. If she couldn't consult a professional, she would have to work with what she had, and that was random stories she had read on the internet.

"Did you ever read the story online about the little boy on the beach who saves the starfish?"

Kat leaned her head to the side to give Mel a baleful look. "I don't exactly have a lot of spare time for web surfing."

"Right," said Mel. "I'll give you the recap. Little boy walks down the beach every day as the tide is going out. Every time he finds a starfish, he throws it out into the ocean as far as he can."

"Please tell me this is a short story."

"Give me a chance, here," said Mel. "One day, a man asks him what he's doing, and the little boy explains that he's saving the starfish. If he doesn't throw them back into the ocean, they'll die before the next high tide. The man laughs and says that there are miles and miles of beaches, and thousands of stranded starfish. There's no way the boy could possibly make a difference."

Tears started leaking from Kat's eyes again. Mel wasn't sure if that was a good thing or a bad thing, but she kept going.

"The boy bends down and picks up another starfish, then throws it as far as he can back into the ocean. 'I made a differ-ence for that one,' he says."

Kat made a choking noise and grabbed the box of tissues. Mel ducked, assuming the box was about to go airborne, but

Kat yanked out several tissues, dried her tears, and blew her nose before thunking the box down on the cushion beside her.

"That's a horrible story."

"No, it's not. It's a story you need to hear." Thank goodness Tessa wasn't here to witness her playing amateur therapist. "You can't help everyone. That would be impossible. All you can do is help one person at a time. It matters, and you know it."

"You shouldn't believe everything you read on the internet." Grabbing another tissue, Kat blew her nose again.

"Well, you shouldn't believe everything you hear inside your head. You are one human being and you make a difference. The world is a better place because you're in it, whether you want to hear that or not."

Kat was quiet for a long time.

"Thanks," she said at last. "I still feel like shit, but better, if you know what I mean."

"I do," said Mel.

Kat wiped her puffy, red eyes and blew her nose yet again.

"You look like shit, by the way," said Mel, and Kat made a sound that was half laugh, half hiccup. "You can't go out in public looking like that. Want to order a pizza and watch a movie?"

Kat nodded. "That would be perfect."

CHAPTER EIGHTEEN

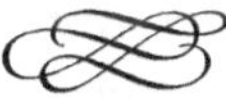

As the movie credits rolled, there was a clatter at the
back door, and Mel jumped up to see who it was.

"Who's there?" she called as she headed toward the kitchen.

Kat got up more slowly and folded the blanket that had
been her cocoon. This afternoon had been exactly what she
needed. They had chosen a classic, *Notting Hill*, which Kat had
never seen. Mel had made popcorn. The movie had relieved all
pressure to talk, and the pizza, when it had arrived mid movie,
had been the perfect comfort food. Kat had managed to shut off
her brain for two whole hours. Sneaking a glimpse in the hall
mirror, she was relieved to see no trace of the earlier breakdown, just a hint of exhaustion.

Following the sound of voices back to the kitchen, she
found Mel and Dora in conversation.

"Next time, give me a heads-up," Mel was saying. "I had no
idea you were coming back today. I could have made dinner."

"That's all right. I love cold pizza. Well, hello, Kat," said
Dora. "What were you girls doing this afternoon?"

"Just watching a movie," said Kat. "I didn't realize how late it
was getting. I should head home, actually."

She grabbed her purse from the kitchen table but paused before heading out the door.

"Thanks, Mel. This was exactly the kind of afternoon I needed."

"Anytime," called Mel as Kat escaped out the back door.

Home felt unusually empty, so Kat turned on the TV and let a home decorating show play in the background while she tackled her slowly shrinking backlog. She deliberately ignored the journal she had set aside on the entryway table. She wasn't ready to go there yet, still too fragile. It was much easier, and more productive, to bury herself in work. She forced herself to make it an early night, leaving only a handful of files for tomorrow.

Maybe it was emotional exhaustion, but she fell hard into a dreamless sleep and woke up at five in the morning, completely alert. There would be no snoozing on this fine Sunday morning.

It was still dark outside, but Kat got up and showered anyway. The time had come to face her demons. She made a cup of coffee, retrieved the journal from the entryway table, and curled up in her favorite chair. A predawn glow warmed the sky through the window—not enough to read by, so she switched on the lamp. Later in the day this spot would be too warm, flooded with direct sunlight, but right now it was perfect. Taking a deep breath to brace herself, she opened up the journal.

Yesterday she had scanned the first few pages, getting a sense of the stories without absorbing all the details. Today, she read more carefully, looking for clues as to the identity of the girls. There were few. The journalist had been careful to use only first names. As for the journalist herself, she never signed her entries, but her name should be somewhere in the church records, given that she had mentioned her husband, Lucas, the minister. As the minister's wife, she would have been well-placed to learn about these situations, and clearly she had been compassionate enough to take action.

As Kat got to know the writer through her words, she realized that these were essentially case notes. The journalist had documented each girl's situation, found a solution unique to the particulars of the case, and followed up afterward to make sure that each girl was doing well in her new life. As word spread of the sanctuary to be found at the church, more girls came. The hardest to read were the cases where she couldn't help, where she was too late. She lost so many girls in childbirth, and so many babies in those first few weeks after birth. It was a miracle that she found the strength to keep doing the work, but then—as Kat knew all too well—there's no way to stop doing the work. There will always be girls who need your help. How can you abandon them just because it's hard?

The difference between her own situation and the writer's was that the writer had support in her work. From what Kat had read, the minister didn't get too involved, trusting his wife to see that the girls were safe, but he deflected the criticism that might have otherwise come her way and lifted her spirits when she lost hope. Kat needed someone like that in her life. It was too easy—and much too early—to speculate on whether or not Rob might be that person, but she felt marginally better knowing the possibility existed.

Kat weathered the second read-through better than the first. The journalist was, in essence, a colleague, part of a long tradition of people who help. Over the course of the entries, Kat grew to understand how much inner strength it must have taken to protect these girls. The inclination of many of the "pillars of the community" had been to shun them, believing they brought trouble upon themselves and deserved what they got. Certainly, bad decisions played a part in some of the cases, but these were young girls. Of course they made bad choices. They had no life experience yet. No judgment. More than half the cases, though, found girls in trouble through no fault of their own. The journal writer helped them all. She didn't judge, and she didn't shame. She simply kept them safe and helped them to make the best of an already difficult situation.

When Kat had finished, she put the journal aside, stood, and stretched. She needed to move, so she threw on some sneakers and headed out the door. Although she had been up for hours, it was barely seven in the morning, the sun just rising. She walked past the diner, which opened at seven on Sundays instead of six, and saw Lucy inside chatting with the handful of early risers. Crossing Main Street, she walked to the library, following the compulsion to visit the graves in person.

Walking the rows of graves, this time she recognized the names, knew the stories, and her heart ached for these girls who hadn't made it, and for their babies, lost too soon.

She thought about her mom, sent away to school in the United States to escape the violence in Colombia, knowing that her family still faced danger at home. Her mother had always insisted that her family was lost, and had refused to discuss Kat's biological father. When pressed, her mother had always promised to tell her more later, when Kat was old enough to understand. All those secrets, all those stories, had died with her. Only in the past few years had Kat begun to wonder if her family in Colombia was truly gone, or if perhaps her mother had cut ties with them rather than admit to a pregnancy out of wedlock.

Kat sat on the bench and stared into the past, wondering if she would have felt the same calling had she lived a hundred years ago. A cynical smile touched her face. A hundred years ago she would have died in childbirth and never had the opportunity to help other girls.

In order to survive the last ten years, Kat had divided her life neatly into "before" and "after." She had even thought of herself as two different people. One had died, so that the other could live. It had all been so clear, and it had worked. But now those clear lines were beginning to blur, and her carefully crafted life was in danger of crumbling. Exhibit number one: yesterday's breakdown. As it turned out, the old, fragile Kitty hadn't died, exactly. She had been hiding, or hibernating, and now as she emerged from that hiding place, her presence undermined the foundations of Kat's life. Standing strong for so long had taken its toll. She was exhausted, wanting more than anything to take a break. But how could she take a break when there were so many people who still needed her strength?

Instead of living in the "after" all these years, it turned out she had been living in denial. There was no "before" and "after" anymore, just Kat, and Kat was a mess.

Rob arrived early for his meeting with the muralist Sunday morning. Kat had called him an hour earlier to share the story behind the grave markers, and he could use the extra time to let it all sink in. As he paced the rows of the cemetery, he thought about the lost girls—children really—and knew that the mural and the garden design would need to acknowledge their stories.

"Hot Muralist" finally arrived, and Rob's reaction upon seeing him was, frankly, disappointment, which was ridiculous. He had assumed, based on Mel and Mary Evelyn's assessment, that this guy would look like some kind of supermodel. In reality, he looked like a regular guy—short brown hair, in decent shape, and not that much older than Rob. He wore khakis and a button-down shirt over a white tee, basically the preppy uniform, which made him look more like an architect than an artist. It was not clear why the ladies were so excited.

He stood up from the bench and extended a hand. "Rob Murray."

"Fitz," said the muralist. "Great to finally meet you. Any updates on the cemetery?"

Rob nodded, and they began to walk toward the graves. "We just learned that the church was also a shelter of sorts for unwed mothers in the late 1800s and early 1900s. Because the girls were so young, many died in childbirth, or their babies didn't make it."

Fitz walked silently along the edge of the cemetery, studying the stones and occasionally looking back toward the library building. Rob didn't rush him. He'd been doing much the same thing himself for the past hour.

"Have you had a chance to share any of this information yet with the community?" asked Fitz.

"Not yet. One of our volunteers found the journal just yesterday."

Fitz stopped and put his hands on his hips as he surveyed the entire site, from the top of the library wall down the gentle slope to the cemetery. He shook his head.

"My initial ideas all seem too lighthearted now."

Rob nodded in agreement. "Mine, too. We can't just ignore the cemetery. It needs to be an integrated part of the design. The church provided a safe haven for these girls and their babies. Maybe we could recreate that feeling in the park."

Fitz nodded slowly. "Bring them back into the community, in a way they couldn't be when they were alive. Maybe even tell their stories."

Relieved that he and Fitz were on the same page here, Rob gave a silent thanks to Mary Evelyn for choosing the right guy for the job. They continued brainstorming, trading ideas and taking notes for almost an hour.

"Let's make sure that people from the church are included

in the community meeting. Is that still planned for Thursday night?" asked Fitz.

"Yep, Thursday night, seven p.m. Mary Evelyn has been talking it up already."

"Typically, I bring some sketches—just ideas, really—to see what resonates with the group. Do you think you could do the same for the landscaping?"

"Absolutely. Once I get my ideas down on paper, it would be pretty straightforward to sketch some elevations for the meetings."

Fitz started walking again, faster now as he circled back around toward the front of the library. Rob let him take the lead, following a few steps behind.

"Did Mel say when she'd be done with the wall?" asked Fitz.

"They finished level two yesterday, so only the ground level left to go."

"Will she continue to help with the project after the wall is finished? I could always use a helping hand with the painting of the mural itself, and I understand she paints."

Fitz was still striding ahead, so Rob didn't worry about hiding his amusement. Someone was awfully curious about Mel.

"I haven't asked, but I will." Rob waited to see if Fitz would ask any more questions about Mel.

"She seems very...competent."

"That she is," Rob agreed blandly. He debated getting involved, then decided why the hell not. "She's still in town today, if you'd like to check in with her yourself. She might be more willing to help with the next phase if you ask her personally."

Fitz stopped at the wall, looked up at the second level. "Maybe I will," he said, "if she's here anyway."

And my work here is done.

"I need to head home," said Rob, "and get these ideas on paper while they're fresh. Is there anything else we need to discuss now, or should we continue via email?"

Fitz turned around. "We're good," he said. "Thanks for meeting me. I'll shoot you some ideas by end of day tomorrow, and we'll go from there."

"Sounds good," said Rob. They shook hands again, and Rob headed for his truck.

On the ride home, he realized that he hadn't looked forward to a project this much in years. Ever since starting his business, he had been flying solo. No colleagues, only clients—and collaboration with a client was a delicate undertaking, the conversations carefully filtered. Sure, he had his crew, and they were great, but they were pretty straightforward guys. They didn't want to debate the different ways that he could handle drainage, or the species of tree that would best suit a particular location. They wanted to do their jobs, be done, and enjoy their nights and weekends.

Not since grad school had Rob brainstormed ideas with a colleague. Until now, he hadn't realized how much he missed it. For the first time in years, someone would challenge Rob to do better.

This was going to be fun.

Kat and Hannah met at the library as they had before, only a little earlier this time. They walked slowly around the corner and up the hill as the church bells tolled eleven. Churchgoers trickled into the parking lot, and Kat now knew that many others would stay inside for coffee and snacks. She hoped to catch Pastor Rachel in the office before the minister joined the social hour.

Sure enough, they found both Irene and the minister in the

church office, along with a few parishioners. They hung back until the parishioners' questions had been answered. Then Pastor Rachel beckoned them into her office, gesturing for them to sit in the chairs opposite her desk.

"I heard you finally found something," she said, "and I've been dying of curiosity. Tell me all about it."

"Hannah is the one who found it, so really she should be the one to tell you."

Hannah shot Kat a look but rose to the occasion.

"I found a journal tucked inside one of the folders, and in it, I found entries from the late 1800s and early 1900s, stories about girls in trouble."

Kat pulled the journal from her purse and handed it across the desk to Pastor Rachel.

"Do we know who the author was?" the minister asked, examining the first few pages.

When Hannah didn't answer, Kat stepped in. "It appears she was the minister's wife. You might be able to verify that with other records. Her husband's name was Lucas."

Pastor Rachel nodded. "We probably can. I'll ask Irene to look into it. What kind of trouble were these girls in?"

This time Hannah was ready with an answer. "Mostly they were pregnant," said Hannah, "although in a few cases they were just getting abused."

"There weren't a lot of programs or resources for young women at that time," added Kat. "This woman was a lifesaver for them."

"Why so many graves?" asked the minister. "If someone was helping these girls, why were they dying?"

"A lot of them were really young," said Hannah. "Way too young to have babies. They died in childbirth, and not all the babies survived."

"If they didn't die during childbirth, some died days or weeks later from complications. Their bodies just weren't ready

for the trauma," added Kat. She clamped down hard on a wave
of memory, forcibly anchoring herself in the present.

"I'd like to read through the journal this afternoon," said
Pastor Rachel. "It's amazing to me that we sheltered so many
young women and yet nobody remembers."

"Any thoughts about next steps?" asked Kat.

"I can come tomorrow after school and make a list of all the
deaths mentioned," said Hannah. "We can compare that list to
the names on the graves."

"Good idea," said Kat. "I can make sure we have a list of all
the names on the graves. Rob may have one already. I'll ask
him." Her behavior yesterday must have confused the hell out
of him. Half of her wanted to offer some kind of explanation,
but the other half wanted to curl up in a protective ball until
the world got back to normal. Unclear at this point which side
would win.

Pastor Rachel leaned back in her chair and steepled her
fingers beneath her chin. "Our real challenge will be to handle
this information in a way that honors both the memory of
these young women and also the privacy of the families
involved."

"I was thinking about that, too," said Kat. "The young
women and their families are long dead now, but some of the
babies may still be living."

"A bunch of the girls changed their names when they went
away to start new lives," said Hannah. "The minister's wife kept
in touch with most of them. She talks about it in her journal
entries, but I haven't come across any actual letters or
addresses."

"Have you finished going through the files?" the minister
asked. Hannah shook her head. "Let's not give up hope, then."

"Families researching their genealogy would be very interested in this information," said Kat. "I'm just not sure how to let
people know that it is available."

"Maybe the library can advise us on that, or someone local who is into genealogy."

"Good idea," said Kat. "I'll ask Mary Evelyn."

"Some of the babies were adopted by local families," said Hannah. "I wonder if they would want to know."

Neither Kat nor Pastor Rachel knew the answer to that question.

"We have a lot to think about," the minister said, "and a lot more to discuss. Hannah, why don't you keep us posted on what you find over the next few days? I'll reach out to other churches to find out how they handle this type of information. I'm sure this is a problem that has been solved before."

"Okay," said Hannah. "I should probably go home now."

"Thank you for coming today, Hannah," said Pastor Rachel. "Please tell your mother and sister that I send my love."

"I will," said Hannah, before making her exit.

Pastor Rachel stared after her, a concerned look on her face.

"I worry about that girl," she said. "That family has experienced so much loss, and I feel like Hannah never really bounced back from it."

"When did her father die?" asked Kat.

"I think Hannah was nine or ten at the time. It was just a few of years into my pastorship. His funeral was one of my first here." She was quiet, thinking back on it. "It crushed all three of them, frankly, and her mother was still very vulnerable when she met her current husband. Before we knew it, she had remarried and they stopped coming to church."

"Did they get married here at the church?"

The minister shook her head. "No, they had a civil ceremony up at the courthouse, without family or friends. I get the sense that Jennifer—Hannah's mom—doesn't see much of her friends anymore." She shook off the dark thoughts and stood. "Maybe this is an opportunity to reconnect with the family, make sure they're doing okay. We do what we can, right?"

Kat nodded, her sense of unease growing. She clearly wasn't the only one who had a bad feeling about Hannah's situation at home, but there was nothing alarming enough to call in the cavalry.

"Would you like to come downstairs for a cup of coffee?" asked Pastor Rachel.

Kat wouldn't have minded continuing the discussion, but she didn't have it in her to make polite conversation with strangers right now, no matter how friendly they might be.

"Thanks, but I've got some work to finish this afternoon. Best to get right to it."

"Of course," the minister said as they walked through the main office and into the hallway. "You're welcome anytime."

They parted ways, Pastor Rachel heading downstairs and Kat heading out the door into the sunshine. She needed to find a way to ask Hannah about those marks on her arm. No more waiting.

CHAPTER NINETEEN

ROB CALLED KAT WHEN HE THOUGHT SHE MIGHT BE HOME FROM her meeting with the minister. He could have waited until Tuesday to give her an update, but he had an idea. More than that, he wanted to know that she was doing okay. She had sounded pretty fragile this morning.

"Hey," he said when she answered her cell phone.

"Hey, yourself."

"How did it go with the minister?"

"Really well," she answered. "She's going to read the journal this afternoon, and Hannah is going to keep sorting through the rest of the files this week looking for related information. I'm going to make a list of all the names on the graves, and we'll see if we can account for everyone in that cemetery."

"I think I have all the names noted down on my site plan, if you want to use that as a starting point."

"That would be great," she said.

"What do you have going on this afternoon?"

"Why do you ask?"

"I was thinking..." he began.

"Always dangerous."

"Funny," he said. "I was thinking that I have a bunch of paperwork to do today."

"I find myself in a similar situation."

"And yet I want to hang out with you."

She laughed. "I've almost cleared out my backlog. I don't want to lose the momentum."

"I know," he said. "That's why I was thinking that we should work together."

A pause, then, "What exactly did you have in mind?"

"We pick a place, yours or mine, or even your office. I don't care as long as there's Wi-Fi. We get all our work done while hanging out in the same room at the same time. I figure it's less lonely that way."

"And you think we'll actually get work done?"

"I promise not to distract you until we're both done."

"Intriguing," she said. "I like to work at my kitchen table, but I'm not sure it's big enough for two people to spread out."

"I don't actually need that much room," he said. "I have one stack of papers on each side of my laptop, and that's all the space I need."

"What are you, a robot?" she asked. "Some of us need piles. Lots and lots of piles."

He knew then, improbable as it seemed, that they would someday argue about her piles and how they were taking over the house. It might, however, be too soon to share that flash of insight with Kat.

"I have a pretty big kitchen table, if you'd rather work here," he said.

"Then I would have to move my piles."

"True."

"Let's work here," she said firmly. "I'll carve out a spot for you."

"Sounds like a plan. Have you had lunch?"

"Not yet."

"I'll pick something up on the way over," he said. "Half an hour?"

"See you soon."

When Rob knocked on Kat's door, he half expected her to send him back home again saying that it was a bad idea and she would never be able to get any work done with him in the same room. She opened the door, and although she didn't immediately kick him out, he could see the wariness in her eyes.

"I come bearing gifts," he said, presenting her with a small aloe plant, its tiny pot adorned with a colorful mosaic. Surprise eclipsed any doubts she might have had. She accepted it with a smile and stepped back to allow him inside.

"Thank you." She seemed unsure of where to put the plant.

"It will do best with some sunshine, maybe over by the window?"

She nodded and moved to follow his suggestion. Curious, he watched as she paused by the kitchen and looked back over her shoulder.

"Do I need to give it water?" She was taking this gift seriously.

"No, it's fine for now. You'll probably need to water it once a week. Oh, and you might want to put a saucer under the pot so it doesn't leak water onto the windowsill."

"Right. Good idea."

While she hunted through the cupboards for a saucer, he took the opportunity to survey the space. No other houseplants, which might explain her uncertainty about this one. Not much of anything cluttered the room. Her space gave him the feeling that she was just visiting—that she hadn't made it a home.

Whatever he had expected to find in her inner sanctum, this wasn't it. In Rob's experience, a person's living space reflected their personality. The things they chose to display, the clutter of life, the choice of artwork or posters for the wall—all of these things provided clues about the occupant of the space. Kat had left no clues. Even the reprints on the walls felt generic, as if she had rented the place furnished, or bought the decorated model unit. Of course this only made him more curious about the real Kat. Maybe her office reflected the real Kat. She did spend most of her time there.

He set down his work stuff and held up the bag of sandwiches. "Hungry?"

"I could eat," she said, adjusting the position of the tiny pot on the windowsill one last time before turning around.

He had forgotten to ask what she liked, so he had ordered an assortment of small sandwiches, all condiments on the side. The bag held enough food for a family of six, but he figured better safe than sorry.

She shook her head when she saw how heavy the bag was, but she smiled, too. "I can't believe you got this much food." After taking the bag from him, she unloaded the contents onto the kitchen counter and opened a bag of chips. "We could survive for days on this. Maybe even a week."

"Just trying to keep you fed," he said. "I heard from Lucy that you're not much of a cook."

Kat tossed a chip at his head and took a seat at one of her two counter stools. "Lucy should know better than to spread rumors about her most reliable customer."

Rather than crowd her, Rob ate his sandwich standing up at the opposite side of the counter. They kept the conversation light, and when he could tell that she was antsy to get back to work, he made it happen with minimum fuss. She kept glancing over at him while they worked, as if she expected him to interrupt her with questions or fidget in creative and annoying ways. He just smiled and kept working. Honestly, he'd never felt more relaxed.

Over the next couple of hours, Kat seemed to relax, too. Taking credit for that would be a bit of a stretch, but he'd provided company without distraction, which had to at least count as a contributing factor. The cemetery stories had really thrown Kat for a loop, and as much as he wanted to ask how she was doing, he didn't want to put that tension back in her shoulders or the line back between her eyebrows.

Late that afternoon, he wrapped up for the day, trying not to make too much fuss about it. If she was ready to stop, she would stop. If not, he would head home and give her the time and space she needed to finish.

"Is it five fifteen already?" she asked. "I would have guessed maybe three."

"Well, you would have guessed wrong," he said. "You've been pretty focused over there among your piles."

She had given him the couch, with room for his two piles, one on either side. Her own stacks of papers and folders filled the entire kitchen table, making it really hard to tell how much work she still had to do.

Kat leaned back in her chair and stretched, and he couldn't help but wonder if she realized how sexy that was. Now wasn't the time to make a move, but it didn't hurt to look.

"Do you have a lot of work left?" he asked.

She shook her head, then started rolling her head from side to side to get the kinks out of her neck. "I actually got a lot done this afternoon, maybe more than I would have if I had been working alone."

"How so?"

She gave a little shrug. "You helped me to stay focused. I didn't take a break to do laundry or get a snack, or put the TV on for background noise." After a pause to consider, she said, "We should probably do this more often."

A bark of laughter escaped him. "So my presence enables

you to work even more than you already do. I don't know if that's wonderful or awful. Maybe a little of both."

She stood up and stretched again. "Come on. Let's go for a walk."

Rob packed up his papers and laptop, leaving them locked in his truck. Then they wandered through the park and down to the lakefront. Even on the weekend, at this time of year the lake was quiet. Only one motorboat disturbed the late-afternoon peace, and they could barely hear it as it raced along the far shore. After strolling to the end of the municipal pier, Kat slipped off her sandals, sat down, and dangled her toes in the water, kicking up a splash each time a larger wave rolled by.

Rob sat beside her, keeping his feet up on the pier. He didn't want to break the mood, but he had so many questions—or really just one big one—for Kat, and this might be his best shot at asking them. He waited in silence until the hard planks of the pier made him shift uncomfortably. Then he asked.

"What happened after you left?"

He let the question hang in the air between them, hoping she would answer, but knowing that she might not. It was a big ask, not just the question itself, but asking her to trust him with the answer.

"It's not a time in my life that I like to revisit."

"I understand," he said quickly. "I shouldn't have asked."

"No...it's okay. I don't mind telling you, but I'm not going to regale you with stories. Just the basics. Can you live with that?"

"Of course."

She pulled her legs up onto the pier and wrapped her arms around her knees, her face serious. "I hope that's true."

Silence fell around them again. Kat looked out over the water, and he started to wonder if she had changed her mind about answering. Then she spoke.

"Tell me the parts of the story that you know."

He hadn't expected a question and had to think for a minute about his answer. "You and I were supposed to work together after school on that art project, but you were freaking out about something and went home instead. The next day, I found out that your stepfather had shot your mother and then himself. They said you were okay, but you never came back to school." Rob swallowed, not sure how to say the next part. "Later, the newspaper called it a murder-suicide. There was speculation about why he did it, that he might have been physically abusive to your mom, but no real answers. They didn't even refer to you by name, probably because you were under eighteen."

Nodding throughout his awkward recitation of the known facts, Kat marveled yet again at the idea that nobody had leaked the details. Not Jack or his father, not Mel or her sisters. Other police officers must have known, but everyone had kept the details private. She had always assumed that everyone knew the sordid truth. This new reality would take some read-justment and might in some ways make life easier. First, though, she needed to tell Rob the truth—at least, the bare bones. She picked up where he left off, her voice very matter-of-fact.

"First I went to a crisis center, where I had to tell my story and they had to figure out what to do with me. From there I went to a group home in Milwaukee. They gave me the option of a foster home back here, but I wanted to be as far away from here as possible."

She looked over, checking in with him. He nodded but didn't say anything, and she looked back at the water.

"I was pregnant."

Rob couldn't help the indrawn breath, but cursed himself when he saw her shoulders tense. It took a minute for her to resume her story.

"The newspaper got it almost right. He physically and

emotionally abused my mom, and he sexually abused me. My stepdad was the father of the baby."

This time Rob controlled his reaction. He kept his breathing even while he waited for Kat to continue.

"I was too far along at that point to end the pregnancy. They had me in counseling, but despite all the therapy sessions, a part of me still believed that everything was my fault and the pregnancy was my punishment."

The hardest part about listening to Kat tell the rest of her story was the knowledge that there was nothing he could do to change the outcome. Her story had already been written, and he could only listen.

"The pregnancy was easy, but the delivery almost killed me. If I had been one of the church girls a hundred years ago, I would have died. Thanks to modern medicine, I'm alive, but the baby didn't make it."

She didn't bother to check on him this time, just paused, took a breath, and kept going.

"My friend Joan up at county was my caseworker at the time. She was amazing, helped me navigate the transition from foster care to being on my own. There was some life insurance money, which funded college. I stayed in Milwaukee for both college and grad school, just kept going to school like it would keep real life from ever happening.

"Somewhere along the way, I found friends and a purpose: I would help kids the way Joan helped me. I worked at a big law firm long enough to pay off my student loans and build a nest egg, and then I quit, came here, started up my own practice."

The silence fell around them again, and this time Rob knew she was done talking. He ached to know more, as she had suspected he would, but also didn't want to hurt her with endless questions. It was time for him to say something.

"I'm sorry I wasn't there for you."

"I didn't give you that option."

"I know. I'm sorry anyway."

"You know the greatest blessing in the whole mess? I never had to watch my mother take sides. My greatest fear, when I imagined telling her what was happening, was that she would believe him and not me. I see it happen to kids all the time. I didn't want to hurt her by telling her, and I was too afraid to find out how she would react. And then I lost her." Kat turned to look at him for the first time in what seemed like hours. "I choose to have faith in my memory of her, to believe that she would have believed me."

Kat would have left Rob at the pier and walked home alone, but he had parked right next to her town house. There was no way to avoid the long walk back home. It wasn't like he was going to leave her alone at the lakefront after everything she had just dumped in his lap.

She was such a coward. The confession had left her feeling vulnerable and exposed, and she hated it. Even as the words fell out of her mouth, she had known that she shouldn't be telling him, shouldn't be talking about it at all. He already made her feel unsteady and too much like the girl she had been before. Now he knew the full story—or most of it, anyway. She couldn't take it back. He would never look at her the same way again, never believe the illusion of the strong and confident Kat. He was a normal guy. He deserved someone balanced and happy and...not broken.

They walked in silence all the way back home, but the anticipated awkwardness never materialized. He simply walked beside her—no pointless conversation, no painful questions. Nothing, really. They just walked.

When they reached her town house, he kissed her gently on the cheek and said, "Thank you for sharing your story with me."

"Thanks for listening," she answered softly.

Was he really going to let her off the hook that easily?

"Are you okay to be alone right now?"

She nodded.

"I'm going to head home, but if you want to talk more about any of this, you call me, okay?"

"Okay."

He leaned in slowly, giving her plenty of time to decline the kiss, but she realized that she wanted it. Even if this thing between them couldn't possibly last, she wanted the kiss. Sinking into each other, she absorbed his quiet strength. If the last couple of days were any indication, she was going to need it.

Too soon, he pulled back and rested his forehead against hers. For a few moments they simply breathed. Then he pulled away, walked slowly to his car, and left.

Mel didn't recognize the number on the caller ID, but the Chicago area code made her pause, then answer. If it was a robocall, she could always hang up.

"Mel." The voice should have been as unfamiliar as the number, but she knew exactly who it was, and the knowledge sent a little shiver down her spine.

"Fitz. To what do I owe the honor?"

"Rob gave me your number. I was hoping we could get together to talk about the next phase of the project."

Her mother was upstairs unpacking, but Mel wouldn't put it past her to eavesdrop if she had any idea who was on the line. Closing her laptop, she set it aside and slipped quietly out the back door and onto the screened porch overlooking the lake. The wicker sofa was tempting, but with most of the windows in the house open, the potential for eavesdropping was still too high. She left the house altogether, heading toward the commons and the lakefront.

"I thought my volunteer stint was coming to an end? Not that I don't love tuck pointing."

"It doesn't have to end." Without the distraction of his physical presence, Mel could appreciate that voice, deeper and huskier on the phone than you might guess from looking at him. Everyone texted these days, making their direct communication feel strangely intimate.

"Tell me more." It didn't hurt to listen, right?

"I was thinking…" He paused. "Maybe we should get together for a drink to talk about it."

A slow smile spread across her face. "I'd love to, although I can't until later. My mom just got back from a trip, and we're having dinner with my sisters tonight."

"And I have to head back to the city in a few hours."

"So tell me more now." Big girls don't pout, she told herself sternly.

"You mentioned that in addition to photography you also paint."

"Yes, I have been known to paint." Mel didn't typically share her work with other people, but she was curious to see where this conversation was headed.

"It's a big wall, and I have a limited window to get the mural finished." He cleared his throat, and it occurred to Mel that he might actually be nervous. "If you have some time to help with the actual painting, I would really appreciate it."

Mel sat on one of the benches down by the shore path while the weight of his words sank in. The reality was that she needed to bank as much cash as she could in the next month, finishing out all her freelance gigs and getting those invoices out for payment. It would be tough to collect unpaid invoices while out of the country, especially with limited internet access.

But his work was amazing, and he was asking her to be a

part of it. It had been so long since she had taken on a project just for fun. If she managed her time well, she should be able to finish her work and also help with the mural. The temptation proved too much to resist.

"I'd love to help." She tried not to let too much giddiness spill into her voice. "I don't have any upcoming location work in Chicago. All my projects are in the editing phase, so I can work from here as easily as downtown."

This could actually come in very handy. Until she came clean with the family about her plans, she needed a believable excuse for living at the lake instead of finding a new sublet. She'd been house sitting and couch surfing since her lease ended, most of her stuff in storage, and she didn't have anything good lined up for these final weeks before the trip. Dora would believe any excuse if she thought her matchmaking schemes were working. Pretending to fall for Fitz wouldn't be a chore. In fact, a fling with an expiration date was just the thing she needed.

"Thank you." He sounded like he meant it.

"My pleasure." Yes, the double entendre was intentional. "When will you be back up here?"

"Thursday."

"I'll see you then."

Operation "Seduce Fitz" was officially underway.

KAT WAVED AT IRENE AS SHE WALKED PAST THE CHURCH OFFICE ON Monday afternoon. At this point, she was becoming a regular. Irene was on the phone, as always. The door to the minister's office was closed, and Kat wasn't sure if that meant Pastor Rachel was busy or not here. Hannah was curled up in her favorite chair, paging slowly through a file. If the stacks of file boxes were any indication, she had made excellent progress today. The "done" stack of files significantly outweighed the "to be reviewed" files.

Hannah looked up as Kat entered the room and gave her a small smile. "Hi," she said.

"How's it going?" answered Kat, absurdly pleased with Hannah's smile. Progress was measured in small steps. Kat hoped they had made enough progress to have a critical conversation today. A little luck would help, too. "Anything interesting?"

"Not yet. I finished the list, though." She picked up a piece of paper from the side table and handed it to Kat. "I can't remember exactly how many graves there were, but the number of names is close to what we need. I hope they match."

"Me, too."

Kat took the list and scanned it. Hannah had added dates of death, where available, or at least the year, and also noted if the lost were mothers or babies. Kat felt the weight of responsibility that she now shared with the long-dead minister's wife to take care of these kids, and to make sure they were not forgotten.

"Her name was Winifred, but apparently people called her Winnie," announced Pastor Rachel from the doorway, startling both Kat and Hannah. Neither of them had any idea what she was talking about.

"The minister's wife. Her name was Winnie. Irene found it in the church records. Her husband held the pastorate during the time period when the cemetery was created."

"Really?" said Hannah. She looked absolutely delighted with the news. Kat couldn't help smiling herself.

"I would not lie to you," the minister said. "How goes the search? Any new information?"

"Nothing new," said Hannah, "but the list is ready."

"Good. We need to know that all the children are accounted for."

"Any luck with other churches?" asked Kat.

"I've found a lot of guidance about when to allow access to our records to people doing genealogy research, that kind of thing, but nothing about making information more public. I have a few leads in the museum world. We'll see what they say."

"From a legal perspective, deceased people do not have a right to privacy," said Kat. "I know it sounds harsh, but that's how it works. We also can't reveal any surnames because we don't know them."

"I suppose the key question is whether or not any of the people mentioned in these records are still alive."

"Good point," said Kat. "The young mothers in Winnie's files are most certainly not living—that would make them over one hundred years old—but I'm not so sure about the babies. Some of them, especially those mentioned toward the end of her records, would be in their nineties now. It's not outside the realm of possibility that they could still be living."

"I think we need another list," said Hannah, "a complete list of all the people Winnie helped. Maybe we can find out what happened to the ones who left, if we can ever find their addresses."

"Good idea," said Pastor Rachel. "You keep up the good work." The minister might have continued, but they were interrupted by the arrival of a woman and a girl who looked about twelve. "Jennifer. Fiona. What a nice surprise. It's wonderful to see you."

Pastor Rachel embraced them both. This must be Hannah's mother and sister. Hannah was already standing and cleaning up her work area. There would be no critical conversation today.

"It's good to see you, too," said Jennifer. She was very soft-spoken, the resemblance to Hannah unmistakable. "Sorry I didn't call you back."

"Not to worry," said Pastor Rachel. "I just wanted to see how you were doing. It's been wonderful to see Hannah again."

"What are you doing, Hannah?" asked Fiona, the younger sister.

"Come see. I'm going through all these old church files trying to solve a mystery."

"A mystery?" Soon the two girls were huddled over the current set of files, Hannah paging through to show Fiona what she was learning.

"I can't believe how Fiona has grown," the minister said to Jennifer.

"I know. I think she might end up taller than Hannah."

"Well, that makes sense. Her father was tall."

Jennifer ducked her head and nodded.

"How is everything with Carl?"

"Fine. It's fine," said Jennifer. She made it a point to look Pastor Rachel in the eye, but Kat could feel the underlying vibe. Things were not fine.

"That's good to hear," the minister said gently.

"We should probably get going," said Jennifer. "Need to get started on dinner."

"Of course," said Pastor Rachel as Jennifer called to Fiona and Hannah to wrap it up. "Remember that you're always welcome here, no matter how long it's been."

"I know," said Jennifer. "Thank you."

She hustled the girls out, but both Pastor Rachel and Kat could hear their conversation.

"Why did you have to pick me up?" asked Hannah, sounding annoyed. "It's only a few blocks. I walk home all the time."

"Your dad asked me to pick you up—for safety."

Hannah made a skeptical noise, echoing Kat's thoughts. "Hidden Springs isn't dangerous."

"Regardless, he asked, so I'm here. Now let's just go home and get dinner—"

The main doors closed behind them, cutting off the rest of the conversation, but Pastor Rachel and Kat had heard enough.

The two exchanged looks.

"You know," the minister said as they slowly followed the family's path down the hall toward the main doors. "I was a social worker for a few years before I became a minister."

"Really? Why the career change?"

"I still wanted to help people, but I needed to do it in another way," she said. "Being a minister creates a different kind of relationship. There's a reason they use the word 'calling' to describe the decision to join the ministry. I had to do it."

"What do you think about the situation with Hannah and her family?" asked Kat.

"Lots of warning signs," said Pastor Rachel, her expression thoughtful, "but nothing concrete. I wish I could do more."

"I have concerns as well," said Kat. "I'm keeping an eye on Hannah, and hope to talk with her about it in the next few days."

"Let me know if there's anything I can do," the minister said. "I hope we can help."

On Tuesday, after all the other volunteers had left, Rob and Kat walked through the cemetery, comparing Hannah's list and Rob's annotated plat to the actual grave markers. He had jotted down the names when they first discovered the graves, but they needed to be sure that every single grave marker had been documented.

Starting in the far corner, they moved through the rows together, with Rob double-checking to make sure that the name on the grave matched the name on his plat, and Kat consulting Hannah's list to see if the name appeared. If it did, she put a small checkmark next to it and noted its location. Rob had come up with a grid numbering system for the graves on his map, so that everything could be easily cross-referenced.

Rob had worried that things between him and Kat would be awkward after Sunday, but they had focused on the work today, rather than each other, and it helped smooth things over. The rapport between them didn't feel as lighthearted as before, but it was better than distance. Rob wasn't sure how to help Kat wrestle with her past or how to put them back on steady footing. All he could offer was his support.

It quickly became clear that they had chosen the right starting point. For the most part, the names on the graves followed the chronological order on Hannah's list. The church must have run out of room and added a final set of graves along the outer edge of the small cemetery.

"Winnie kept excellent records," said Kat as they reached both the end of the cemetery and the end of Hannah's list. "Every single grave is accounted for."

Rob contemplated the graves. "I feel like we should be happy that we've accounted for them all, but all I feel is sad."

"I know," said Kat. "I can't imagine how hard it must have been for Winnie to watch this cemetery grow over the years."

"Maybe that's why it was forgotten."

Kat looked over at Rob, as if startled by the idea, but then back at the graves.

"You may be right," she said thoughtfully. "I wonder who died first—Winnie or her minister husband."

"You know, after both of them were gone, the graves would only be a painful reminder to the rest of the community of how they had let these girls down. Not a lot of incentive to remember them."

Kat was quiet for a moment. "I never thought of it that way. Forgotten on purpose."

"Fitz and I have been kicking around some ideas about how to help people remember."

"And? Anything good so far?"

"We'll know more after the community meeting Thursday night. Speaking of which, he's coming up on Thursday afternoon and wants to meet with the volunteer crew before we finish up," said Rob.

"I need to ask Hannah if she wants to share the story of the graves on Thursday night, or if she would rather Mary Evelyn do it. I'll ask her before we get started on Thursday."

There was his opening.

"Want to grab dinner in between?"

Kat nodded, rewarding him with a small smile. "That would be great."

And just like that, all was right with the world again.

CHAPTER TWENTY-ONE

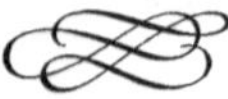

herself up on the second level of the scaffolding, doing a final
inspection and taking some aerial shots of the project. This
gave her a unique perspective on the arrival of Fitz, who didn't
seem to realize he had achieved rock star status in the eyes of
the volunteer crew.

Only a few people paid attention to the car pulling into
the last empty parking space. When he stepped out of the car,
though, someone spotted him, and she watched the news
ripple through the group of volunteers. They didn't swarm
him, thank goodness, but the change in the atmosphere could
be felt even up here. Mary Evelyn had stepped outside a few
minutes prior, no doubt anticipating his arrival, and he
walked over to greet her first, Rob joining them a moment
later.

She should probably go down and say hello, but she was
enjoying the view from up here, watching the people watch
Fitz. He didn't seem to notice the attention, or if he did, he took
it in stride. She wondered what it would be like to be that
comfortable in your own skin. Mel considered herself pretty

grounded, overall, but even she would have been self-conscious on the receiving end of that much admiration.

As if he could hear her thinking, Fitz looked up and met her eyes. She brought the camera up and snapped his picture before he could duck his head, then turned away to make her way down to ground level. While she was doing that, he separated himself from Mary Evelyn and Rob and met her as she descended the ladder.

She lifted her camera again, but he caught her wrist.

"No close-ups, please."

"Feeling shy?"

He didn't bother to answer, just circled his thumb over her pulse, which she felt in all sorts of interesting places.

"Thanks again for agreeing to help with the next phase," he said. "It's a tight timeline, and I can't do it alone."

"I wanted to spend some time up here anyway. It's no hardship." She didn't bother to hide her interest, and she saw the answering heat in his gaze.

"I appreciate you going the extra mile."

Her smile widened. "Community service is my passion."

Mary Evelyn reclaimed him, saving him from her open flirtation. Not that he seemed to mind. Mel leaned back against the ladder. Damn, but the man could rock a polo shirt like nobody's business. She watched as Mary Evelyn walked him around the site, starting with the graves and likely filling him in on all the latest news. Mel occupied herself by inspecting the ground level of the wall, making sure that it was as ready as she knew how to make it.

If the photography thing didn't work out, she definitely had a future in tuck pointing.

A few minutes later, Mary Evelyn called everyone over. Mel chose a spot in the sunshine, which offset the recent chill in the air. Once everyone had gathered around, Mary Evelyn formally introduced Fitz, and then asked Hannah to kick off the meeting by updating everyone on what she had learned about the graves. Mel groaned silently. She hadn't realized that Fitz's visit would merit a formal meeting, or she might have been tempted to skip it. But then, of course, she would have missed Fitz. Resigning herself, she decided she might as well make the most of it. She was as curious about the graves as everybody else, so she moved closer. Hannah wasn't the loudest kid in the bunch.

"The last time I gave an update," she was saying, "we had only found regular church records, nothing related to a cemetery. That all changed on Saturday."

Mel was impressed. Hannah had really grown in confidence over the course of this project, and she was speaking loudly enough for everyone to hear.

"We found a journal written by someone named Winnie, who turned out to be the wife of the minister here in the late 1800s and early 1900s. Winnie worked for more than thirty years to help girls who were in trouble, starting with a girl named Rose. Some of the girls were getting abused at home. Some were pregnant and the boy wouldn't marry them. There were all sorts of stories. Winnie made it her mission to help them. Some of the girls died in childbirth, probably because they were so young. Sometimes the babies were lost with them. In other cases, the girls made it through but the babies died later. Of course, not everyone died. Many of the girls and babies went on to lead new lives in new places. They had a chance to start over. The ones who didn't make it were buried here."

Hannah's audience buzzed with excitement. They started to pepper her with questions. "Do you know the stories of all the graves?" "Where did the girls go—the ones who didn't die?" "How many girls did she help?"

Mary Evelyn stepped in to act as moderator, which helped Hannah keep her cool in the face of a million questions. She was able to answer most of them, with some noted down for later.

"Now," said Mary Evelyn, "let's take advantage of the time we have today with our muralist, Mr. Fitzsimmons. He'd like to do some brainstorming to gather ideas for the design."

She continued in her role as moderator, asking Fitz to briefly talk about his process. Most of what he said was familiar to Mel, either from her research or their conversations. She enjoyed watching him, though. He was good with people, good with the small crowd, soft-spoken but intense. He didn't spend a lot of time talking about himself. Instead, he focused on the role of the community in sparking the concept for the mural. She scanned the group and realized that he had their full attention, even the teenagers.

As he transitioned into brainstorming, he asked them to first wander around the space, including the cemetery, and consider how the space related to the community, and to the community's past and future. In about ten minutes, they would come back together and share their ideas with each other.

While the group of volunteers got up and milled around, oddly silent, Fitz wandered over toward Mel.

"You're supposed to be walking around," he said softly.

"I've been thinking about this for weeks," she answered. "I've got my ideas all ready."

He shook his head in mock despair before changing the subject. "You doing anything after this?"

"Nope," she said. "You?"

"I was thinking about getting out on the water before the community meeting tonight. We're not going to have a lot more beautiful days like this, and I'll probably be spending them painting this wall."

"Seems a shame to waste the sunshine."

"Let's talk after," he said. "We still have some brainstorming to do."

Fitz wandered away to check in with Mary Evelyn, and Mel pretended to check the wall while she simultaneously resisted the urge to do a happy dance. Fitz was probably thinking of going out on a boat, but she would see if she could talk him into some stand-up paddleboarding. It was still plenty warm, and it wasn't too windy today. Besides, she liked keeping him off balance.

When they came back together, Mary Evelyn took more of a backseat role, while Fitz focused on drawing ideas out of the crowd. He started with those people least likely to speak up, which was brilliant. By speaking first, they couldn't compare their ideas to anybody else's and decide not to say anything.

The high school girls were among the first that Fitz called on for their ideas, and they talked about making the space welcoming for children, where they didn't have to be quiet. The high school boys said pretty much the same thing, with the hackers adding that they'd like to see the outdoor space connect with the indoor space. And then it was Henry's turn. He couldn't resist joking around, saying that the area was already haunted. They should focus on the spooky aspects and use it for Halloween events. The graveyard would be the center-piece, and the mural should be full of skeletons and witches.

The group would have laughed and moved on, but Hannah wasn't willing to give him a pass. Even from across the way, Mel could see that she was practically vibrating with anger.

"That is a horrible thing to say," she said sharply, her voice pitched low but it carried easily to the whole group. "These were actual human beings who died, and you just want to make jokes about it. Do you even realize that stuff like this still happens today? You're just like the boys who would get a girl pregnant and then leave them in the lurch."

She stormed off, disappearing around the front of the library. Before Fitz could say anything, Henry stood up. He looked shaken, but determined.

"I'm sorry," he said. "That was just a dumb joke. I'll go after her."

The group was quiet as he left, and then Mary Evelyn stepped in to get them back on track. "Let's continue brainstorming while they take some time to work it out."

As the discussion continued, even the adults agreed that the mural and garden area needed to be designed for children. Not a playground, exactly, but a space where they would enjoy spending time, and where they would feel welcome.

The discussion took on a life of its own after the last volunteer had spoken. At one point, someone said they wanted to learn more about Winnie's efforts on behalf of young girls. Programs like hers would have been relatively uncommon at the time. One of the teenage girls—was her name Paola?—said something about it being too bad that there weren't programs like Winnie's today, because she knew of more than one girl who could use some help.

Kat didn't let that remark go unanswered. "There are lots of programs now to help kids who are in trouble."

"Well, I've never heard of them." The skepticism in her voice was pure teen. "What good is a program if nobody knows about it?"

"I work with a lot of people at the county who run programs specifically for teens in trouble."

"Yeah, that sounds like a good way to get sucked into the system." Shaking her head, the girl turned away.

Mel couldn't blame her for the attitude. She hadn't heard great things about the system either. For a minute it looked like Kat wasn't going to let it go, but she pressed her lips together and the conversation moved on to other topics. To Mel's surprise, she realized that Kat was no longer an enigma. They had spent enough time together that Mel could read her pretty well, and not just when she was having a crisis. Never in a million years would she have predicted the friendship, but Mel found she was grateful for it.

· · ·

Kat wanted to finish the discussion about "the system," but the person who really needed to hear about the resources available to her hadn't rejoined the group yet. Only after the brainstorming session had wrapped up did Hannah and Henry emerge from the back door of the library. Whatever had been said, they had clearly made their peace. The two joined in the cleanup, and some of the volunteers began to head home.

This was Kat's opportunity to talk with Hannah before she left for the day. Rather than confront her directly about the marks, Kat had decided on a more indirect approach, at least to start. Mary Evelyn was assembling an exhibit inside the library to complement the mural and garden outside. Mel's photo series showing the different stages of the project would be displayed there, as well as historical information about the site and excerpts from Winnie's journal. Kat planned to add information relevant to girls today—exactly the kind of information Hannah needed—and she was going to ask for Hannah's help in compiling the information.

Before she could approach Hannah, a squad car pulled up. Rob stepped up beside Kat, and he identified the driver for her. "That's Carl, Hannah's stepdad."

"You've met him?"

"Just once, last Saturday, when he stopped by looking for her."

Kat and Rob walked together over to the squad car. Hannah had also spotted her stepdad and hustled over. They arrived at the squad car at about the same time.

"In the back, Hannah," said Carl.

Hannah climbed into the back without argument. Kat watched her closely, looking for clues as to her feelings, but she had shut down completely, her expression blank.

"Hi, I'm Kat Rodriguez." Best to go on the offensive in these situations. Her intro forced Carl to acknowledge her presence. "I'm sure you remember Rob Murray from last weekend."

Carl nodded curtly.

"Hannah has been a real asset to the project," said Kat, undeterred by Carl's lack of response. "She took the lead on research into the cemetery and has discovered the stories behind each of the graves. We really appreciate her efforts, and her willingness to go the extra mile."

"That's great," said Carl, although his voice didn't match his words. "She's been falling behind on her homework, though, so she won't be able to spend as much time here anymore."

Kat met Hannah's eyes, and the girl looked like she was going to object but thought the better of it and kept her mouth closed. Kat found it hard to believe that Hannah was behind on anything. The girl was incredibly conscientious. More likely, Carl was lying, but she wasn't in a position to call him on it.

"Of course," said Kat carefully. "School comes first."

She hated seeing them drive away, Hannah a prisoner in that back seat. Kat knew that the back doors only opened from the outside. The girl would be stuck in there until Carl let her out.

"Hannah's great, but I'm not a fan of the stepdad," said Rob.

"Me either," said Kat. "Me. Either."

Kat thought about what Jack had said about Carl, that he was always checking in with his wife, making sure he knew where she was. And now he was picking up Hannah, a junior in high school, because he didn't seem to trust her to walk three or four blocks home. Hannah's mom no longer brought the girls to church, which would be no big deal if it didn't seem to isolate her from people she cared about, and who cared about her. All of this in combination with the marks on Hannah's arm, and all of Kat's alarm bells were ringing.

Her instincts hadn't been particularly reliable these past few years, often leading her to see threats when there were none, but the evidence was adding up in this case. If she couldn't trust herself, she could trust the evidence.

It wasn't enough to make a report yet. Not without something really solid. Things could go sideways too easily when the person involved was a part of law enforcement. No, her best bet was to make sure that both Hannah and her mother had access to information. They needed to know how to get out of a bad situation, assuming this was, in fact, a bad situation. If not, no harm, no foul. Information never hurt anyone.

And if Kat could get Hannah talking about those marks, then maybe she would have something concrete enough to go ahead and file a report.

"What are you thinking?" asked Rob.

"Nothing," said Kat. She wasn't ready to share her suspicions yet, not when it could all be a reaction to her own demons. "Like you said, I'm just not a fan of the stepdad."

"Isn't there something we can do?"

"About what? It's not illegal to be a jerk. Technically, Carl hasn't done anything wrong, or at least, nothing worth causing a fuss over. So what if he occasionally makes his kid ride in the back of the squad car? That's not going to get him in any real trouble. Reporting it would only piss him off. No need to make it worse."

"Shouldn't we talk to Hannah?"

This time Kat did laugh, and it sounded cynical, even to her own ears. "I'm not sure we'll have the chance. Carl just implied that Hannah wouldn't be back."

Rob just shook his head. "I'm not a parent, so I know I can't really understand, but I feel pretty confident saying I would never do that. Make my kid ride in the back of the squad car, I mean."

The words sank in, making it hard for Kat to breathe. She really hoped Rob would get the chance to be a father someday. Unable to form words properly, Kat simply nodded in agreement. She would have to tell him at some point. Not now. Now she would focus on pulling together information for Hannah and her mother, and if Hannah didn't show up on Saturday morning, she would figure out another way to get that information to both of them.

"I have to go." The panic building in her chest would not allow her to stay. Not for dinner with Rob, and not for the community meeting. She needed to be home. Safe. She needed to get away—from Rob, from the graves, from her own powerlessness. "See you Saturday," she said, and she made her escape.

Mel arrived early for the community meeting, hoping that the lighting would be decent. This would be a great opportunity to get some shots of the project that showcased the larger process, not just the manual labor. Without a boost of daylight from the front windows, she worried that she would be reliant on aging fluorescent fixtures. Thankfully, someone had replaced the old fluorescents with newer LEDs. No flicker, and the color temperature was in the mid 3000s. Not too blue, not too yellow. There were even some standing lamps providing midlevel lighting. She could definitely work with this.

As she checked angles and lighting levels in different corners of the room, she admitted to herself that she might possibly have come early in the hope of catching Fitz. Their last-minute plans to go out on the water had been superseded by a summons from his mother to join the family for dinner. Apparently, his family had a summer place on the lake (which explained how her mother knew his mother), and his sister and her family were also in town tonight. His disappointment in missing out on their lake time went a long way toward soothing Mel's instinct to sulk.

No sign of Fitz, though, and it was almost time for the meeting to begin. No sign of Rob or Kat, either, and she thought they planned to come, even though they had brainstormed this afternoon. Weird. Mel drifted over to the circulation desk, where her mother and Mary Evelyn were chatting.

"Nice turnout," observed Dora. "And people are still arriving."

Mary Evelyn nodded, surveying the crowd. "I had hoped for fifty, but the project hasn't stirred up any real controversy, so I may have been overoptimistic. Still, I thought people would be curious about the cemetery." She paused, then stepped sideways in order to get a better view of the main door. "Excellent. We have a couple of people from the village board. We'll need their approval before we start painting the actual mural. The village owns the building," she explained.

"Which ones?" asked Mel. "I'll be sure to get a picture of them."

Mary Evelyn pointed them out, and Mel made a mental note of where they chose to sit. Chairs filled the open area between the circulation desk and the magazine displays, with a few extra rows tucked in between the low shelves nearby. A bulletin board blocked the view of the magazine covers, and a lectern stood just to the side.

"Is there anybody else I should be sure to photograph?"

"Make sure you get a glamour shot of Prudie," said Dora. "We can feature her in a media release. Put the gossip train to work in our favor."

"And Prudie is...?"

"Front row, red sweater." Mary Evelyn grimaced. "Make sure she knows you're taking her picture. That will take her mind off any nitpicking she has planned."

"Understood."

"I see the minister from the church." Dora pointed out a group of women just entering through the main doors. "She's got a couple of other ladies with her, probably also from the church."

"It's good that they're here," said Mel. "I wonder how they're feeling about all the dead bodies in their backyard."

"Mel." Dora's voice held the all-too-familiar mom edge that told Mel her mother was not amused.

"What? It's literally true."

Dora just shook her head. Mel glanced over at Mary Evelyn, but the librarian had looked away from the front door and wasn't paying attention to their conversation at all. Instead, she was looking at her watch.

"You worried Fitz is going to be late?"

"He said he might get here at the last minute. Family thing."

At that moment, Fitz arrived, and the game was on. He and Mary Evelyn ran the meeting much as they had the afternoon session with the volunteers. They used a few different techniques to draw out ideas from the assembled group, but the general idea was the same.

Mel haunted the edges of the room, catching those moments where people were talking in small groups, their faces animated and their hands caught on film midgesture. Under normal circumstances she wouldn't call attention to herself, but when she reached the front of the room, she took a different approach. Most of the attendees were absorbed in their small-group discussions. Approaching Prudie's group, Mel asked them to lean in close and smile, staging the shot so that there could be no complaints later. Prudie smiled for the camera. Mary Evelyn caught Mel's eye immediately after and gave her the thumbs-up.

Easing her way toward the fringes of the crowd, Mel made sure to get a shot that included the group from the church. One of the women in the group caught her attention as she zoomed and focused. Her face looked familiar, and yet Mel could swear she had never seen her before. Taking a few extra shots of the group, including one close-up of the mystery woman, Mel hoped that her subconscious would figure it out overnight.

Fitz called for everyone's attention, and as the crowd settled back into their seats, Mel found a good spot to focus her attention on the man of the hour. She got a good shot of him gesturing toward the bulletin board, another of him answering an audience question with intensity and focus. The man was too hot for his own good. She took more shots of him than strictly necessary—not that she planned to build a private collection of Fitz photos. That would be weird and stalker-y. She just wanted to make sure she had a good selection to choose from, given all the publicity Mary Evelyn wanted to do.

Was she crazy to want to hook up with him? She was leaving the country in a month, which meant that anything she started could have no future. She would be gone for too long. On the one hand, he seemed amazing, and she might never have the chance to cross paths with him again—not casually, anyway. On the other hand, he seemed almost too amazing. What if she fell for him? These things happen, and she wasn't going to let anything jeopardize her plans. Not even a little unplanned tumble into infatuation.

The meeting wrapped up before she could reach any kind of decision. To fling or not to fling, that was the question. He was mobbed by the crowd, of course, but they eventually thinned out. Most were older, and it was getting close to bedtime.

Dora and Mary Evelyn were back at the circulation desk. Mel joined them, just as Mary Evelyn asked her mother a question.

"I never asked you about your trip. How was New York City?"

Mel didn't hide her curiosity. Her mother had told her and her sisters the bare minimum about her mysterious old friend and the sudden trip to visit her. When Dora didn't immediately answer Mary Evelyn's question, Mel raised an eyebrow and leaned on the circulation desk. "Yes, Mother. Please, tell us about your trip."

Dora shot Mel an annoyed glance before composing her answer for Mary Evelyn.

"I didn't see much of the city, really. An old friend of mine was in the hospital, and it seemed the right time to visit." The normally voluble Dora simply closed her mouth after one sentence, leaving Mary Evelyn blinking in confusion.

"I don't remember you ever mentioning friends in New York City," said Mary Evelyn.

"We had fallen out of touch."

Dora had clearly been practicing her answers, and she didn't appear to feel an ounce of guilt for stonewalling Mary Evelyn. Mel would continue her quest for answers later. Maybe wine would loosen her mother's tongue.

Finally, the last of the adoring fans left, and Fitz came over to thank Mary Evelyn and say his farewells.

"I thought it went really well," he said. "Thanks for organizing everything."

"My pleasure," said Mary Evelyn. "I took a bunch of notes. Lots of good ideas. I'll get those typed up and email them to you tomorrow."

"That would be wonderful. Thank you."

"I'm afraid I have to head out—" began Fitz, but Dora interrupted before he could finish.

"Of course you do," she said. "We don't want to keep you. Mary Evelyn and I have a few things to discuss before she closes up for the night, so why don't you two run along?"

"But all the chairs—"

"We've got this," said Mary Evelyn firmly.

Mel fought back a laugh. They could not be more obvious in their matchmaking. However, since she was thinking of falling in with their plan, she didn't protest, instead taking Fitz by the arm and leading him toward the door.

"See you later," she called over her shoulder.

Once they had made it safely outside, she released his arm. It would have been weird to continue to cling to him without an excuse, no matter how flimsy.

"Sorry about them. They mean well."

"What just happened?"

"A little matchmaking." At his startled expressions, she said, "Don't worry. It's harmless. They'll be easier to manage if we pretend to cooperate."

He stared thoughtfully back into the library. "As long as my mother isn't in on it."

"Not as far as I know, although I wouldn't put it past my mother to rope her in."

"Sorry we couldn't go out on the water earlier. I'd suggest a rain check for tomorrow, but I have to head back to the city tonight."

"Why do you have to go back?"

"Big meeting tomorrow about a project that I'm involved in. Can't phone it in."

"That's unfortunate." She smiled crookedly at him.

"See you Saturday?" he asked.

She nodded.

"Until Saturday, then."

CHAPTER TWENTY-TWO

Kat parked at the library on Saturday morning, hoping
that she would find Hannah up at the church as usual. After
Carl's remarks on Thursday, however, she would not be
shocked to learn that Hannah couldn't make it.

More leaves had curled up and fallen to the ground. They
crunched beneath her feet as she walked over to Rob, who was
giving the volunteers their instructions for the day. At this
point, their work-in-progress was nearly complete. They would
probably finish the job today. Only the careful cleanup work
around the graves remained, the wall crew having finished up
on Thursday.

Kat waved to Rob, letting him know she was headed up to
the church rather than staying to help. They hadn't spoken
since her abrupt departure the other night, and she could feel
the distance growing between them. As much as it hurt, she
had come to a painful realization over the past few days. There
was no sense pretending to be normal, or attempting to build a
normal relationship. Better to nip this budding connection
than to let it take root. It would only hurt more to end it later.

Today, after the other volunteers left, she would end things with Rob.

In addition to her turmoil over Rob, a knot of dread had been growing in her stomach about Hannah since Thursday, and it tightened as she walked around the block. Joan had tried to talk her down, but Kat's instincts were screaming at her that something was *very wrong*, and she needed to take action *now*. Joan had advised the opposite, and the rational part of Kat's brain knew she was right. Act too soon, without evidence or cooperation, and you risk making things worse. Her gut, however, did not respond well to reason.

To her relief, Kat found Hannah curled up in her usual chair paging through yet another folder. She was down to the last four boxes, which meant she might finish the work today, particularly if Kat helped. The downside of this excellent progress, from Kat's perspective, was that Hannah's volunteer stint would likely end today as well.

"Thought I might find you here," said Kat from the doorway.

Hannah looked up, her expression serious. "I wanted to finish these last few file boxes before I have to stop volunteering."

Kat mentally cursed Carl, but she kept the anger off her face.

"It's a good goal. Can I help?"

Hannah nodded, gifting her with a small smile, and Kat breathed a sigh of relief. They would at least have this chance to work together, and hopefully to talk. She took her place at the table and chose one of the remaining boxes. They worked in a companionable silence for a few hours, sorting through those last boxes. After the contents had been annotated and all the boxes stacked, Kat and Hannah stood side by side to appreciate the mountain of work that now filled the "completed" wall.

"Nice job," said Kat.

"You helped, too."

Kat gave her a sideways look. "You did the majority of the work. Don't be afraid to take the credit."

"Thanks," said Hannah, ducking her head. The praise wasn't comfortable, but at least she owned her accomplishment.

Still looking at the wall of boxes, Kat eased into the critical conversation. It would be easier for Hannah to answer without direct eye contact. "Why did you volunteer for this project? I know you're not required to do community service like the other kids."

"I needed something to do," answered Hannah, tugging on one of her long sleeves. "This was walkable, so I didn't need to be driven anywhere. I also—I found out about it down at the station, and I volunteered."

Given what Kat had seen of Carl's controlling behavior, she wondered if Hannah's on-the-spot volunteering had been strategic. By offering to help in public, with witnesses, she made it harder for Carl to say no. But, as with all the other warning signs, it was all speculation.

"What will you do after school if you're not working on the project?" Kat straightened the stacks of boxes as she talked, trying to make the line of questioning feel bland.

"Watch my sister. Focus on my homework. I've been falling behind."

Turning slowly to face Hannah, Kat offered her first challenge to Hannah's story. "And if I speak with your teachers, will they also say that you've been falling behind?" In reality, they wouldn't talk to Kat at all, since Kat wasn't Hannah's parent or guardian, or even her guardian *ad litem*. But Hannah didn't know that.

The girl didn't answer, which was enough of an answer for Kat.

"Can we talk about the marks on your arm?"

Hannah stiffened, then her face settled into the impassive mask Kat had seen on Thursday. "No."

"If you're a danger to yourself, I need to make a report." She said it gently, but firmly enough that Hannah would know she was serious.

"Go ahead," said Hannah, crossing her arms. "It was just an accident. An injury on my arm isn't going to change anything."

"It could."

"It won't." Her voice didn't leave room for objections. "I won't let anything separate me from my family. From my sister. No matter what you think."

Her words shredded Kat's carefully worded script. Kat had never considered how a younger sister could change the dynamic. She had been so alone, all those years ago, hadn't had to worry about anybody else.

Taking a step toward Hannah, Kat said, "I know this can be a scary conversation to have—"

"You know nothing. Leave it alone."

Hannah inched backward, poised to make a run for it.

"I *know*," said Kat, more certain than ever that Hannah needed a way out. "Ten years ago, I was you, and I'll tell you what it felt like. You desperately want someone to know, but you don't. As awful as things are, at least they're predictable. If people knew, then everyone would know, and your life would be over. At least now, you only have a couple of years left, and if you can just get through it, you can escape, and nobody ever needs to know what happened. But it's poison, the secret, and as scary and awful as it is to imagine life with people knowing, it's also horrible thinking that nobody will ever know. That he'll never be punished. You're angry. So angry at him for hurting you, and at your mother for letting him. She must know. How could she not know? The house just isn't that big. So it's not only his fault. It's her fault, too. The only person with no blame here is you, no matter what your mother might tell herself to make herself feel better."

Hannah had grown more and more pale while Kat was speaking, and now she looked like she might throw up.

"You can't know," she whispered.

"I do know."

Hannah closed her eyes, and a few tears leaked out.

"I can't leave, not until Fiona is safe."

"Fiona will be safe."

She opened her eyes, anger easily overpowering the tears. "Don't do that," she snapped.

"What?"

"Don't make promises you can't keep. You don't know what will happen. You don't know how good my stepfather is at working the system, or how far my mother will go to protect him. So don't tell me that everything will be okay. You don't know that."

Kat nodded slowly. "You're right. I shouldn't make promises. I know that things can go wrong, and the system doesn't always work as it should."

For a second, Hannah looked like she was going to ask about that, but she shook her head. "I need time," she said.

"Why don't we meet here tomorrow after church? We can talk to Pastor Rachel. She can help figure out the right thing to do."

Hannah thought about it for a minute, then nodded, still wary.

"Okay."

Before Kat could say anything more, Hannah turned on her heel and left.

Kat blew out a breath and sank into Hannah's favorite chair. The memories boiled and churned, threatening to drown her, but Kat fought to keep her head above water. It took fifteen minutes of breathing exercises and a whole lot of determination, but she squashed them back into the mental closet that had held them so well until recently. Then she locked the door.

Nothing could change Kat's story. Hannah's story, however, could have a happier ending.

Rising from the chair, Kat slipped out of the church without running into anyone and walked slowly around the corner back to the library, where a few stragglers were helping to tidy up. She slowed her steps, giving herself some extra time beneath the canopy of an old oak before talking to Rob.

She would tell him that Hannah had finished the project, but she debated sharing their more important conversation. Kat's first instinct was to keep the information to herself. Confidentiality had become so ingrained that any sort of disclosure felt uncomfortable. But nothing about her relationship with Hannah required confidentiality. When she thought about Winnie, and how the minister's wife had been able to help so many girls in part because she had someone to share the load when it got too heavy, Kat realized that she wanted to share her load, too. So badly.

Kat would give Hannah until tomorrow to come to terms with the fact that someone knew she was in trouble. Depending on what Hannah was willing to share with her, she would make her report on Monday, and things would unfold from there. In the meantime, while she was stuck in the in-between, she really needed a partner. She didn't want to carry this burden alone.

She had arrived this morning determined to end things with Rob before anyone got hurt. Now here she was, not even three hours later, wavering, talking herself out of a painful but sensible choice. As frustrating as the confusion and indecision were, they were not the real problem. Deep down, beneath all the chaos, she finally recognized the fear, and it pissed her off. Kat had promised herself years ago that she would not let fear drive her decisions or shape her life. Fear was a slippery enemy, though, disguising itself as pragmatism, whispering that she needed to be realistic, to stay safe.

She didn't want to be safe. She wanted to take risks and live her life—preferably not alone.

And that decided it. Someday, she would share her life fully, and in order to get there, she needed to take the first step. Just a baby step. She would share her concerns with Rob, even though they couldn't take action yet, and maybe the sharing would help her find the patience to wait until tomorrow.

The last of the volunteers headed home. Rob walked to meet Kat by the front corner of the library.

"I'm guessing she was there?" he asked.

Kat nodded. "We finished going through all the boxes. It was important for her to finish, because today will be her last day helping."

"You're sure?"

"She seemed very sure."

He scuffed his work boot on the ground, clearly frustrated.

"It just feels wrong. Isn't there anything we can do?"

"Nothing but wait."

"For how long?" The challenge in his eyes echoed her confrontation with Hannah.

"At least until tomorrow. There's no point in trying to 'save' her if she actively works against us."

"Why would she do that?"

"To protect her sister."

"Oh." Kat could feel his anger fade. Rob was the kind of guy who understood the need to protect.

"We actually talked about it today, indirectly. She was very careful not to say what was going on, but she acknowledged that something was wrong. We're going to meet again tomorrow after church and figure out next steps."

"I don't like it."

Kat stopped herself from lashing out. He wasn't supposed to argue with her. He was supposed to offer unquestioning support.

"I don't like it either, but there's nothing else we can do right now."

Rob looked like he was going to swear, started to say something, but stopped. Finally words burst out of him.

"We need to talk to Jack."

"Absolutely not," Kat snapped. "He'll feel obligated to take action immediately, and it's too soon for that. Besides, he works with Carl. His loyalties aren't clear."

"He saw what happened with you, and he learned from that. I think we can trust him."

Kat absorbed the blow without flinching.

"And I don't."

They stared at each other for a moment, stuck in the unexpected standoff. Kat couldn't stop him from talking to Jack, and he knew it. This wasn't how it was supposed to work. They were supposed to be on the same page. She took a deep breath and tried to stay calm.

"Please don't do anything until after I talk with Hannah tomorrow."

"But—"

"Please. I told her I would give her time."

"Are you sure?"

"Positive."

"Fine." Rob did not sound happy, which was just fine with Kat. She wasn't happy either.

· · ·

Rob kicked the dirt a few times after Kat drove away. Correction: after he had driven her away.

He would never lie to her, but in this situation, honesty might have been the kiss of death for their chance at a future together. Maybe he was an idiot for speaking his mind, but he couldn't let her make a bad decision without saying something —and this was a bad decision.

Everyone seemed to agree that Hannah was in trouble. They needed all the help they could get to figure out a solution, and that included Jack. This wasn't something Kat needed to tackle alone.

And what if Hannah didn't show up tomorrow? They needed to take action now.

He stalked back to his truck, climbed in, and slammed the door. He had told Kat that he would wait until tomorrow, and he would keep his word, but he didn't have to like it.

In what was becoming something of a habit, Kat met Mel at The Beach that evening. Saturdays got pretty crowded at the popular bar, so they went upstairs to the deck overlooking the water where it was easier to talk. Somehow they ended up on the subject of Hannah, and Kat's concerns, and Rob's reaction.

"I just don't want to see history repeat itself, you know?" Kat shook her head. "This time we need to get it right."

"What happened that night?" asked Mel. "They never told us." The silence stretched thin between them, as Kat considered whether she wanted to open that door again. "Never mind," said Mel. "I don't need to know."

Maybe talking about it would help them figure out Hannah's situation. "It was a long time ago. Most of the time it feels like it happened to somebody else." Kat was silent for a moment, then continued. "You read my journal, at least enough to know that I was in trouble."

"I read the whole thing."

Kat choked out a laugh. "Of course you did."

"Curiosity has always been a problem for me. Also taking action without thinking about it first."

"I told you about the one thing I didn't write down in the journal. Looking back, I don't know what would have happened when I finally had to tell someone I was pregnant. Even if people assumed I'd gotten knocked up by a boyfriend, there were paternity tests. Eventually, the truth would have come out."

"Oh, God. I never thought of that."

"It was pretty much all I was thinking about in the week or two before everything went south. I'm glad my mother never found out. It would have destroyed her."

Silence filled the space between them. Kat felt the thump of the bass from the music downstairs, and the cool breeze off the lake on her face, reminding her that she had made it out of that house.

"She stayed with him for me, you know," Kat continued. "She never was very comfortable being on her own, and she thought that he would protect us from the world. Later, when it got bad, she made sure to keep his focus on her. She tried to protect me." Kat swallowed hard. "The least I could do was protect her, too."

"Where were you that night?"

"I was at home."

"But—how did you...?"

"Why am I not dead?" asked Kat.

"Well, yeah."

She sighed. "I was in my room doing my homework."

Sprawled on her stomach on the bed, Kitty struggled to focus on the textbook in front of her. The knot in her stomach might be nerves, or it might be how it feels when you have a baby growing inside you—a baby that was going to blow up the world. If only she were better at making friends, maybe she would have a girlfriend she could call, someone who would help her think of a way out of this that didn't end in disaster.

Flopping over onto her back, she pressed hard on her eyes to keep the tears from falling. Her mother already suspected something was wrong. If she caught Kitty crying, she wouldn't leave it alone until she knew. And Kitty couldn't bear to tell her.

And now her journal was missing. She had double-checked in all the places it should be. Her locker. Her bedside table. It hadn't fallen under the bed. It was nowhere, and the sense of dread intensified. What if her mother had found it? Or, more terrifying, what if her stepfather had found it? Her words implicated him in a crime, one he would never allow to come to light. Worse, what if someone at school had found it? She had treated the English project—write at least a page a day, whatever you want, the teacher will only count the pages—as a real journal, and those pages reflected the real Kitty, not the face she showed the world.

She had to leave. There was no other solution. She looked old enough that she should be able to get a job in the city, disappear into the thousands of people who wouldn't know or care who she was. Just another face in the crowd. Just another single mom. Choking back a sob, she forced herself to sit up and think—really think—about how that might work. Pulling her knees into her chest, she rocked slowly and started to formulate a plan.

The sounds of her mother puttering in the kitchen were interrupted by the screech of tires, the sound of her stepfather yelling her mother's name. Her mother appeared in the doorway of the bedroom, turned off the light.

"Under the bed, Kitty. Ahora."

*Kitty scrambled to comply. Spanish words only slipped out
when her mother was very, very upset.*

"My stepdad came home. Mom could tell he was upset, told me
to get under the bed, pretended I wasn't home. It was like she
knew what was going to happen." Kat took a deep breath, let it
out slowly.

*Holding herself very still, barely breathing, Kitty listened with
every cell in her body. Had he found the journal? What story would
he tell her mother? Would she believe him?*
"Where is she?" he demanded.
*"Out with friends." Kitty had never heard her mother lie with
such confidence, and her heart broke at her mother's attempt to
protect her.*

"The hardest part was staying quiet. I can still remember
the dust, and how I had to stop myself from sneezing."

*The crack of a gunshot made Kitty jump. The thump that followed
had her pressing a hand over her mouth to keep from crying out. A
second gunshot. Another thump. Tears streaming down her face,
Kitty pressed herself against the wall and stared at the six inches of
the doorway that she could see from under the bed.*

"It happened so fast, like he had planned it. There was no
hesitation. I waited for what seemed like forever, but it was so
quiet, I couldn't stay under the bed forever.

"After that it's a bit of a blur. I found them in the living
room. Called 911. Everyone I talked to that night was very
gentle, as if I were a grenade that might explode." Kat shook
her head. "I wasn't going to explode. I was a ghost. The old Kitty
was dead, and nobody was there to take her place. Not yet. That
took some time."

"I had no idea," said Mel, completely at a loss. She had always assumed that Kat had found out later, been whisked away to somewhere safe.

Kat lifted a shoulder and tucked the memories back in the box where they belonged. "I'm alive, right? My mother's instincts saved my life. I need to do that for Hannah. I'm getting the same vibe from Carl that I remember from my own step-dad. I need to find a way to help her before something goes wrong."

CHAPTER TWENTY-THREE

Sunday morning, Kat arrived at the library at the usual time, expecting to find Hannah on the bench, but there was no sign of her. Thinking back to their conversation yesterday, Kat realized she had used the phrase "meet here," so Hannah was probably waiting for her in the workroom at church.

A leaf fell on her shoulder as she walked around the block, startling her out of her thoughts. She smiled, looking up at the fall color overhead and taking a deep breath of the crisp air. This would always be her favorite time of year, even if she hadn't worked in a garden since she was small. The act of planting bulbs and perennials, hoping that they would emerge the following spring, had always struck her as a leap of faith— more magic than science. She loved the wonder of watching those first bulbs peek through a thin layer of snow. Now, for the first time in years, Kat contemplated putting in a garden of her own. A small one, nothing too crazy. Just a bit of earth.

The eleven o'clock bells tolled as Kat approached, followed soon after by a trickle of congregants heading to their cars. Kat didn't see Hannah outside, so she checked the workroom. Empty. Irene, bustling around the office, hadn't seen her either.

Kat went outside and sat on the steps to wait. *Hannah is coming,* she reassured herself. *Of course she's coming.*

But what if she wasn't? What if she couldn't? How could she help Hannah get out of this situation if she couldn't give her the information she needed? If Kat called Child Protective Services and let the system do its thing, Hannah would lie through her teeth in order to stay with her sister. The system would fail, and Hannah would be stuck.

As the minutes ticked by, Kat's stomach solidified into a heavy stone, and with that weight came the knowledge that she had made the wrong call. Tortured by the thought of all the missed opportunities, all the times she could have equipped Hannah with the information she would need to escape, Kat pressed hard on her temples, wishing that she could start over.

A vehicle pulled into the parking lot, crunching the carpet of fallen leaves. She looked up, saw Rob climbing down from the cab of his truck, and straightened her shoulders. He was going to be upset. Their eyes met across the parking lot, and his expression settled into grim lines when he saw that she was alone. Guilt made it difficult to maintain eye contact, so she watched the leaves skitter over the pavement until he stopped in front of her.

"No Hannah?"

Kat shook her head.

"What now?"

Standing slowly, Kat brushed off her pants. "Let's go talk to Pastor Rachel."

They found both Irene and Pastor Rachel in the office. Kat introduced Rob and asked if the two of them could speak privately with the minister. She looked at them curiously but ushered them into her office without further questions.

"What's wrong?" Her face had settled into lines of deep concern.

"Hannah was supposed to meet me here after church today to talk more about her situation."

"So she admitted that there was a situation?"

"Not in any detail," said Kat, "but she did at least acknowledge that things were bad, and that she wouldn't do anything that would result in being separated from her sister."

Pastor Rachel nodded slowly. "The girls have always been close. I can see where Hannah wouldn't want to abandon Fiona."

"I'm concerned that her stepfather isn't permitting her to leave the house," said Kat. "Once he isolates her it will be difficult if not impossible to get her out. She's already said that she's willing to lie to stay with Fiona."

After a moment, the minister replied, "We can still file a report."

"I'm concerned that would make things harder for Hannah."

"You think we should watch and wait?"

Rob shook his head. "I don't understand. We know something is wrong. We need to do something now, before it gets worse."

Kat leaned back in the chair and closed her eyes, letting the minister explain. Maybe Rob would believe a neutral third party, one without Kat's troubled history.

"The system is set up in such a way that every report will be investigated, but not automatically believed. If the family puts on a good show, meaning that Hannah plays the part of the dutiful daughter, confused by the inquiry and perfectly happy at home, there's no reason to believe an outsider. Not without other evidence."

"And the marks on her arm?"

"Conveniently explained as an accident."

"I can't believe you would both just give up."

"Nobody is giving up," snapped Kat.

Of course Rob was frustrated and itching to take action. The anger in his voice was palpable. If only he understood that she was angry, too. Hannah's impossible situation notwithstanding, Kat hated feeling powerless because it knocked her right back into the headspace of the girl she had been, trapped and alone. Pushing back against the memories, she scrambled to think of something they could do without making things worse. Passive acceptance wasn't going to cut it.

"I understand your frustration," said Pastor Rachel, "but we need to be realistic."

Rob stood up and stalked over to the window, staring at the parking lot outside.

"So we wait?" asked Kat, praying that the minister would disagree.

"We wait."

A commotion in the outer office cut off Kat's objection. Pastor Rachel stood, but before she could investigate, the door to her office burst open.

"Where are the girls?"

Hannah's stepfather Carl filled the doorway, his stance that of a drunk looking for a fight. No, not drunk. Wild. They were going to need to talk him down. Irene hovered behind, looking frantic. Pastor Rachel paused halfway around the desk as Rob moved to place himself between Carl and Kat, physically shielding her from Carl's anger.

"I'm Pastor Rachel," said the minister calmly. "Who are you?"

"You know damn well who I am."

Rob stepped into the breach.

"This is Carl, Hannah and Fiona's stepfather. Carl, what are you talking about? Where are the girls?"

"They disappeared from the house in the middle of the night. The girls would never do that on their own. This is all your fault." The accusation was directed at the minister. "Filling Hannah's head with ideas."

Pastor Rachel didn't seem to take offense. In fact, a tiny part of Kat, the part that could stand back and watch the scene unfold without freaking out, was impressed with the smooth transition into conflict mediation mode. The minister had been out of the social work game for years, but there must be enough drama in the congregation to keep her skills sharp.

"Now, Carl, why don't you take a seat and we'll figure this out together?" Gesturing to the seat that Rob had just vacated, she leaned against the desk, kept her body language relaxed. "We've welcomed Hannah's help in recent weeks in going through old files, but I certainly haven't had time to fill her head with any ideas. If the girls are missing, we need to focus on finding them. Have you reported them missing yet?"

"I know they're here." Carl wasn't accepting the minister's invitation to sit, instead becoming more agitated.

"I haven't seen Hannah since yesterday when she finished going through the last file box. Irene, have you seen her?"

"No, ma'am," said Irene from behind Carl. His startled glance over his shoulder betrayed a lack of awareness of his surroundings. His eyes took on a hint of cornered animal, surrounded on all sides and ready to fight his way out.

"Carl." The minister's voice was low, soothing. "I promise we haven't seen them. If it would make you feel better, you're welcome to search the church. When did you first realize they were missing?"

He couldn't seem to focus, his gaze shifting constantly, but at least he answered. "I've been working second shift, so I sleep in." Kat noted the defensive tone in his voice. "When I woke up this morning, I assumed the girls were in their rooms doing homework. Jennifer made my breakfast. When I asked about the girls, she said they were both still sleeping, so I told her to wake them up. She came running back into the kitchen saying they're gone, and she had no idea for how long or where they might be." His mouth settled into a flat line. "She might be clueless, but I know exactly where they are. I came straight here."

Pastor Rachel held out a hand in an effort to calm him. "Carl, I think it's time to report them missing."

"They're here," he insisted.

"They're not. The church is locked overnight. How would they have gotten in?"

"It would be easy enough if you let them in."

She sighed.

"I live half an hour away. I did not get up in the middle of the night before a Sunday service and drive over here to let them in. Please, Carl, let's go down to the station together to report them missing."

"This isn't police business. It's family business, and you need to stay out of it."

"You brought me into it, Carl." The minister's voice was firm, her expression immovable. "If you won't go down to the station and report them missing, I will."

"You can't do that."

She raised an eyebrow. "Yes, I can."

Carl looked like he was going to explode. Turning, he pushed past Irene.

"Never mind," he said as he stalked toward the door. "I'll take care of it."

Kat, Rob, Irene, and Pastor Rachel just blinked at each other after he had left the office. They could hear him peel out of the parking lot.

"I really hope he's going down to the station," the minister said.

"Me, too," said Rob, dropping into the vacant chair.

"Would you like me to call down to the station to confirm?" asked Irene.

"Yes, thank you. Let's give him fifteen minutes, then make the call."

"Will do, Pastor."

They were silent for a moment, then Rob spoke. "Are we sure the girls aren't here? Could they have snuck in at some point this morning?"

"We can certainly check."

The four of them split up. Rob checked the secondhand shop. Kat checked the workroom and the bathrooms. Irene checked other closets and likely hiding places. Pastor checked the sanctuary, including the balcony and the choir loft. They met back in the entryway.

"Did you check the hidden closet?" asked Kat.

Pastor Rachel nodded. "I didn't open it, but the candelabra is still in front of the access panel and the door is latched."

"So," said Kat, "waiting is no longer an option. We need to file our reports with CPS. If Hannah has taken matters into her own hands, we need to give her all the backup we can."

"Agreed," said Pastor Rachel. "Let's each make separate reports. It will help to bolster her case when they're found."

Kat looked up at the ceiling as if it could offer forgiveness. "This is all my fault. I should have found a way to talk her through the process. She didn't have to run away. She had options. Allies." She turned to Rob. "You were right. We should have talked to Jack yesterday."

His hand engulfed hers, and the comfort offered in that gesture made her swallow hard, her eyes prickling with tears.

"Stop blaming yourself." The minister had no patience for hand-wringing. "You did what you thought was the right thing at the time. That's all you can do. Now that circumstances have changed, we'll try to do the right thing again."

Kat nodded, then stood and looked out the window at the parking lot, itchy to get going—to do something. This was not the time for tears.

"What matters now is that we find Hannah and Fiona and keep them safe." Pastor Rachel grabbed a sticky note and a pen and scribbled on it. "Here's my cell phone number," she said, handing it to Rob, who stood within arm's reach. "Let me know the minute you hear anything, and I'll do the same. What's your number?"

Rob rattled off his number and Kat followed suit. She was going to need to get her shit together if she was going to be any help to Hannah. The girls were out there alone, and they needed help.

"Irene." Pastor glanced at the secretary who still hovered in the doorway. "Can you look up Jennifer's phone number for me? I need to check on her, just to make sure she's okay. She may be safer here or down at the station rather than at home."

"Good idea," said Kat. "I'm going to call in that report." She stood abruptly and made her escape before anyone could stop her.

CHAPTER TWENTY-FOUR

She hadn't realized she was practically running to her car and forced herself to slow her steps. Why was she always running away from Rob?

The man was impossible to understand. He should be angry with her, but he wasn't. He should be frustrated. He wasn't. How could she build a relationship with someone if she didn't understand the rules?

In this case, she was running not just from Rob but from her own mistakes. She should have asked Hannah about the marks the first day she saw them. She should have given her the information she needed right away, even if the girl didn't want to hear it, so that when she reached the breaking point she would have known what to do. Now Hannah and Fiona were out there somewhere on a night that might bring the first frost of fall.

If they were really lucky, Hannah had found shelter with friends, someone who would help the girls rather than sending them back home, but Kat wasn't optimistic. She had seen first-hand Carl's isolationist tactics, separating both his wife and the girls from the world. The chances of the girls having another trusted adult in their life were slim.

Too bad Carl hadn't been right. If the girls had come to the church for help, they would have found the safe haven they needed. Pastor Rachel would have known exactly what to do.

"Where are you going in such a hurry?" Rob looked concerned, but Kat couldn't tell if he was worried about her or the girls.

"I need to make that report, and then I'm going to make some calls. Joan will have suggestions for what to do after we find them. Nobody works the system better."

Left unsaid was the fact that she would be making these calls on her own. The confusion and hurt in Rob's eyes gave her another reason to run. He deserved someone who didn't fall apart at the slightest provocation, or shove him away when all he'd ever done was be there for her.

She climbed into her car and started the engine, refusing to meet his eyes as she backed out of the parking spot and drove away. If leaving hurt this badly now, think of how much worse it would feel after months of trying to make it work.

Once safely home, Kat took some deep breaths and acknowledged that she was going to hurt for a while. Luckily, she had worked through pain before. She could do it again. Turning on the television, she let the noise fill the room while she searched for something—anything, really—to calm her down.

She ended up at the window, staring out at the trees and the road beyond, her fingertips absently stroking the spiky leaves of the aloe plant. She checked the soil with her fingertips and found it dry. God knew how long it had been that way. She should give it a little water, but she didn't know how much would be too much. Why had Rob left her in charge of keeping a plant alive, when she was failing so badly at her own life?

If only she had made the report at the first red flag. If only she had gotten to know Hannah faster. But of course, "if only" wasn't going to help anyone right now. Was there even a point to calling in the report today? Nobody on the weekend and after-hours hotline was going to initiate an investigation until the girls were found.

She pulled out her phone to call Joan.

Rob walked slowly back to his truck as he watched Kat drive away. The rejection hurt, an unexpected kick in the teeth when he had hoped for reconciliation. She was shutting him out and he wasn't sure what to do next. If he pushed too hard, she might build even higher walls. If he did nothing, she would think he was the type to give up at the first sign of trouble. There must be another way.

Maybe he had been delusional to think they had a shot. He still wanted to believe it, but he couldn't do it alone.

He drove aimlessly around town, mulling his options and hoping to catch a glimpse of Hannah or Fiona, or at least some sign of their presence. It didn't take long to realize the pointlessness of the exercise. Stopping at Lucy's for lunch, he found that she already knew about the situation, her husband having heard it on the scanner.

"You look strong. Help me move these tables."

Command central, it appeared, would be here at the diner. He didn't object to her orders. It felt good to be doing something, even if it was just rearranging some furniture. When she instructed him to call his crew and any other local friends to spread the word, he did that, too, hoping his small contribution could make a difference. It sucked to feel powerless, making him remember all too clearly how he had felt when Kat had disappeared ten years ago.

This was a small town. Somebody should have seen the

girls by now, unless— He stopped himself midthought, refusing to go down that rabbit hole. If they had gotten a ride out of town, then this thing had just gotten a whole lot worse. He had heard too many stories of young girls swept up by bad people. Shaking his head, he forced his thoughts back to the present, his focus on helping Lucy. Dwelling on the worst-case scenario would help nobody.

His stomach growled, reminding him to eat. Lucy was more than happy to throw a sandwich his way. More and more people trickled in, wanting to help, and Lucy handed out search assignments. Rob took one group out, needing to be doing something so that he didn't go chasing after Kat and scare her off even more. The search for Hannah would bring them together again, and when it did, he would find a way to make her understand that he was still here, waiting, when she needed him.

Mel was in the middle of a late breakfast (technically a lunch) when Dora came in the back door.

"Do you know a girl named Hannah who's been helping out at the library?"

Mel nodded, her mouth full.

"Well, apparently she's gone missing. Parents woke up this morning to find her and her sister gone. Lucy heard it on the scanner at lunchtime, told me about it just now when I was down there for coffee. Mary Evelyn is beside herself, and nobody really knows what to do. This is a small town. It's not like there are a lot of places to hide. Not for long anyway. I mean, think about it. Where would you go if you needed to run away? I wouldn't stick around. I would head for the city. Sure, it's more dangerous, but it's also a lot easier to disappear. If the older girl was smart enough to squirrel away some money, the two of them could manage for at least a week, I would think."

Dora paused to take a breath and Mel dove in.

"Mom, back up. Hannah is missing?"

"That's what I said. Missing, along with her younger sister."

Mel had never met the sister. "How young?"

"You know, I didn't think to ask, but I don't think she's very little."

"Does Kat know?"

"Honey, I have no idea. Lucy was just repeating what they said on the police radio."

"I need to call Kat." Mel was already up and moving. Her cell phone was still in the bedroom upstairs.

"Lucy is sending volunteers out to search different areas. I was going to head back over to help after I change clothes," called Dora after her. "Do you want to come with me?"

"Maybe," yelled Mel as she pounded up the stairs. "I'll let you know."

Mel burst into her bedroom and grabbed her phone from the nightstand. Kat answered on the first ring.

"What's up?"

"Did you hear that Hannah is missing?"

"Wow. News travels fast. How did you hear about it?"

"My mom, via Lucy, via the police scanner."

"Makes sense," said Kat. "I was about to go out looking for her—for them. I can't sit at home any longer. You want to come?"

"Absolutely. Do you have any ideas about where to start?"

"Nothing concrete. I just have some idea of who she's running away from."

"Who?"

"Her stepdad."

"Ugh, the cop?"

"You know him?"

"I saw him roll by, asked one of the other volunteers about him. I hear he's an asshole."

"I can confirm that based on personal experience this morning."

"Is that how you found out?"

"Yep. Hannah and I were supposed to meet at the church this morning, but she never showed. I was talking to Pastor Rachel about it when Carl—the stepdad—stormed in, demanding to see her, saying that he knew she was there at the church. Of course she wasn't, and he looked like an idiot. I think he went from there to the police station to report her missing."

"What about you?" Mel was still trying to process the news and had just realized the implications for Kat. "This all must be hitting a little too close to home. How are you doing?"

A brief silence on the other end of the line.

"I've been better."

"I'm coming over," said Mel.

"You don't need to do that. I'm fine. Really. I'll feel even better if I'm out there doing something. Why don't I come pick you up and we'll go out looking?"

"Give me twenty minutes," said Mel.

As promised, Mel was showered and dressed and ready for pickup fifteen minutes later. Dora joined them on the ride over to Lucy's, and she would have joined them in their search assignment, too, but Mel suspected Kat was close to the edge, so she encouraged her mother to work the phones instead and make sure everyone in town was on the lookout for the missing girls. Lucy agreed that she could use the backup.

"Where should we start?" asked Kat.

"We've already got a few crews out there," said Lucy. "Why don't you two go up on the bluff. I remember a tiny shed in the woods up there. If it's still standing, they might be hiding out in it."

"We're on it," said Kat. "I know where that is. And after that?"

"Check the outbuildings at the high school, then come back here. In the meantime, I'll find out where the police are searching, make sure we coordinate."

They checked the shed, then the outbuildings between the grade school and the high school, next to the athletic fields. Nothing.

Sitting in the car in the school parking lot, they debated the feasibility of checking all the vacation homes close to the lake. Second homes outnumbered the year-round homes by a wide margin, and the prospect was daunting.

"I think we should at least walk along the shore path and check the boathouses," said Mel. "Some of them may be unlocked, or easy to break into. If I were running away, that's probably where I would start. There are hardly any summer people around this late in the season, so nobody would see me down by the lake, and nobody would need to get stuff out of their boathouse."

"Let's check back in with Lucy and grab some food. She may have people searching the boathouses already, and if not, we can suggest it."

"Good idea," said Mel, but although Kat had started the car, she didn't immediately start driving. "You thinking about your mom?" Mel didn't want to poke around too much, but Kat probably needed to talk about it.

Staring at the tennis courts, Kat nodded slowly.

"We'll find them before anything bad happens," said Mel with a confidence she didn't really feel. Kat's mouth hardened into a firm line.

"Yes, we will."

CHAPTER TWENTY-FIVE

QUIET FILLED THE CAR ON THE WAY TO LUCY'S. IN THAT QUIET,
Kat faced the fact that she owed Rob an apology. He had been
nothing but patient with her, and she had shoved him away.
She owed him the words: *I'm sorry. I'll try to do better.*

Hannah's situation had dredged up memories and opened
scars she had thought long healed, but that was no excuse for
her behavior. What was the point of all that therapy if it crum-
bled at the first real challenge?

As soon as they knew the status of the search, she would
call him.

Parking spots in front of the diner were all full, so Kat
parked at home and they walked the couple of blocks over. At
Lucy's, they found half the town had come to help with the
search. The police, undoubtedly, were running their own operation from the station, but Lucy had to beat them on sheer
manpower. People were jammed into booths or huddled
around a giant table in the middle of the room. Kat had to
swallow a lump in her throat. If Hannah could see how many
people cared about her and her sister, she would never feel
scared again.

A quick scan of the room turned up a lot of familiar faces, but Rob's wasn't among them.

"Can you find out if there's any news?" Kat asked Mel. "I'm going to step outside and make a quick phone call."

She slipped out without waiting for an answer and put through the call to Rob.

"Hey."

"Hey," she replied, but then realized she didn't know what to say next. Sidestepping the hard stuff, she started with the practical. "Mel and I are at Lucy's. Do you want to come join the search?"

"I'm out searching right now."

Of course he was.

"When you're done with your current run, maybe we could go out together."

A pause before he answered. "Are you sure that's what you want?"

His voice didn't sound angry, exactly, just tired.

"I am." Kat tried to put all the things she wasn't saying into that simple answer.

"Then I'll see you soon."

"Thank you."

After they hung up, she leaned against the side of the building and looked up at the sky. Maybe an apology would be easier face-to-face. A cynical part of her wondered how many times she could push him away before it finally worked and he stayed gone. The hopeful part of her didn't want to learn the answer to that question.

Maybe this was what people meant when they called someone their "rock." The metaphor had never really made sense to her until now.

The midafternoon sun held back the autumn chill, for now. The crisp air helped Kat regain her equilibrium, but also reminded her that tonight it would likely drop below freezing.

Those girls needed a safe haven. Kat didn't pray often, but today she prayed they had found one.

Hannah, where are you?

Slipping back inside Lucy's, Kat found Mel and asked for an update.

"Lucy found a map of the area—a real paper map—and she's been taking calls and crossing off all the places people have looked for the girls. She's also got her husband listening on the scanner so we can cross off the places the police have checked. I gave her our update."

"Has anybody searched the boathouses yet? Or the vacation homes?" asked Kat.

"Nobody has checked the boathouses. The police are doing a visual scan of the outside of the houses known to be empty, looking for evidence of a break-in."

"If the girls have broken into an empty house, at least they'll be warm and safe tonight." Kat actually hoped they had taken that route, rather than making a run for the city. "Did Lucy agree about the boathouses? We should head out soon to check as many as we can before sunset."

"She did. You ready to get back out there?"

"Just a couple more minutes." Kat said the words with a small smile. "Rob is coming, too."

"Good. He'll be helpful." Mel looked over Kat's shoulder. "Speaking of which...."

Kat turned slowly, her stomach tightening, and saw him in the doorway.

"Give me a minute," said Kat. "I just need to—"

"Go," said Mel. "I'll get us a snack."

"Thanks."

Before Rob could take more than two steps into the room, Kat appeared in front of him. She was looking at him like she actually wanted to see him, which was a nice change from their last few encounters.

"Hi," she said, matching his slow smile with one of her own.

"Any sign of the girls yet?"

Kat shook her head. "Mel and I were just going to grab some food and then go out again. Will you come with us?"

He nodded, happy to see her smile, but cautious. As she watched his face, her smile slowly faded.

"I'm sorry. This whole thing with Hannah has really thrown me for a loop, and I shouldn't be taking it out on you."

"It's not that..."

"I'd like to explain, if you'll let me, but later, when we've found the girls."

This time he did smile. "Okay."

Her impulsive kiss on his cheek was unexpected, and before he could register that it had even happened, she was pulling him through the crowd toward Mel, who had claimed a booth at the back. The table in front of her was completely covered with plates of food.

"Hungry?" asked Rob.

"Smart-ass." Mel gestured to the seat across from her. "Sit, both of you. Eat some of this food. I think Lucy is cooking as a coping mechanism. She just keeps bringing more and more plates."

They sat as instructed and ate what they could, but Rob was anxious to get out there before the sun went down and the temperature dropped any further. They were just about to clear their table and head out when Jack came in the door. The room quieted as he stepped up to the counter to address the crowd.

"Hi, everyone. First, I want to thank you all for helping with the search. Jennifer, the girls' mother, also asked me to share her gratitude. She's with us down at the police station, trying to brainstorm new places to look. Lucy, thank you for keeping us up-to-date on where you all have searched so we can coordinate our efforts. Second, I want to let you know that we do not currently have any leads—no sightings in town or anywhere nearby. It's as if they disappeared into thin air, and it's incredibly frustrating." He ran a hand through his hair, leaving it sticking up in all directions. "That's all I've got for now, folks. Keep up the good work and we'll let you know the minute we hear something."

He answered some questions, then conferred with Lucy for a few minutes as they examined the map. After that, Jack made a beeline for their table.

"Have a seat," said Mel, scooting over so that he had room to sit. "Do you need food? We have way too much."

Jack eyed the food, then shook his head. "In a minute. First I have a question for Kat. Earlier this afternoon, I had a chance to talk with the minister over at the church. She mentioned that she had called in a report to CPS regarding Hannah's situation, and she mentioned that you were going to do the same. Is that correct?"

Kat nodded. "I called about an hour ago. Right now they're not in the home so they're not considered to be in imminent danger. The folks at the after-hours crisis hotline took the report and they'll give it to an IA on Monday morning."

"Thank you for doing that. I need to be prepared to take appropriate action to protect the girls when we find them."

"Jack, I don't know if—"

"Please, Kat, trust me on this. I need to make sure this time is different."

She swallowed, looking over at Rob and then back at Jack. Rob put his arm around her shoulder and gave a squeeze, but he didn't push her. She needed to decide to trust Jack on her own.

"How?" asked Kat. "The police don't usually get involved until much later—*after* an investigation."

"Let's assume we find the girls today." Jack leaned forward, his expression intense. "If there are already two reports on file, and I make a third the minute the girls are found, then their situation can meet the standard of 'imminent danger,' and we can get the on-call IA to come out and investigate right away."

"What's an IA?" asked Rob.

"Initial Access worker," she answered. "The person who investigates the reports." She turned her attention back to Jack. "And their mother?" She watched Jack closely, trying to read his intentions. She understood that he was trying to make up for what had happened to her, but she wanted more than good intentions. She wanted to be sure his plan would work. They were all so scarred by what had come before, and they all needed things to go right this time, but she worried that Jennifer would side with her husband, for whatever twisted reason, and that Hannah would have to witness as her mother chose Carl over her daughters.

Kat had never reached that point, but she had feared it. Her mother had refused to see what was going on for so long that when Kat had tried to imagine telling her, she just hadn't been able to do it. It had been too easy to picture her mother dismissing her confession as a dramatic stunt, or accusing her of making things up to cause trouble. Kat might not be able to protect Hannah from everything, but she wanted to spare her this one betrayal.

And yet, what if it wasn't a betrayal? What if her mother chose Hannah over her husband?

"The IA could interview the girls without the influence of their parents, and could insist on talking to Jennifer without Carl present. She's safe now at the station, but Carl is stuck to her like glue. If we can bring in the right resources, someone who specializes in domestic abuse, we might have a chance of convincing her to tell us what's really going on. I know it could backfire. She may refuse to speak out against her husband, but if there's a chance of helping her, too, I think we need to try."

Kat nodded. "I understand what you're trying to do."

Jack leaned back, obviously relieved.

"Does Carl know that you suspect him?" asked Rob.

Jack shook his head. "I had to tell the Chief, of course, but for now we're treating him like we would any parent. He's pissed that he's on the sidelines, but there's no way he can be involved in the search in an official capacity."

"I'm glad you're prepared to take action when we find the girls," said Rob. "I can't imagine sending them home with him."

"You should revisit all the areas that have been searched," said Kat. "Just in case."

"Why?" asked Mel. "That seems like a waste of time."

Kat met Jack's eyes, hating the cynicism that had caused her to make the suggestion. She could see the same bleak understanding in his expression. He answered Mel.

"This may look like a clear-cut case, but there's always the possibility that the girls didn't run away. If someone else was involved in their disappearance, that person may have used the search to cover their tracks. All the search areas will be double-checked by someone unrelated to the first search team. Even if it is just a runaway situation, fresh eyes may catch something the first team missed."

"Well, that's awful," said Mel. "I get it, but it's still awful." She gestured to all the food on the table. "You should eat. We're going to search the boathouses along the shore path, but we can wait a few minutes and keep you company."

Jack waved them off. "Don't wait for me. I need to talk with Lucy again anyway, prioritize the next few search areas, make sure she's tracking who did which searches. We need people out there."

"Yes, sir," chirped Mel. "We are on it." She waited while he stood up, then slid out of the seat herself. "We'll report back by sunset."

· · ·

As they headed toward the door, Dora emerged from the back room and intercepted them, enfolding Mel in a hug. Mel waited patiently until her mother had hugged her fill, patting her on the back throughout. Her mother was a hugger. There was no avoiding it. To be honest, right now she didn't want to escape.

Dora released Mel but didn't completely let go, holding her at arm's length.

"No news yet? I've been on the phone in back."

"Nothing," answered Mel. "Jack just gave us all a report, and he said it's like they disappeared into thin air."

"Don't say that."

"They're fine," said Mel firmly. "Hannah is a smart girl. She won't let anything happen to Fiona."

Mel had watched enough true crime shows to know that very bad things could indeed happen. Girls can be taken far from home by total strangers, or killed and buried in their own backyards by people who are supposed to love them. In this case, however, she absolutely refused to believe either of those outcomes was possible. Not today. Not here.

Dora finally released Mel's shoulders.

"Are you kids heading out to search?" she asked. "You'd better get going. Only a few good hours of sunlight left, and then the temperature is going to drop like a rock." She realized what she had just said, and what it might mean for the girls, and her expression turned bleak. "Go. Find them. I need to tell Lucy about my progress."

"Wait," said Mel, realizing that she hadn't seen any young people here at Lucy's, only the older crowd. "Has anybody reached out to the community service kids yet? Or any high schoolers, for that matter?"

Kat and Rob just looked at each other, but they didn't know any more than Mel did. Dora took Mel by the arm and marched her over to Lucy, where Mel repeated the question.

Lucy cocked her head to one side, forehead wrinkled, as if checking a mental list. Then she shook her head.

"I'm not sure," she said. "Mother—Mary Evelyn—said that she had contacted all the volunteers, but I don't know if that included the kids. Let me call her. She's still at home, making calls from there."

While Lucy called her mother, Mel turned around to talk to Kat and Rob. "Maybe you two should start checking the boathouses while I get this sorted out. As long as someone has phone numbers for the kids, I can call them. I think most of them know me by now."

"I have their phone numbers," said Kat. "Let me know if you need them, okay?"

"I will."

Mel waved them off, and then turned back to Lucy, who was on the phone with Mary Evelyn.

"You are a genius," said Lucy. "She hasn't called them yet. I guess their contact list was in a different folder."

"I'll call them," said Mel.

Lucy relayed the offer to Mary Evelyn, then nodded back at Mel.

Through the front window of the diner, Mel could see that Kat and Rob were just pulling away in Rob's truck. She quickly texted Kat, who texted back the ten contact records in quick succession. Thus armed, Mel retreated into a corner and started making calls.

Half an hour later, Mel couldn't have been more pleased. Not only did she have the community service kids assisting with the search, but they had also started posting on social media. The kids weren't on Facebook; the adults had that one covered. They used all sorts of other apps to communicate, and Hannah and Fiona's disappearance was now big news on all of them.

Shortly after that, Mary Evelyn came into the diner to join

the larger group. She had been busy, working from home on Facebook and the phone to make sure that everyone was helping to spread the word and keeping a lookout for the two girls. Jack called over to say that the Milwaukee news programs had asked for details and photos, so their pictures would soon reach even more people. Mel didn't like to think about the girls out there on their own. She still hoped they would find them somewhere in town.

Dora was sitting next to Lucy, helping her to answer the phone and mark off areas as cleared. After they had brought Mary Evelyn up to speed, Dora asked her a question.

"Mary Evelyn, you once told me that you ran away from home as a teenager. How far did you go? Where did you hide?"

When Mary Evelyn's expression darkened, Lucy put her arm around her mother's shoulders and gave her a squeeze.

"I was very lucky," she said. "I didn't have to go far. The family of a good friend took me in, and I was able to continue my life pretty much as usual. Things weren't quite so formal then. My father was happy to be rid of me, so he never protested my departure. My friend's family was happy to have an extra set of helping hands in the house, so they never minded me being there. Even the school didn't worry too much about who was signing off on my paperwork, as long as I was in school."

"Do you think maybe Hannah and Fiona are with a friend?" asked Mel.

Mary Evelyn shook her head. "I stopped at the police station on the way here to ask, and they confirm that they've checked out that possibility. Unless someone is lying, which is always possible, the girls didn't turn to anyone else for help."

"We'll find them," said Lucy. "I know it."

"I hope so," said Mary Evelyn. "No matter what happens, I'm glad they're together. When I left, my younger sister refused to come with me. Leaving her was the hardest thing I've ever done."

"You have a sister?" asked Dora. Mel could practically sense the avalanche of questions that was about to follow, and one look at Mary Evelyn's face made her realize this wasn't the time.

"Mom, let's stay focused on the search."

"I am focused," she replied, indignant. "We have two young girls to find. If you're done calling the teenagers, then maybe you should get back out there and look before the sun goes down."

"Yes, ma'am."

CHAPTER TWENTY-SIX

Kat and Rob had made it nearly a mile down the shore path, checking what seemed like hundreds (but was probably more like fifty) boathouses with no luck, before the sun finally sank behind the trees. The light painted beautiful streaks across the lake, but it didn't do much for visibility. After tripping for the third time, Kat decided to call it.

"We need to head back. We're going to kill ourselves stumbling around in the dark."

Rob stopped walking and turned around. "I could use my phone as our flashlight."

"I know," said Kat, "and if you really want to keep going, I will, but I'm afraid we'll miss clues in the dark."

"Why don't you call Mel and see if she's got any news?"

"On it."

Kat dialed Mel and had her on the phone a few rings later.

"Anything?" asked Kat.

"Nothing here. You?"

"Still nothing, and we can only check one or two more before heading back. We're losing the light."

"Want me to come pick you up?"

"That would be great, actually. We could keep moving forward instead of heading back. Give it fifteen minutes. We'll check as many more as we can before full dark and then head up to the road. We'll be on the north shore, about a mile down."

"Got it," said Mel. "I'll go grab my car. See you in a few."

Kat hung up and told Rob the plan. Then she turned on her phone flashlight and they continued down the path, checking four more boathouses before stopping. Kat wrapped her arms around herself and shivered. Dora had been right. The temperature was dropping fast. She should have brought a jacket, or at least a sweater.

Rob wrapped an arm around her. "Don't give up hope. It hasn't even been twenty-four hours yet. We'll find them."

She leaned her head against his shoulder, absorbing his strength as they both looked out over the water. "I need to believe that."

They stood in silence for a few minutes, watching the sun's fire slowly fade from the surface of the lake. Then they trudged up a brick path, skirted one of the empty lake houses, and followed the driveway to the road.

Rob squeezed himself into the passenger seat of Mel's tiny car while Kat slid into the back, doing a little human origami to fit in the child-size seat. All three were quiet on the ride back to Rob's truck, which they had parked right near the beach.

"We'll meet you back at Lucy's," said Rob before hauling himself and then Kat out of Mel's car. He ducked his head back in before closing the door. "Hopefully there's a plan for searching overnight."

"I'll find out," said Mel. The defeated slump in her shoulders was hard to miss.

Rob turned up the heat in the truck as soon as he got in.

The dropping temperatures hadn't bothered him so much, but Kat was shivering.

As they drove back over to Lucy's, their route took them past the library. Eyes scanning the area almost reflexively at this point, Rob was about to roll past when he caught sight of the side door in the shadow of the scaffolding. He slammed on the brakes.

"What the hell?" Kat yelped.

"I think I know where they might be."

He backed up the truck and then pulled into a parking space at the library.

"It's a long shot, but we should at least check." It took only seconds for him to slide out of the truck and run around to the passenger side. Kat was already opening her door.

"You think they're behind the library?"

"I think they might be *inside* the library."

"But how...?"

"I'll show you," he said, grabbing her hand as she hopped down onto the pavement. Leaving the passenger door open, Rob jogged toward the side door of the library, tugging Kat alongside him. The flashlight on his phone seemed too bright in the gloom beneath the scaffolding, but it did a good job of illuminating the door handle. All it took was one firm shake and the door popped open.

"You're kidding me," said Kat.

"It's been broken for a while."

"We're going to need some backup. There are a lot of places to hide in there, and I'd hate for the girls to get spooked, have them slip outside while we're looking some-where else."

"Agreed."

Kat called the diner, reported in, and requested backup. The waiting sucked, but what felt like hours was probably no more than five minutes. As tempting as it was to begin the search without them, Rob didn't want to scare the girls—if they were even there. This could all be a wild goose chase.

The sound of running feet heralded the arrival of the first wave. The group streamed over to the side door and began to pepper Kat and Rob with questions. He demonstrated the faulty door handle twice before Mary Evelyn arrived and started organizing everyone.

"Rob, you and Kat take the first group in through the side door and carefully search each room on the lower floor. One member of the team needs to stay by the door. The rest of you, follow me. We'll go in the front door and start the search on the main level. Lucy is calling the police to let them know what we're doing. They'll be along soon."

Rob wondered if Mary Evelyn would consider moonlighting as one of his crew leaders. Her level of efficiency was almost scary. After giving her a minute to get to the front door, he pulled open the side door and the group filed quietly inside, ready to search. Kat stayed back, in case the girls made a run for it. With so many helpers, it took less than fifteen minutes to search every inch of the library.

No sign of the girls.

Rob found Kat talking with Jack just inside the back door. He broke the frustrating news, and together the three of them trudged upstairs to where the searchers had gathered by the circulation desk. Mary Evelyn tried to raise everyone's spirits, but it was a losing battle.

"I want to thank Rob for the idea that the girls could be hiding in the library. I've always thought of the library as a safe haven for people from all walks of life, and I hope the girls think of it that way, too. I know we're all disappointed that they're not here, but let's use this as inspiration to think of all the other possibilities we've missed. What other buildings could they access?"

People shouted out ideas, like the school and the rec center.

Jack added several of the suggested locations to the overnight search plan, others having been crossed off the list earlier in the day.

"It's been a long day, everyone." Jack's matter-of-fact voice carried well in the crowded space. "I know you'd all like to keep searching, but if you don't take time to rest, you'll miss something, and we can't afford to overlook any clues. Go home. Have some dinner, if you haven't eaten. Go to bed early and then come back tomorrow morning to continue the search. In the meantime, add your name and phone number to this clipboard. If we find the girls overnight, we'll call you first thing in the morning."

Kat turned to Rob, determined to keep going, no matter what Jack said, but Rob took one look at her face and shook his head.

"No."

"What? I didn't say anything yet."

"I can tell by your face that you want to keep searching, but Jack is right. You need to rest. We both do."

"But the girls—"

"I know," said Rob gently. "Nobody is giving up. Remember that we're not the only ones looking. We have to take turns, and now it's our turn to rest."

She pressed her lips together, but she had stopped arguing, so he took that as acceptance, if not full-out agreement.

"Let me drive you home."

She let him lead her out of the library and away from the chattering crowd. He could feel exhaustion weighing him down. She must be wiped out as well. They both needed a little food, and then as much rest as they could manage before morning.

CHAPTER TWENTY-SEVEN

Kat barely had the energy to climb back into Rob's truck. He didn't bother to turn on the radio, and a defeated silence filled the cab as he drove toward her place. They both needed to rest, but she didn't want him to leave. Not yet. Not until she had a chance to apologize properly.

"Come inside," she said as he pulled into the parking space in front of her garage door. "We can scrounge something to eat. If nothing else, I have a few frozen dinners."

Heart thudding in her chest as she awaited his answer, she wondered why time always seemed to stretch out in moments like this. Five heartbeats. Six.

"You sure?" So cautious. She had done that—made him cautious.

She nodded. Exhaustion had her close to tears, but they didn't fall.

"Okay."

She got out of the truck and unlocked her front door, and they stepped into the semidarkness. Instead of turning on a light, she waited for him to close the door and then wrapped her arms around him.

"Thanks for coming back."

The strength and comfort of his embrace was pretty much the only thing holding her up, and when he shifted his hands to rub her shoulders, she actually moaned out loud.

"You can do that for as long as you want," she mumbled, and he did, kneading those ridiculously strong hands up and down her back until all the defeat had drained right out of her.

It was amazing, the joy to be found in leaning on another human being. The physical comfort was only a part of it. The idea that she could lean on him in the metaphorical sense, that other people out there in the world experienced this level of support every single day—it boggled the mind. She must be very, very careful not to get used to it, because the only thing worse than never knowing this feeling would be to rely on it and then lose it. No wonder her mother had hated being alone, after she had known and lost this everyday wonder.

She would be careful, but maybe it was okay, just this once, to lean.

They ate frozen dinners on the couch with their feet up. Rob flipped through the channels on the TV, but after catching the report of the missing girls on two different news programs, he turned it off. It didn't seem right to watch a sitcom or a movie when the girls were still out there.

"I'm sorry." Kat's voice, soft in the silence, caught him by surprise. "I've been awful to you these last few days, and you don't deserve that. I need to explain."

"You don't owe me any explanations. This whole thing with Hannah is way too similar to what you went through. It's got to be messing with your head. I get that."

"It's more than that," said Kat. She twisted around so that she faced him, one leg bent and hugged close to her chest.

"When I told you my story, I left something out. Something important."

She had shared a lot on the pier that day, filled in a lot of gaps in a story that was already hard to hear. He squeezed her shoulder. "Tell me, then."

"The day that I gave birth, it didn't go well."

"You did tell me that," he said softly. "The baby didn't make it."

"It was more than that." She took a deep breath, visibly steeling herself to say more. "There were complications. It took them a while to realize that something was wrong—apparently it's not a common problem, especially in someone young—and by then things were very wrong. I told you that the baby didn't make it. Neither did my uterus. It ruptured."

He cocked his head to one side, trying to make sure he understood what she was saying.

"They had to do a hysterectomy. I have no uterus. I can't have children."

Rob nodded slowly, not sure what she needed him to say. Something, obviously. "Okay," he began, feeling his way in the dark. "I can see that this was, and still is, really hard for you."

She nodded, her continued silence suggesting that she hoped he would say more.

"And since we're dating..." he continued. "Is it too soon to say we're dating?" She shook her head emphatically. "Since we're dating, you want me to know this important fact in case things get serious." She nodded slowly, gaze steadfastly on her knee. "Because it feels like this could get serious." She kept nodding, and her mouth started to hint at a smile. He took a breath, hoping that he was on the right track here.

"I'll be honest," he continued. "I haven't spent a lot of time thinking about marriage and kids and all that. I've been really focused on my business, and my attempts at dating haven't led me to daydream about the future. However." He reached over and stroked her cheek, startling her into meeting his eyes. He wanted to know she was with him for this next part, because it was important. "I do hope to get married one day and build a life with the woman I love. Maybe kids will be a part of that life and maybe they won't. It's not a deal-breaker for me."

She studied him intently for a solid minute before the deep furrow in her forehead smoothed out and her shoulders relaxed.

"I like how you're thinking long term," he said, reaching out for her hand.

"You deserve a family, if you want one," she said, her voice tight. Rob gave her hand what he hoped was a reassuring squeeze. She continued, "I think it's really important to be up front about this from the start, to avoid hurting you later."

Not to downplay what had happened, but Kat was being incredibly thickheaded about this. She, more than most, should know that there is more than one way to build a family.

"Let's say, hypothetically, that we keep dating, and things get really serious." At Kat's raised eyebrow, he continued. "We start talking marriage, and then we get married, and then finally we decide that we would really like to start a family, because kids would complete the picture for us."

"Hypothetically."

"So we know that we can't have our hypothetical children the old-fashioned way."

"Right."

"So we talk through all the other options available to us, because there are a lot of options these days. Way more than there used to be."

This time her response was slower in coming. "True."

"Just to be clear," he said, "we could use a surrogate, or we could adopt, or we could foster, or—hell, I read a news story the other day about a woman who had a baby after a uterine transplant. This is the future we're talking about. Pretty much anything is possible."

Kat leaned forward and snagged a tissue from the box on the coffee table so she could blow her nose and wipe her eyes.

"You know, you're pretty amazing," she said.

He grinned at that. "So I've been told," he said, which earned him a watery laugh. "And my amazing suggestion for today is that we not worry about having kids. Let's try this dating thing first and see how it goes. I don't want to miss any of the good stuff along the way."

She nodded. "Amazing suggestion."

"Would this be an appropriate time to make out?"

She sputtered, caught between outrage and laughter.

"We're supposed to be resting until they let us search for Hannah and Fiona."

"I know," he said, a hint of mischief in his eyes. "I'm just trying to think of something super-distracting—to take our minds off the search."

"And that's the only thing you can think of?"

"Yep."

Kat laughed.

If anyone had tried to tell her that, after confessing her deepest, darkest secret, she would be laughing out loud imme-diately afterward, well—that would have made her laugh. Because it was impossible, of course. Except it wasn't. Not with Rob. With him, it seemed, anything was possible.

He gave her a minute to process, but even as she caught her breath, she could read the intent in his eyes. He reached for her hands, pulling her closer even as he leaned back, until she lay on top of him on her tiny couch. It wasn't the most comfortable couch of all time. His head was jammed up against the armrest, his feet spilling off the other end, but he didn't seem to mind. In fact, he seemed pretty happy about the situation. And that was the last coherent thought she had.

The world shifted into slow motion: His hand sliding into her hair to cup the back of her head, drawing her closer. His body warm and strong beneath her. His arm wrapped around her back, holding her gently in place. His mouth, finally meeting hers in a very intimate demand. This was no gentle coaxing. They picked up right where their last kiss had left off and went deeper, until they both needed to come up for air, foreheads together, eyes closed, both a little overwhelmed by the heat between them.

Feeling a flutter of panic at the back of her mind, Kat ruthlessly shoved it back and out of the way. Her past would not intrude on this moment. She wouldn't let it.

His hand stroked down her back, over and over, until the tension drained from her body.

"I should go," he whispered, and she could feel his breath on her lips.

"Don't go."

He shifted position slightly, so that her head rested on his chest. She could hear his heart beat strong and steady.

"If I stay, I'm afraid we'll rush things, and then I'll lose you. I won't let that happen."

She lifted her head and rested her chin on her hands, looking him straight in the eye. "What if I want to rush things?" His caution made her bold. That, and the fact that he couldn't exactly hide the evidence of his raging desire when it was pressing into her belly.

"I did not wait ten years for this moment only to screw it up."

"So serious…" She leaned forward to kiss the corner of his mouth. "Are you sure there's nothing I can do to persuade you to stay? What if I promise we won't go past second base?"

She had his interest now, and she was an excellent negotiator.

"Clothes stay on."

"Until we go to bed, of course."

"I'm sleeping on the couch."

"If you like," she said, kissing her way along his jawline. "My bed is much more comfortable. It's a queen-size bed. No footboard." She had reached his earlobe, and he groaned in a combination of appreciation and, apparently, frustration. "You could sleep on top of the covers."

"I could..."

She had definitely won this round.

CHAPTER TWENTY-EIGHT

KAT OPENED HER EYES TO SEE ONLY GRAY. BLINKING A FEW TIMES, her ceiling came into focus, shadowy in the predawn light. The earliest of birds chattered outside. She licked her dry lips, rolling toward the nightstand where she normally kept a water bottle, but the duvet didn't move with her. Turning slowly back the other way, she realized she was not alone.

Brain still foggy with sleep, it took a few minutes to sift through the events of yesterday. The search. The hollow sense of defeat. The tearful discussion with Rob. Their interlude on the couch, and Rob's willingness to stay, though the idiot had insisted on sleeping on top of the covers. It had felt selfish to snuggle into his warmth when the missing girls were most likely uncomfortable and cold, but she hadn't realized until that moment how much she craved the comfort of simple human contact.

No memories after that. She must have fallen asleep. Now, mind alert but body heavy, Kat wondered if her residual fatigue was more emotional than physical. When they found the girls she would be able to truly rest. Not before.

After rolling back toward the nightstand, careful not to

disturb the covers or shake the bed, Kat took several sips from the water bottle and then checked her phone. No missed calls. Either they hadn't found the girls overnight, or they hadn't started making phone calls yet. Anxious to know which, she glanced over her shoulder at Rob. Despite her attempts not to disturb him, he was blinking the sleep out of his eyes and looking at her with a bemused expression on his face.

"Morning," she said, her voice sounding both scratchy and overly loud in the stillness.

"Already?" he asked, and she chuckled softly.

"It's just after six."

He rolled onto his back and rested his forearm over his eyes. Taking advantage of the opportunity to study him unobserved, Kat marveled at his strength. It wasn't just physical, although that was obvious from the size of his arms and the breadth of his shoulders. He was solid, through and through. The mattress dipped beneath his weight, tempting her to let gravity pull her to his side. Even more compelling than his sheer presence, though, was the inner strength that she was just beginning to understand. "Strong and steady." The phrase might have been invented for him. He didn't get angry; he simply took action. She trusted him in a way that she hadn't trusted anyone in a long time.

"Today will be a better day," said Kat.

"You sound very sure," he said as he lowered his arm.

"I am," she said simply. "I refuse to be pessimistic about this. We're going to find the girls, and we're going to keep them safe. End of story."

He smiled. "I like your attitude."

Giving in to temptation, she scooted closer, until she was tucked up against his side. He rolled back onto his side and kissed her forehead, running a hand through her hair. If it weren't for the missing girls, she would stay here all day.

"My attitude will only improve with a little breakfast.

Should we stop lazing around and go see what's happening at Lucy's?"

On a typical day, Lucy opened at six. They couldn't count on today to be typical, but neither could Kat imagine Lucy opening late when there was work to be done. It was more likely she had opened early.

Rob only lived about ten minutes away, so he drove home to shower and change while she did the same. His crew cut gave him an advantage in terms of speed, and he was knocking on her door again before her long hair could dry completely. They left his truck at her place and walked the short distance up to Lucy's. Even from outside, they could tell it was hopping, which suggested that the search had resumed. The parking spots along the road in front of it were full again, and it looked like standing room only through the windows. Kat took the stairs two at a time and pulled open the door, eager to get some food in her stomach and get back out there.

They were lucky to find a small table for two in the back, and their waitress filled them in on the overnight developments in the search. Nobody local had turned up any clues, but the story on the TV news, amplified by all that social media sharing, had brought in a couple of hundred leads for the police to sort through. Kat and Rob each rearranged their workday as they ate, clearing their schedules so they could continue the search. As soon as they were done, they headed out to resume the boathouse search. This time, they parked farther down the north shore road, looped back down the driveway that they had walked up the night before, and double-checked that last boathouse in the light. It was still as tightly locked and cobwebby as the night before, only this time they also noticed the windows on the sides and checked those as well. No sign of the girls.

After two more hours of boathouse checking, Kat and Rob

admitted defeat. The girls had gone missing in the early hours of the morning, and they would have needed to find shelter before sunrise, or soon after. The likelihood that they had come this far down the path was slim. Rob slung an arm around Kat's shoulder and together they doubled back, heading for the diner to report in and get a new assignment.

"I'm starting to think that they left town after all," said Kat as they walked. "I don't think they could stay hidden with everyone looking for them."

"Unless someone is hiding them."

Kat pondered that for a moment. "It's possible, but it seems so unlikely. I mean, what's the long term plan there? Hide them forever?"

"Depends on who's doing the hiding. If it's a teenager, they may not have thought much about the long term."

"True," Kat mused. "Maybe our next step is to visit each of the community service kids at home, see if one of them is playing the hero."

"It's worth a shot," said Rob. "Let's check in first at Lucy's and see what's going on."

If they had thought that Lucy's was crowded before, it was now somewhere beyond that, making it very difficult to move through the room or hear yourself speak. They did eventually find Lucy and update her on their nonprogress. She crossed off the boathouses on her oversize map, then told them to hang out for a bit. Officer Jack was supposed to stop by at about nine to update them on the police progress and let them know what would change when they hit the twenty-four-hours-missing mark.

They grabbed a cup of coffee from the communal pot at one side of the room and then leaned against the wall in the far back corner, right by the hallway leading to the restrooms.

"After the break we should head down the lake path in the

other direction," said Kat. "I don't think anybody has been checking over there. I know it's less likely, because the girls would have had to cross a lot of open ground, including the beach, but who would have seen them in the middle of the night?"

"Unless someone has a better lead, I think you're right."

"I just hope they didn't find a way to get out of town. If somebody gave them a ride to the bus station, or the train station, they could be impossible to find. It's a lot easier to disappear in Chicago or Milwaukee than it is here."

Rob was quiet for a minute. "A friend would be more likely to give them a ride than to try to hide them. And the train station is only fifteen minutes away."

"The girls would only have had to hide for a few hours until the first morning train."

"We need to ask Jack if they've already checked the bus and train stations. Two young girls traveling alone would have been unusual, especially first thing in the morning."

Kat nodded, now antsy for Jack to arrive. She didn't want to get too wound up about a possibility that had already been eliminated, but she didn't want to miss a second of search time if the girls were already in downtown Chicago. It was too easy to imagine them getting off at the train station downtown and—

Train station. Train. Railroad.

"Rob, I think I know where they are."

Rob stared at her, waiting for her to explain. She took his cup of coffee instead and turned to weave through the crowd, trusting him to follow. She passed by Lucy at command central and said, "Lucy, we're going to check out an idea. We'll be back in a few minutes."

Lucy nodded without looking at Kat, so she continued on,

setting the coffee cups on the counter as they passed by. In another minute, she and Rob were out the door. Once clear of the crowd, she started jogging down the street to where Rob's truck was parked in her driveway. He caught up and matched her pace.

"You going to explain?"

She grinned. "Not yet."

To her delight, he didn't press for answers, just ran beside her until they reached the truck. They both climbed in, and he asked, "Where to?"

"Back to the church."

They were there in a heartbeat and parked in the nearly empty parking lot. Not completely empty, though. If Kat remembered the schedule correctly, both the office and the secondhand shop would open at nine. Before Kat could check the time, the church bells announced it for her, and she laughed.

"What?"

"If I believed in signs, that would be a really good sign," said Kat as she grabbed Rob by the hand and pulled him toward the main entrance. Hopefully, either the minister or Irene would be here. Sure enough, both women were in the office and awfully surprised to see them.

"Have the girls been found?" asked Pastor Rachel.

"Not yet," answered Kat, "but I just thought of a place we need to double-check."

"Where?" asked Pastor Rachel and Irene in unison.

"The closet."

"You think they snuck into the church later?" asked the minister.

Kat shook her head.

"I think they were in the hidden closet when we did our search."

"But Pastor checked the closet," said Irene.

"She didn't actually open the door, because it was latched on the outside, but I have a theory."

The minister and Irene looked at each other as understanding dawned. "You think there's a way to latch it from the inside." Pastor Rachel was already moving toward the door, with Kat, Irene, and Rob close behind.

"I hope so," said Kat. "We're running out of places to search."

"Do you think they could have slipped in on Sunday morning?" said the minister as they entered the sanctuary. The organist was practicing, filling the large, open space with music. Kat's heart raced. After all the disappointments of the last twenty-four hours, she desperately wanted this hunch to be right.

"If they timed it just right, they could have hidden outside, then come in after I unlocked the doors, but before anybody else started to arrive. Or maybe they snuck into the building during the service and waited until the sanctuary was clear to slip into the closet."

The hope in Irene's voice made Kat bite her lip. Please, please, please let her be right about this.

The minister opened the door of the outer closet, then looked at Kat.

"Hannah is most comfortable with you," she said softly, and gestured for Kat to step inside.

Kat stepped into the shadowy space. Her hopes notched upward when she noticed that the candelabra didn't sit squarely in front of the panel as it had before. She slid the candelabra out of the way and crouched down, knocking softly on the access panel. No response. She lifted the lever from the latch and pulled, and the panel swung to the side. Sure enough, there was a lever on the inside as well, so that people hiding inside could latch or unlatch the door as needed. From the shadowed interior Kat heard a scuffling noise. Praying that it was human and not rodent, she leaned forward into the darkness.

Her heart stopped when she saw the two pale faces peering at her from the far corner. Then it started up again in double-time.

"Hannah, it's me. It's Kat. You're safe now. Fiona is safe. Pastor Rachel and I are going to help you."

Hannah had her arm around her sister, and Fiona turned to hide her face in Hannah's shoulder. She was shaking. Kat met Hannah's eyes and spoke in her strongest and most reassuring voice.

"You don't need to hide anymore. It's time to come out."

Hannah gave a small nod, barely a movement at all, but Kat saw it and acknowledged it with a nod of her own. Then she backed up so that the girls could get out. She stood and turned to see Pastor Rachel, Irene, and Rob all hovering in the door-way. Rob took one look at her face and smiled. Kat grinned back.

"We found them," she said, then laughed. "They're safe. We found them."

"I'll call Jack," said Rob. He waited for Kat to respond, and she realized that it was really a question, not a statement. He was checking in to make sure she still trusted Jack to help them handle the situation.

She gave a firm nod. "He'll know exactly what to do."

Rob disappeared just as the girls emerged from the small space. They were covered in cobwebs but otherwise seemed healthy and unharmed.

"Would you girls like to get cleaned up before we talk about what happens next?" asked Kat.

The girls nodded, then followed Kat to the washroom. The music faltered as they paraded back through the sanctuary, but Pastor Rachel must have signaled the organist somehow because she got back on track right away, the music sounding even more joyful as their little group exited via the side door. It took a solid fifteen minutes to clean the cobwebs off both girls, but they seemed more relaxed afterward. Hannah straightened her shoulders and met Kat's eyes in the mirror above the sink.

"We're ready."

CHAPTER TWENTY-NINE

Rob stepped outside the church to make the call to Jack, who answered on the second ring.

"We found them."

"Where?"

"Hiding in some kind of secret closet in the church."

"They're okay?"

"Dusty and scared, but otherwise unharmed." Eyes on the sky, Rob sent up a quiet thank-you. "They were safe and warm last night. No worries on that front."

"Give me ten minutes to set a few things in motion, and then I'll be over there to explain what happens next."

"No worries. It will take at least that long for them to get cleaned up."

"Don't let them leave."

"Carl still at the station?"

"Yep, and I'll make sure he stays here for the time being."

"Word might be out already. The organist was practicing and saw us find them. I'll check in with her, ask her to keep it under wraps for now. Should I give Lucy a call?"

"I'll do it, tell her they've been found but not where. That might buy us a little time. The last thing we need is for a huge crowd of people to descend on the church. We can give the girls more privacy than that."

Rob headed back inside after talking with Jack and found Irene in the office crying at her desk. She waved him in.

"Don't mind me. I'm just so happy that we found them, and they're safe." A pause to blow her nose. "I didn't sleep much last night. It was so cold outside, and I kept imagining the girls hiding out somewhere with no heat."

Unsure how to respond to the tears, Rob made noises of general agreement and hoped Kat and the girls would emerge from the bathroom soon. Pastor Rachel came out first, so he gave her the update.

"Regardless of where the girls go next, they need food. They brought some snacks with them, but they haven't had a proper meal for more than twenty-four hours. Irene, could you call over to Lucy's and order some sandwiches to go?"

"Wait," said Rob. "Jack's trying to keep the girls' location under wraps for a few hours, thinks it might turn into a circus if people know they're here. When you place the order, don't mention who it's for."

"Got it," said Irene, her tears clearing up in the face of the task at hand. "Any special requests, or should I just get an assortment of sandwiches?"

"Keep it simple," Pastor Rachel said. Her gaze shifted to the window behind him, and the parking lot. "The police are here."

Turning to look, Rob said, "That's Jack Emerson." He glanced back at Pastor Rachel. "Do you know him?"

She nodded. Rather than waiting in the office, they walked out to the foyer to intercept him.

"I'll order the food," Irene called after them.

Jack's expression was grim, and one side of his face was a mottled red.

"You okay?" asked Pastor Rachel.

"Carl and I had a disagreement."

"Ah."

"The girls?"

"They're still getting cleaned up—" A commotion in the hallway behind her cut the minister off midsentence. "It appears they're finished. Give me a minute to get them settled in the workroom. We've got food on the way. Once they're fed, you can take them down to the station."

"They can stay here," said Jack, "as long as they're comfortable. The station doesn't seem like a good choice. That's Carl's turf and will probably make them nervous. Joan from county is heading over here now with an Initial Access worker."

Pastor Rachel's expression eased. "Good. I hate to let them go so soon after we found them. Why don't you come explain the process?"

Rob trailed behind both Pastor Rachel and Jack, hanging back until the traffic jam cleared in the narrow hallway and he could enter the workroom. File boxes covered the back wall. Those must be the boxes Hannah had sorted. Two comfortable chairs sat in the corner, each holding a pale and anxious-looking girl. Hannah's face had the determined expression of someone who has passed the point of no return. Fiona just looked lost.

Jack, with his policeman's uniform, had their full attention. He appeared to understand that the uniform might be a disadvantage in this situation because he had crouched down in front of them. It didn't do a lot to make him less intimidating, but every little bit helped.

"Hannah, Fiona, we're so glad you're safe. Pretty much the entire town has been looking for you." The tinge of green on Hannah's face had Jack quickly backtracking. "Don't worry. You don't have to deal with any crowds or anything like that."

"Are you here to take us home?" Fiona's question hit Rob right in the gut.

"No."

Fiona sagged back in her chair, visibly relieved, but Hannah sat up straighter, ready to do battle.

"There are some things we need to figure out first," Jack continued. "Kat's friend is coming to talk to you, to understand whether or not home is the best place for you to be. After you talk to her, we'll know more about what comes next."

The rumble of an empty belly filled the room, and Fiona blushed.

"First things first," said Pastor Rachel briskly. "You ladies need to eat something. We've ordered sandwiches. They should be here any minute. Is there anything else you need?"

Two heads shook in unison.

"Okay, then. Rob, Jack, why don't you keep an eye out for Kat's friend? Kat, why don't you and the girls come with me? We'll see if they have sweaters in your sizes over in the second-hand shop. You both look a little cold to me."

Rob followed Pastor Rachel's instructions, understanding the need to give the girls some space. As he and Jack retreated to the foyer, he gave the side of Jack's face a second look.

"You're going to want to get some ice on that."

"Eventually."

The girls preceded Pastor Rachel and Kat through the door of the secondhand shop, and Kat marveled all over again at the amount of stuff they had managed to squeeze into the space. At first the room appeared deserted, but then Kat spied one of the older ladies on the far side of the room, pulling clothing out of a large box. Which one was she? Letty? No, that was the one with the tea. At that moment the woman looked up, and Kat remembered.

"Mary Catharine," the minister said, "we're hoping you can help us find some warm sweaters for these girls. They didn't get much sleep last night, and they're really feeling the change in the weather."

The girls emerged from between two clothing racks, and Kat could see the moment Mary Catharine realized who they were, although she hid her reaction well.

"Of course. Let's see, Hannah will probably need something from the adult section," she said, gesturing vaguely toward the far wall, "and Fiona will probably have more luck right here in the kids section."

Pastor Rachel helped Hannah to hunt through the adult-size sweaters, while Mary Catharine started showing Fiona the sweaters on a table just behind Kat. Within minutes, both girls had found something warm and comfortable.

"Thank you so much, Mary Catharine," the minister said. "This is just what we needed. Now, I wonder if Irene has had a chance to pick up those sandwiches?"

They turned toward the door only to see Mary Evelyn standing there, frozen, holding a large brown bag. Kat glanced back and forth between Mary Evelyn and Mary Catharine, noticing the resemblance for the first time. Mel had told her the surprising story yesterday, that Mary Evelyn had run away from home as a teenager, and she had left a sister behind.

With a start, Mary Evelyn unfroze and stepped into the shop, weaving through the racks toward the group of them. The tense determination on her face found a mirror in Mary Catharine. Glancing at Pastor Rachel, Kat quickly realized the minister had no idea that anything might be wrong.

"Pastor Rachel, why don't we have the girls eat in the other room?" Taking the brown bag from Mary Evelyn, whose attention focused solely on her sister, Kat led the retreat. "Thank you so much, Mary Evelyn."

Glancing away from her sister only briefly, Mary Evelyn said, "My pleasure. I'm just so glad the girls have been found safe, and that they were together."

Kat could only assume that last zinger had been directed at Mary Catharine, who dropped her gaze and began refolding the clothing on the table in front of her. She looked up from her busywork to glance at Fiona.

"You were very brave to leave with your sister. Not everyone has that kind of courage."

Mary Evelyn pressed her fingers against her lips, then cleared her throat and spoke to Fiona. "Leaving a sister behind hurts you in a way that never heals."

Finally, Mary Catharine looked at her sister. "Being left behind hurts worse. If you had only waited another week—"

"Then what?"

Kat had tried to signal Pastor Rachel and the girls that they should head toward the door and give these two some privacy, but they were either ignoring her or were too caught up in the moment to notice. Giving up, Kat tried to fade into the background.

"Then you could have come to live with Aunt Bea, too."

Mary Evelyn sighed. "Aunt Bea only came to get you because I told her if she didn't, I would tell everyone in town what was going on. She had you out within the week."

"Why didn't you come, too?"

"Bea wouldn't have me. Called me a traitor to the family. Said it was all my fault."

Mary Catharine's lower lip quivered. "I didn't know."

"We both got out. That's what matters."

"I'm sorry." Mary Catharine's voice was barely above a whisper.

"Me, too, MC. I should have waited until you were ready."

Pastor Rachel looked over at Kat, as if she had suddenly clued in to the fact that they were intruding on a private moment. Moving toward the door, she coaxed Hannah and Fiona out as well, so that they could give the two sisters some space. They had a lot of catching up to do.

CHAPTER THIRTY

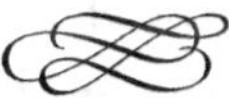

Soon after the girls finished eating, Joan arrived with the Initial Access worker from county. After making introductions, Kat studied Hannah's face to make sure that she felt comfortable. The girl had been working in this room for weeks, so it should feel like her territory, but confirmation would be nice. A small smile and nod from Hannah reassured Kat that she could leave them to it.

Kat closed the door behind her and found the hallway quiet. The murmur of voices from the secondhand shop suggested that Mary Evelyn and her sister were still talking, and the organist was still doing her thing in the sanctuary. After slipping past the office, Kat splashed water on her face in the restroom before stepping outside into the crisp fall morning. She found Rob sitting on the steps.

"Hey, you." She said it with a small smile and took a seat beside him, leaning her head on his broad shoulder.

"You found them."

"We found them," she corrected.

Leaves had only recently begun to fall, and a small breeze chased them around the parking lot. So many girls had found sanctuary here. She was so very grateful that Hannah and Fiona had found it, too.

"What happens now?"

"They're with the IA."

"What's that again?"

"Initial Access worker. Unless Carl has adopted the girls, and I don't think he has, it should be fairly straightforward to keep him away from them. It's not like he has parental rights. A lot depends on their mom. Speaking of..."

A squad car rolled into the parking lot, Jack at the wheel. As soon as he parked, Jennifer burst out of the passenger seat and rushed toward the door, her face red and puffy but her expression determined.

"Where are the girls?"

Kat and Rob had stood, and now Kat reached out to clasp Jennifer's hands.

"The girls are safe. They're meeting with the interviewer from the county right now, so you can't see them quite yet. Do you want to wait here with us?"

Jennifer looked panicked, her attention shifting from Kat to Rob to Jack, who took his time walking over from the squad car.

"I can't see them now?" Her voice a high-pitched squeak, the girls' mom was—understandably—having trouble keeping it together.

"Just a few more minutes," said Kat in a low, soothing voice. "Not long at all. Here, sit down."

Kat sank down onto the top step and patted the spot beside her. After a fraught moment, Jennifer followed suit. She looked at her hands, rubbing them as if they hurt, and began to rock. Jack leaned against the side of the church building, and Rob stayed on his feet, the two speaking in low voices.

"It's all my fault." Jennifer's whisper carried easily to Kat, who wasn't quite sure how to respond.

"You're not responsible for the behavior of other people."

That had been a favorite of one of Kat's therapists. Even if all that counseling hadn't really "taken" with Kat, the wisdom might be helpful to Jennifer—although it wasn't clear whether or not the distraught woman was listening.

"I was so alone, and Carl was so sure of himself. He had all the answers."

Jennifer seemed to be talking to herself, directing the words at her tormented hands, but just when Kat thought she was lost in her own world, the woman looked Kat right in the eye.

"I let my girls down."

Agreeing was probably not the right thing to do. Instead, Kat searched her mind for another pearl of wisdom. "Nobody can be strong all the time."

"No," answered Jennifer, "but I should have done better."

A commotion in the entryway behind them ended with the doors bursting open and the girls rushing to their mother, who was just coming to her feet. They met in a tangled hug that lasted a long time.

As they began to pull apart, their mother said, "I'm so sorry. I thought—it doesn't matter. I'll do better."

They squeezed tight again, and Kat stepped back, both to give them room and to speak to Joan, who had trailed them out the door. The IA was right behind her, gently separating Jennifer from the girls and inviting her inside for an interview. Jennifer clearly didn't want to be separated from her girls, but she seemed to understand this was important, too.

Joan threw an arm around Kat's shoulders and squeezed. "How's my girl?"

Kat relaxed against her, grateful for the solidity that was Joan. The woman was a force of nature, loud and loving, strong and fierce. You couldn't ask for a better champion in your corner when life knocked you sideways.

"Better now that we have two girls safe and sound."

One last squeeze and Joan dropped her arm, turning to face Kat so they could speak more privately.

"You sure you're okay?"

"Weirdly, yes. I have...someone to lean on."

At Joan's raised eyebrow, Kat found herself at a loss for words, which led to an expression on Joan's face that Kat knew all too well. Mama Bear had questions. Glancing over her shoulder at Rob, then back at Joan, she figured the best she could do was delay.

"It's been an interesting few weeks. Maybe we could grab coffee soon?"

"Very soon," replied Joan, before stepping away to answer a question from Jennifer. Kat took advantage of the break to speak with Hannah.

"How do you feel about all this? You okay?"

"Mostly I'm relieved. No more secrets."

"Good. You understand the next steps?"

Hannah nodded.

"You know you can always call me, day or night." Kat fished a business card out of her purse, scribbled her cell phone number on the back. "You have a lot of people looking out for you, but if you ever feel like things are heading in the wrong direction, you let me know."

"Okay."

"Promise?"

Hannah smiled this time, and Kat could sense the implied eye roll. "Yes. Promise. Got it."

As the group loaded up and rolled out, headed for the county offices, Kat hung back with Rob. He put his arm around her, and she leaned her head on his shoulder. It felt different now, leaning. Kat knew she could stand on her own, but sometimes she might choose to lean on a strong shoulder. It didn't make her weak. It made her human.

After turning to wrap his arms around Kat, Rob rubbed her

back and shoulders for a minute before stepping away from the embrace.

"Should we go grab a coffee at Lucy's and fill everyone in on the details? I bet they're dying to know how we found them."

"Absolutely."

Rob took her hand, the action completely unselfconscious, and together they walked over to his truck. She looked down at their clasped hands, the connection natural and easy, and smiled.

That evening Mel found herself once again at The Beach. She wondered if she could be considered a regular at this point. Unlike Saturday night, it was quiet, not surprising for a Monday. Mel spotted her friends right away and headed over to their table. The oddity of it all struck her, the fact that she had made friends with Kat of all people, and soon she might be able to say the same of Rob and Jack. A year ago, she would have laughed in the face of anyone who raised the possibility. And yet—

A lot can change in a year. One sister practically married, the other head over heels. Her dad starting a new life, her mom revisiting an old one. And a new adventure waiting around the corner for Mel, an adventure that she should definitely tell her family about very soon. Nothing like a plane ticket to give you a firm deadline.

Mel had barely poured herself a beer from the pitcher when the guys decided on a game of pool, leaving her alone with Kat.

"You and Rob seem pretty solid."

A series of expressions flickered across Kat's face, the most interesting one being surprise. "I guess we are," she said, her tone cautious. "I'm sure I'll find a way to screw it up, but for now, we're good." She took a sip of her beer. "What about you? Is there something going on with the very attractive muralist?"

Mel couldn't help the smug smile on her face. "As it happens, I am entertaining the idea of a fling."

"You haven't decided yet?"

"It's early days yet," said Mel with a shrug.

"Why just a fling? He seems like the kind of guy who might be a keeper."

Swirling her beer, Mel considered avoiding the question. She was going to need to talk about her plans sooner or later, but until now, later had always seemed like the better option. With the clock ticking, though, she could probably use some practice in talking about it.

"I'm leaving town soon, so it doesn't seem like a great idea to start anything serious."

"Where are you going?"

It was a perfectly natural, sensible question, but Mel tensed all the same. She had rehearsed this conversation in her mind too many times, and her family always reacted badly. Maybe a friend would do better.

"Central and South America. I've got a freelance photography assignment that will last two years, working for a nonprofit, documenting their work in different countries."

"That sounds amazing."

"It is," said Mel. It really was amazing, and she needed to remind herself of that every time she freaked out about telling her family. "I haven't had a chance to tell my family, though. Could you keep it confidential for now?"

Kat nodded her agreement. "When do you leave?"

"Before Thanksgiving." Her answer almost earned her a spit take from Kat, who clearly had been expecting a longer time frame.

"That's coming up fast."

"Tell me about it."

"Why haven't you told your family yet?" Kat seemed curious rather than judgmental, so Mel didn't mind answering.

"Mostly I'm a big chicken. Everyone is used to me being the sister who is always available, and I'm about to change all that. And then there's my mom. She's never been a big fan of my vagabond lifestyle, so she's started planning out my life, hoping that I'll just fall in line. I'm afraid she'll see this plan as a slap in the face, instead of just me following my dreams, you know?"

Kat nodded, even as Mel realized the ridiculousness of that remark.

"I'm an idiot," said Mel. "I should be grateful that I have a family to worry about me, instead of turning this into a lot of drama."

"You can have as much family drama as you want, and I can imagine what it's like to be a part of that. In fact, I can use my vivid imagination to offer you some advice." Mel raised an eyebrow at that confident statement from Kat. "Tell your family now, because if you wait until the day before you leave, they are *definitely* going to freak out."

Mel hung her head. "I know, I know. I'll tell them tomorrow."

Mel and Kat joined the guys for their second game of pool. This time around it was girls versus guys. Kat moved to stand beside Jack, giving Rob room to line up his shot.

"Thanks for everything you did today for the girls." Kat needed to let Jack know that she didn't blame him for what had happened to her.

"Just doing my job."

"It was more than that and you know it." He could have used his discretion to steer the course of events in a completely different direction. "You found a way to keep the girls safe." He opened his mouth, and she could tell he was going to object or deflect. "Just say, 'You're welcome.'"

He paused, gave a little laugh, and then said, "You're welcome."

"See? That wasn't so hard."

"Hannah was lucky to have you looking out for her."

Kat shook her head. "I should have acted sooner. I should have trusted my instincts when they screamed that something was very wrong. The girls should not have had to run away to get the help they needed."

Jack had been studying Rob's shots, but after listening to Kat's self-flagellation, he turned his full attention her way.

"You proceeded with caution, and in most cases, that's the right thing to do. There was no way to know things would blow up so fast. Stop beating yourself up and just be happy that it worked out." He held up a hand when she would have objected. "Just say, 'Yes, Officer Jack.'"

She laughed before parroting back his words.

"Much better," he said, and moved toward the pool table to take his shot.

Rob offered to walk Kat home before it got too late, conscious of the fact that they both had to work the next morning. As they approached her front door, the dark silence wrapped them in a private cocoon, full of unasked questions and unspoken feelings. He wanted, more than anything, to sleep with her again, to wake up and have breakfast again. And yet, the crisis had passed. It was just another Monday night with the rest of the workweek stretching before them. He should go home. They both needed a good night's sleep. And yet....

"I don't want you to go home." The vulnerability in her voice was a punch to the gut. He reached out to cradle her cheek in the palm of his hand, his fingers sliding back into her hair.

"And I don't want to leave." He leaned closer, his forehead coming to rest on hers.

"So stay," she whispered.

CHAPTER THIRTY-ONE

Kat stretched in her office chair and tilted her head from side to side, trying to work out the kink that had developed over the course of the afternoon. If only she could recapture the boneless relaxation of early this morning, when she had woken to find herself tangled with Rob, warm and deeply comfortable and...content. Snuggling close, they had dozed until her alarm went off, and he had rumbled in protest.

They hadn't talked about it, or overanalyzed. He seemed to understand that she needed to take things slowly, so he let her take the lead and set the boundaries on intimacy. Just thinking about it made her shiver. His ridiculous patience would be her undoing—or perhaps her remaking.

Sticking with the theme of not overthinking things, she reached for her phone and called him.

"Hey."

"Hey, yourself."

"Do you want to sleep over again tonight?"

"Hell, yes."

She grinned.

"I could cook."

Silence on the other end of the line, then, "Why don't I pick up some supplies on the way over?"

This time she laughed.

"My reputation is that bad, huh?"

"Maybe I just think that cooking together is more fun that cooking alone."

"Sounds great to me. Six o'clock?"

"I'll see you then."

Her smile stuck around for the rest of the afternoon. She liked having someone in her space, someone in her kitchen—someone in her life. Sure, she was still pretty screwed up, but Rob didn't seem to mind taking things slowly. There was no pressure. They could simply...be together.

The following weekend, Mel observed the party below from her perch on the scaffolding. The wall didn't need any more work. It was ready and waiting for its mural, and Mel would be helping to paint that mural starting on Monday. The painting should take only a few weeks, which fit in perfectly with her travel timeline. And sometime during the next few weeks, she would find the perfect moment to tell her family about her plans.

Mary Evelyn, typically at the center of these things, was instead standing off to the side talking with her sister, Mary Catharine. Mel had been perhaps a little less surprised than everyone else at the revelation that the two were sisters, having noticed that Mary Catharine seemed familiar at the community meeting, even if she hadn't been able to pinpoint why. It was funny how, after years of silence, knowledge could fade into obscurity. Like the cemetery. People had known it was there. They had simply forgotten to tell the next generation. Mary Evelyn and Mary Catharine may not have spoken for close to fifty years, but their sisterhood had never been a secret.

Mel sincerely hoped that it didn't take her family fifty years to forgive her for leaving them. Which she would definitely tell them. Soon.

The unveiling of the mural and garden design had drawn not only all the volunteers, but also the crowd from the community meeting and even a few new faces. Hannah and her sister Fiona, along with their mother, Jennifer, were there. Mel didn't know the mother or sister, but Hannah looked much more relaxed than she had before. Even from a distance, Mel saw her smile once or twice.

Fitz and Rob emerged from the side door of the library carrying a freestanding bulletin board between them. They had covered it with a sheet to keep curious eyes away, although she had snuck into the library earlier to peek. Just a little quality control on her photos. One side of the bulletin board displayed the plans for the mural and garden, but the other side featured photos documenting their progress so far. The photos of the teenagers carefully clearing weeds from the small headstones were some of her best work, and she reminded herself to be grateful for this project—and for the time with Fitz—before her next adventure began.

As if he could sense her thoughts as well as her location, Fitz looked up at her and motioned for her to come down. It must be time. Mel clambered down the scaffolding, careful not to bang her camera against the ladder. As Mel emerged from the shadow of the scaffolding, Mary Evelyn was calling everyone together.

"On behalf of the library, I'd like to thank all our volunteers again for the hard work that has brought us to this point in the project. Both your labor and your ideas have helped to shape the site, and we couldn't have done it without you."

Without further ado, Rob and Fitz removed the sheet to reveal the design. On the bulletin board were two large images. The first was a detailed full-color sketch of the future mural to be painted on the side of the library. The second was a 3D rendering, also in color, of the garden and cemetery. Fitz addressed the group.

"I'll echo Mary Evelyn's thanks, and I hope you'll stay involved in the project as we move forward. Let me tell you a little bit about the process that brought you the design you see here."

Fitz talked about the volunteer and community meetings, the ideas that had emerged from them, and the influence of the cemetery on the final design. Not that the theme would revolve around death—far from it. Everyone wanted to remember the potential of those young lives, and to envision the library as a place that all children could feel safe.

"For those who are not close enough to see the detail, our concept for the mural is a giant bookcase full of children's books. Each story of the building will be a shelf on the bookcase. Playing among the books will be children of all ages, from babies and toddlers up to teenagers, as well as characters from the books."

From the oohs and aahs and excited chatter, the concept seemed to be going over well. Mel moved closer to Kat, who stood off to one side next to Mary Evelyn and Officer Jack, and found a great angle for taking reaction shots. She snapped away as Fitz continued talking.

"The garden will include cement sculptures in the shape of books that are sturdy enough for children to climb on, a tree stump transformed into a sleeping bear with a chainsaw, an outdoor story time area inside a living wicker shelter, and a small stream with a book-themed bridge. The cemetery will be protected by a low wrought iron fence, and we will install a plaque that tells the story."

The crowd was getting restless, those farther away from the bulletin board wanting a closer look. Fitz wrapped up quickly, and then Mary Evelyn organized a line so that everyone would have their chance to see the detail. She made sure the line wrapped around the back of the bulletin board so that everyone would have a chance to see the work-in-progress photos as well. Mel blew her a kiss in thanks.

"You ready to get to work?" asked Fitz as he came to stand beside her.

"Yes, sir." Mel gave him a crisp salute.

He watched the crowd closely, studying their reactions to the design, but she could see the slight uptilt at the corner of his mouth.

"I hope you're willing to follow orders," he murmured.

"Of course, sir." He glanced over at her suspiciously compliant tone of voice, and she could tell that he wasn't buying her innocent act, so she let it go and grinned. "Will we have a safe word?"

He shook his head with a laugh. "I'll probably need one."

Kat stood beside Rob, helping with crowd control while he answered questions about the design. She hoped he would have a lot of opportunities to collaborate after this, because she could see how much he had enjoyed it. They had talked just last night about the downside of having your own business. Loneliness was the worst.

"Joan, I'm so glad you could make it." Kat touched Rob's arm to let him know she was abandoning him to his fans, then she and Joan moved to a quieter spot. She and her mentor still needed to get together for that cup of coffee.

"Wouldn't miss it," answered Joan. "Thanks again for agreeing to coordinate the community service program in this area. You have a real knack for working with teenagers."

"That sounds suspiciously like the lead-up to an ask."

Joan's laugh boomed out over the crowd. "Not this time, although I do have a suggestion."

"Let's hear it."

"Sometimes the hardest part about running a community service program is coming up with new projects. Maintaining this garden should definitely go on your list."

Kat surveyed the progress they had made in one short month, and couldn't think of a better way to honor the lost girls and their babies.

"You're right."

"Of course I am."

Kat smiled, shaking her head.

"You going to give that boy a chance?" asked Joan, her eyes on Rob, who was caught up in conversation with one of the parents of the community service kids.

Nodding slowly, Kat said, "I'm thinking he's worth the risk."

Joan put her arm around Kat's shoulder and squeezed.

"That's my girl."

Rob was still deep in conversation, so Kat checked in with Hannah, who was showing the different grave markers to her mother and sister.

"Hannah, it's great to see you."

"I was just telling my mom the stories. Well, some of them." Her eyes landed briefly on her sister, and Kat realized Hannah was still playing the role of protector. It was part of her nature, but Kat hoped that Jennifer would be strong enough to shield both Hannah and Fiona from now on, so that Hannah didn't always have to be the strong one.

All three of them looked lighter, the weight of Carl having been lifted from their shoulders—at least for now. As of yesterday, he was stuck in jail, unable to organize bail, having been arrested and charged with sexual abuse of a minor. Kat didn't have a lot of sympathy for his plight. If he did get out, he was no longer welcome to stay in the family home, which, as it turned out, belonged to Jennifer. Her mother, the girls' grandmother, had come to stay with them for a while, until their case had worked its way through both the legal system and the child protective services system. Jennifer would need to demonstrate that she could keep her girls safe. Kat had no doubt she could do it.

"I was just talking with my friend Joan about the future of the garden," said Kat. "We're going to need some help taking care if it. Any interest?"

"Sure," said Hannah with a shrug.

Kat suppressed a smile at the show of indifference. The answer was still yes.

"Can I help, too?"

The question earned Fiona a classic annoyed-big-sister look from Hannah, and a quick intervention by their mother.

"Maybe Hannah can help on the days when it's just teenagers, and we can all come when they need community volunteers."

A brilliant solution. Kat appreciated the save, since she would have been scrambling for a diplomatic answer otherwise.

"That sounds perfect," she said. "I'll let you know the schedule."

Kat retreated, allowing Hannah to resume the role of storyteller. It was such a relief to see them taking small steps toward normalcy. She would do everything she could to prepare them for the difficult legal and emotional hurdles to come. But not today. They deserved this moment of peace in the sunshine.

Dora and Lucy stood under the shade of the scaffolding, analyzing the reactions of different people to the mural design.

"Verdict?" asked Dora.

"Well-received." Lucy crossed her arms in satisfaction. "I have to say, I'm relieved it all worked out. My mother put a lot of time and energy into this project, and it would have broken her heart if people didn't like the design."

"I still can't believe your mother has a sister." Dora stared in open fascination at the two women standing near the bulletin board. "You have an aunt."

"I know, right?" Lucy shook her head. "No wonder my mom never wanted to go to church."

"I'm glad they reconciled. It's sad that they missed all that time together."

"Speaking of time together," said Lucy, "any progress on your mission to get Mel to move here full time?"

Dora's half-smile had a hint of the diabolical. "I'm making progress. If we can just find the right studio space, I think she'll be able to envision how it would work."

When Lucy didn't immediately respond, Dora pulled her attention away from the reconciling sisters to face her friend. A very skeptical eyebrow greeted her.

"What?" demanded Dora.

"Are you sure it's the right move for her?"

"She's been spending a lot of time up here lately. I think she wants to be here, but she just can't admit it to herself. This is a problem I was born to solve."

Lucy chuckled. "With Luke starting a new life and the other two girls settled, you might possibly be getting overinvolved in Mel's life." At Dora's instinctive protest, Lucy held up a hand. "I will take it upon myself to find you a distraction, so that Mel can figure out her life without your interference."

"Lucy, I hardly need you to—"

"I already have someone in mind."

At that moment, a small child tugged on Mary Evelyn's sweater.

"Miss Mary Evelyn?"

"Yes, dear?"

A tiny hand held up something round and metal.

"Your door handle fell off."

Thank you so much for reading *Love Me Not*!

If you loved Kat and Rob's story, return to Hidden Springs in *Love Letters* to find out what happens between Mel and Fitz and what comes next for Dora. Or go back to the beginning and see how it all began with Callie and Adam's story in *Love Song (Instrumental)*, followed by Tessa and RJ's adventure in *Love Story (Confidential)*.

SIGN UP for Lisa McLuckie's eNewsletter (signup link at www.LisaMcLuckie.com) to receive new release alerts, insider information, and bonus content.

THANK YOU for helping to spread the word about *Love Me Not*. Reviews help readers discover new authors, so please pay it forward by leaving a review on your favorite book site, and be sure to tell your book-loving friends if you enjoyed the story.

And now, an **EXCERPT** from *Love Letters*.

One week ago

Dearest Dora,

Early this morning we lost Lauren. She slipped away just before sunrise. I'm thankful that both the kids had a chance to say goodbye, and so grateful that I chose to stay at the hospital last night to be with her in those final moments.

She asked for you. She was confused at the end, remembering that you had been here but not that you had left. I hope you'll come back to New York to join us for the memorial service. You must be curious to see the twins again, now that they are all grown up. I would like you to know them.

Lauren shared something with me before she died that I can't quite bring myself to believe. You are the only one who will know the truth of it. Although you avoided me during your visits this summer, you cannot avoid me forever. We have much to discuss.

Yours,

Barrett

Today

Dora had started and discarded a dozen replies to Barrett's letter, but she couldn't decide what to say. Too many emotions battled for her attention. Impatience with herself for waffling. Irritation that she didn't know her own mind. Fierce protectiveness of both his family and hers. What was he thinking, bringing her into the mix when the children were still reeling from the loss of their mother? Anger, old and deep, that he would try to control her life again. But beneath it all was fear, and she hated that it still lurked after all these years.

Of course, Luke had to be away this week, so he wasn't here to talk her through the problem. Husbands were supposed to be your rock during tough times, but Luke was falling down on the job. She could wait until he came home, perhaps, but she wasn't some helpless neophyte. Waiting would just make her feel foolish.

As she paused, pen poised and ready for attempt number thirteen, impatience and irritation won the day and she scribbled her answer without second-guessing her words. No matter how much she and Barrett might have to discuss, now was not the time. As far as Dora was concerned, never would be a great time. Immature? Yes. Honest? Also yes.

The unsent reply would torment her until the moment she dropped it into a mailbox, so she addressed, stamped, and sealed it before she lost momentum. Even better, she had to leave immediately for the unveiling of the mural design over at the library. She would drop the letter at the post office on her way and the torture would end. She wasn't one to ruminate over things that could not be changed. Best move the letter into that category immediately.

Today

~~Mom,~~

   ~~I've been trying to tell you something important, but it never seems to be a good time, which is why I'm writing this email. Email can't be interrupted, or~~

~~Mom,~~

   ~~There's something I need to tell you.~~

~~Mom,~~

   ~~We need to talk~~

~~Mom,~~

   ~~I know you don't think I have a plan for my life, but I do. I just haven't told you yet.~~

Mel zoomed in, tightly framing the shot so that it captured the intensity of the conversation. Midmorning light, filtered through a screen of reddish-brown oak leaves, illuminated her subjects without washing them out or creating awkward shadows. If she could just get them to open up... Now. She held the shutter button down and her camera took a burst of photos in rapid succession. Smiling, she lowered the camera and scanned the crowd for her next opportunity.

The unveiling of the design for the new mural had drawn a decent crowd by Hidden Springs' standards. More than forty people filled the freshly cleared area between the library building and the church that would soon become a small park. The newly uncovered cemetery adjacent to the church might deserve some of the credit for the crowd, but most of the truly curious had stopped by to see it already. Some of the attendees, like Mel, had volunteered during the first phase of the project, preparing the brick wall of the library for the mural and clearing the underbrush. Friends, family, and neighbors had come to offer support and hear all the latest gossip. If a freshly tuck-pointed wall and a newly cleared lot could draw this kind of crowd, then the big reveal of the mural itself in a few weeks should be a blowout.

From her perch on the first level of the scaffolding that covered the side of the library building, Mel had a clear view of the crowd, while most of them remained unaware of her presence. She preferred to work this way, an invisible witness to the lives of others. Maybe it made her a voyeur, but she didn't care. People were a mystery to be solved, and they were more likely to reveal their true selves when they thought themselves unobserved.

The creak of the ladder pulled her attention away from the scene below. Instead of the teenager she had expected, the head that popped up through the square opening in the floor belonged to her sister, Tessa, blond hair pulled back in a knot that was looser these days than it used to be. Callie, their other sister, followed on Tessa's heels. She had tamed her own long blond hair into a messy braid today. Mel wondered if she would ever lose the habit of differentiating herself from her sisters by dyeing her hair. She never ditched the blond completely, and she didn't like the idea of cutting it short, but she had always played with color and style. Right now, for example, her hair featured a bright pink streak and matching tips. It had always been important to Mel that people could tell the triplets apart.

"You ladies lost?" she asked.

Ignoring the question, Tessa asked, "What did we miss?"

"Pretty much everything," said Mel, still irritated that her sisters had sidestepped the guilt trip that had roped Mel into helping. Who cared if Mel had enjoyed the work so far, or made new friends, or met a hot muralist? What mattered was that her sisters had weaseled out of it.

"And by everything you mean…"

"Well, let's see," said Mel, letting exasperation color her voice. "You've both managed to avoid more than a month's worth of weed-whacking and tuck-pointing."

The innocent expressions on her sisters' faces fooled no one.

"The end of the sailing season has been really busy," said Tessa.

"And things are crazy for me working on the new album," added Callie. "There was no way to fit it in."

"You two also missed the excitement last weekend."

"Mom told us all about it," said Tessa. "Runaway girls, found safe. Do you know them?"

"The older sister was working on the project, so yes, I know one of them. You would know her, too, if only you had squeezed in an hour to help."

Matching grins were their only reply. Callie sank down onto the floor of the scaffolding and dangled her feet over the side. Tessa followed suit, patting the spot next to her for Mel, who took her time accepting the invitation.

How many times had they sat like this down on the pier, dipping their toes into the water and kicking up spray? Far too many to count. In this case, they had to be more careful, or they might brain someone walking below. The cool October air reminded Mel that there wouldn't be many good days left to get out on the lake. Before she could suggest a paddle-boarding session to her sisters, Tessa spoke.

"So which one is the hot muralist?" she asked.

Thanks to a great publicity photo, Fitz had been dubbed "Hot Muralist" long before he arrived on the scene. Mel had been the first to meet him in person, happily reporting that the reality more than justified the hype. However, hearing

Tessa use the nickname roused Mel's protective instincts. The hint of a spark between herself and Fitz would need shelter to achieve flame status. It did not need interference from her sisters.

At Tessa's questioning glance, Mel realized she hadn't answered the question. She scanned the crowd and picked him out with embarrassing ease.

"He's over by the bulletin board," said Mel as she lifted her camera. "Dark green polo shirt, khaki pants, crouched down by a small girl. It looks like he's explaining the mural design to her."

The angle couldn't be better. Focusing on the energy in Fitz's delivery and the rapt expression on the girl's face, Mel took a burst of photos just as the girl broke into a wide smile.

"I see him," said Callie. "Nice shoulders."

"Interesting," murmured Tessa. Mel felt her own shoulders tense at her sister's deliberately neutral tone. Anytime Tessa used her therapist voice, the sisters knew to be wary.

"What's interesting?" Mel couldn't help asking.

"He's much more clean cut than I would have expected. Less artsy." Tessa turned to Mel and cocked her head. "Not your preferred type."

It's hard to argue with facts, so Mel kept her mouth shut.

"Like I said, it's interesting."

Tessa's slow smile made Mel nervous.

"Is he a good kisser?"

Callie's question caught Mel by surprise and she choked on a laugh. "Seriously?"

"You seem to like him a lot." Her grin was pure mischief. "I thought you might know."

Mel had forgotten the joy and pain of hanging out with both her sisters at the same time.

"Well, I don't. There has been no kissing."

Callie's grin grew even wider. "Yet."

"Are we twelve?" asked Mel. "I can't believe we're having this conversation."

"We are mature adults, and it was a simple question." Callie seemed to know exactly which buttons to push. "No need to get all huffy, especially since nothing happened."

"Yet," said Tessa with a high-five for Callie.

"We're here whenever you're ready to talk about your boyfriend," said Tessa.

"He's not my boyfriend." Mel clapped a hand over her mouth, but the words had already tumbled out, and Tessa was all over it.

"Maybe you wouldn't call it that," she said in that irritatingly superior voice, "but he could be, right?"

"I'm not interested in a boyfriend right now."

"Why not?" Callie asked.

This was it, the perfect moment to tell her sisters about her plans. Maybe not perfect, because she couldn't tell the whole family at the same time, but close enough.

"It's complicated," Mel began. "I've got this gig in the works that will require some travel—"

"Mom, incoming, ten o'clock." Callie's alert derailed Mel's big news. Their mother was headed their way, and she was on a mission.

"She has 'the look,'" Tessa stage-whispered.

Mel groaned. "Is it too late to hide?"

"Way too late," said Callie.

Dora came to a stop directly below them, hands on hips, looking very displeased. Mel suddenly felt seven instead of twenty-seven.

"Girls, get down here. You're going to kick someone in the head sitting like that."

She was right, of course, so the three of them clambered down the ladder to meet their fate. As it turned out, their fate was hugs from their mother.

"Mel, honey, I'm glad I found you. Of course, I'm happy to see all my girls, but Mel, I was looking for you particularly. I've got some leads on commercial spaces that might work as a photography studio for you. We need to see them this week, because they'll go quickly. We don't want to miss the perfect one."

"Mom, I really don't think this is the time...."

"Why not? You're in between apartments, your work hours are flexible, and we're living in the same house for the first time in years. When could it possibly be more convenient?"

Her mother had a point. Even her sisters looked at her curiously.

In every other aspect of her life, Mel would describe herself as bold, assertive, and confident. Those qualities had led to success in her career as a photojournalist, turbulence in romantic relationships, and lots of fun along the way. Within the family, she was the mischief-maker—the one who could make everybody laugh. What her family didn't know, and what she herself hadn't realized until recently, was that her family was her kryptonite. She wasn't happy unless her family was happy, and she found it physically painful to let her family down. This was information that she would never, ever share, of course. Her mother couldn't be trusted with that kind of power. It was a weakness she needed to manage, now that she had figured it out.

In this moment, despite the fact that her future plans did not include a photography studio in Hidden Springs, Mel couldn't bring herself to crush her mother's enthusiasm. That would come soon enough. Maybe she could buy herself some time instead.

"But I said I would help with the mural." Even to her own ears, the excuse sounded weak.

"It's a volunteer project. If you need to take a morning off to focus on your professional future, I think Fitz will understand.

Right, Fitz?" The question was directed at someone standing behind Mel.

"Of course," replied Fitz.

Mel spun around and tried to catch his eye, but he was too busy looking from sister to sister. Maybe she should have given him a heads up that she was an identical triplet. When his gaze finally rested on Mel, he registered the plea in her eyes.

"What did I just agree to?" he asked.

"I was telling Mel that if she needs to take the occasional morning off from mural painting, you won't object."

Fitz looked from Mel to Dora and back to Mel. His expression clearly said, *How can I object to that?*

Mel tried to telegraph *Find a way!* with angry eyebrows and a tiny shake of the head, but it was too late.

"Well, actually," began Fitz. Mel could tell that he was scrambling for an excuse, anything that would help her out.

"I knew you would understand," said Dora before Fitz could come up with a plausible reason to say no. "Don't worry. I'll set up all the appointments for the same day so that you don't lose too much work time. How about Thursday morning?"

Mel opened and closed her mouth, then gave Fitz a shrug. If she couldn't delay, then she might as well enjoy the outing with her mother. Maybe it would help make up for the fact that she would miss both Thanksgiving and Christmas this year.

Dora took Mel's silence for agreement. "Excellent. Now, Fitz, I need you to come with me. There's someone you need to meet."

Fitz allowed himself to be led away, his rueful smile the only hint that he was going under duress. As soon as he was out of earshot, Callie said, "I totally get the nickname."

"Was that a tattoo I saw in the shadow of his collar?" asked Tessa.

"We'll have to get to know him better if Mel is going to date him."

"I'm right here, you know," said Mel, crossing her arms.

Tessa slung an arm around Mel's shoulders and gave her a squeeze. "Maybe it's a good thing that you're exploring your options here in Hidden Springs instead of down in Chicago. With a guy like that on the line, at least Mom will ease off on the blind dates."

Leaving the country would also solve that problem, although it wasn't the only reason she was going. All her life, Mel had wanted to explore the world, and if she didn't go now, it might never happen. The longer she stayed here in Hidden Springs, the more she could feel invisible vines creeping up out of the earth and winding themselves around her feet, trying to tie her down. For years, she had tried to be here for her parents, with Callie off chasing fame, and Tessa absorbed in grad school and then work. Someone needed to check in on Mom and Dad and make sure that they were doing okay. Now that Callie and Tessa planned on spending more time here, Mel could finally explore the world without the tether of worry. It was Mel's turn to fly.

~

Want to read more? Find *Love Letters* at your favorite bookseller.

ACKNOWLEDGMENTS

Most people think of writing as a solitary affair, but in reality it takes a village. I'd like to take a moment to acknowledge all the people in my village who helped to make this book happen.

Kat first appeared as a secondary character in *Love Song (Instrumental)*. In preparation for that book, I talked with my friend, Pete Wilson, about his work as a guardian *ad litem*. He helped me to get the details right for that book, as did attorney Shannon Wynn. Together, their insights helped me to build the character that became Kat. For this book, I also relied on Karin Slayton to help me understand "the system" and how it works. Her perspective as a social worker was invaluable. If, despite their best efforts to educate me, I've still managed to screw something up in the final version of the story, it is entirely my own fault.

Rin Olsson, Vicky McHugh, Karishma Petersen, and Sandra Ogle also contributed their expertise to help get this manuscript over the finish line. Their insights were incredibly helpful.

Special thanks to my family for their patience. This book

took a particularly long time, with a few detours along the way. Let's hope the next one is more cooperative.

With love and gratitude,

Lisa

ABOUT THE AUTHOR

Lisa McLuckie was born a wanderer. She has lived in four states and two foreign countries, had twenty-four different addresses, and explored five of the seven continents. Her debut novel, *Love Song (Instrumental),* earned two honors from the Independent Book Publishers Association in 2015: the Benjamin Franklin Gold Award for Romance Fiction, and the Bill Fisher Silver Award for Best First Book (Fiction).

She currently lives on the fringes of Chicagoland with her husband, three sons (sizes medium, large, and extra-large), and a ridiculously adorable dog named Daisy. Learn more at LisaMcLuckie.com.

Books by Lisa McLuckie
Love Song (Instrumental)
Love Story (Confidential)
Love Met Not
Love Letters

ABOUT HIDDEN SPRINGS

Growing up, I spent a lot of time in the lake country of southeastern Wisconsin. This area may not be quite as famous as the Finger Lakes region in upstate New York, or Lake Tahoe out west, but for me that makes it better. A little more down-to-earth. A little less crowded. The fictional town of Hidden Springs is a wonderful mash-up of all the different lake towns I love, past and present, large (relatively speaking) and small.

If you want to know more about the real-world lakes of southeastern Wisconsin, these web sites provide a great starting point.

- http://www.travelwisconsin.com/southeast/walworth-county
- http://www.visitwalworthcounty.com/
- https://www.visitlakegeneva.com/
- http://www.discoverwhitewater.org/
- http://www.cruiselakegeneva.com/
- http://www.atthelakemagazine.com/

I'll see you at the lake!
Lisa